Wilkins Mary E. Freeman

The Shoulders of Atlas

Wilkins Mary E. Freeman

The Shoulders of Atlas

1st Edition | ISBN: 978-3-75236-504-7

Place of Publication: Frankfurt am Main, Germany

Year of Publication: 2020

Outlook Verlag GmbH, Germany.

The Shoulders of Atlas

A Novel

By
Mary E. Wilkins Freeman

Chapter I

Henry Whitman was walking home from the shop in the April afternoon. The spring was very early that year. The meadows were quite green, and in the damp hollows the green assumed a violet tinge—sometimes from violets themselves, sometimes from the shadows. The trees already showed shadows as of a multitude of bird wings; the peach-trees stood aloof in rosy nimbuses, and the cherry-trees were faintly a-flutter with white through an intense gloss of gold-green.

Henry realized all the glory of it, but it filled him with a renewal of the sad and bitter resentment, which was his usual mood, instead of joy. He was past middle-age. He worked in a shoe-shop. He had worked in a shoe-shop since he was a young man. There was nothing else in store for him until he was turned out because of old age. Then the future looked like a lurid sunset of misery. He earned reasonably good wages for a man of his years, but prices were so high that he was not able to save a cent. There had been unusual expenses during the past ten years, too. His wife Sylvia had not been well, and once he himself had been laid up six weeks with rheumatism. The doctor charged two dollars for every visit, and the bill was not quite settled yet.

Then the little house which had come to him from his father, encumbered with a mortgage as is usual, had all at once seemed to need repairs at every point. The roof had leaked like a sieve, two windows had been blown in, the paint had turned a gray-black, the gutters had been out of order. He had not quite settled the bill for these repairs. He realized it always as an actual physical incubus upon his slender, bowed shoulders. He came of a race who were impatient of debt, and who regarded with proud disdain all gratuitous benefits from their fellow-men. Henry always walked a long route from the shop in order to avoid passing the houses of the doctor and the carpenter whom he owed.

Once he had saved a little money; that was twenty-odd years before; but he had invested it foolishly, and lost every cent. That transaction he regarded with hatred, both of himself and of the people who had advised him to risk and lose his hard-earned dollars. The small sum which he had lost had come to assume colossal proportions in his mind. He used, in his bitterest moments, to reckon up on a scrap of paper what it might have amounted to, if it had been put out at interest, by this time. He always came out a rich man, by his calculations, if it had not been for that unwise investment. He often told his wife Sylvia that they might have been rich people if it had not been for that; that he would not have been tied to a shoe-shop, nor she have been obliged to work so hard.

Sylvia took a boarder—the high-school principal, Horace Allen—and she also

2

made jellies and cakes, and baked bread for those in East Westland who could afford to pay for such instead of doing the work themselves. She was a delicate woman, and Henry knew that she worked beyond her strength, and the knowledge filled him with impotent fury. Since the union had come into play he did not have to work so many hours in the shop, and he got the same pay, but he worked as hard, because he himself cultivated his bit of land. He raised vegetables for the table. He also made the place gay with flowers to please Sylvia and himself. He had a stunted thirst for beauty.

In the winter he found plenty to do in the extra hours. He sawed wood in his shed by the light of a lantern hung on a peg. He also did what odd jobs he could for neighbors. He picked up a little extra money in that way, but he worked very hard. Sometimes he told Sylvia that he didn't know but he worked harder than he had done when the shop time was longer. However, he had been one of the first to go, heart and soul, with the union, and he had paid his dues ungrudgingly, even with a fierce satisfaction, as if in some way the transaction made him even with his millionaire employers. There were two of them, and they owned houses which appeared like palaces in the eyes of Henry and his kind. They owned automobiles, and Henry was aware of a cursing sentiment when one whirred past him, trudging along, and covered him with dust.

Sometimes it seemed to Henry as if an automobile was the last straw for the poor man's back: those enormous cars, representing fortunes, tyrannizing over the whole highway, frightening the poor old country horses, and endangering the lives of all before them. Henry read with delight every account of an automobile accident. "Served them right; served them just right," he would say, with fairly a smack of his lips.

Sylvia, who had caught a little of his rebellion, but was gentler, would regard him with horror. "Why, Henry Whitman, that is a dreadful wicked spirit!" she would say, and he would retort stubbornly that he didn't care; that he had to pay a road tax for these people who would just as soon run him down as not, if it wouldn't tip their old machines over; for these maniacs who had gone speed-mad, and were appropriating even the highways of the common people.

Henry had missed the high-school principal, who was away on his spring vacation. He liked to talk with him, because he always had a feeling that he had the best of the argument. Horace would take the other side for a while, then leave the field, and light another cigar, and let Henry have the last word, which, although it had a bitter taste in his mouth, filled him with the satisfaction of triumph. He loved Horace like a son, although he realized that the young man properly belonged to the class which he hated, and that, too, although he was manifestly poor and obliged to work for his living. Henry was, in his heart of hearts, convinced that Horace Allen, had he been rich,

3

would have owned automobiles and spent hours in the profitless work-play of the golf links. As it was, he played a little after school-hours. How Henry hated golf! "I wish they had to work," he would say, savagely, to Horace.

Horace would laugh, and say that he did work. "I know you do," Henry would say, grudgingly, "and I suppose maybe a little exercise is good for you; but those fellers from Alford who come over here don't have to work, and as for Guy Lawson, the boss's son, he's a fool! He couldn't earn his bread and butter to save his life, except on the road digging like a common laborer. Playing golf! Playing! H'm!" Then was the time for Horace's fresh cigar.

When Henry came in sight of the cottage where he lived he thought with regret that Horace was not there. Being in a more pessimistic mood than usual, he wished ardently for somebody to whom he could pour out his heart. Sylvia was no satisfaction at such a time. If she echoed him for a while, when she was more than usually worn with her own work, she finally became alarmed, and took refuge in Scripture quotations, and Henry was convinced that she offered up prayer for him afterward, and that enraged him.

He struck into the narrow foot-path leading to the side door, the foot-path which his unwilling and weary feet had helped to trace more definitely for nearly forty years. The house was a small cottage of the humblest New England type. It had a little cobbler's-shop, or what had formerly been a cobbler's-shop, for an ell. Besides that, there were three rooms on the ground-floor—the kitchen, the sitting-room, and a little bedroom which Henry and Sylvia occupied. Sylvia had cooking-stoves in both the old shop and the kitchen. The kitchen stove was kept well polished, and seldom used for cooking, except in cold weather. In warm weather the old shop served as kitchen, and Sylvia, in deference to the high-school teacher, used to set the table in the house.

When Henry neared the house he smelled cooking in the shop. He also had a glimpse of a snowy table-cloth in the kitchen. He wondered, with a throb of joy, if possibly Horace might have returned before his vacation was over and Sylvia were setting the table in the other room in his honor. He opened the door which led directly into the shop. Sylvia, a pathetic, slim, elderly figure in rusty black, was bending over the stove, frying flapjacks. "Has he come home?" whispered Henry.

"No, it's Mr. Meeks. I asked him to stay to supper. I told him I would make some flapjacks, and he acted tickled to death. He doesn't get a decent thing to eat once in a dog's age. Hurry and get washed. The flapjacks are about done, and I don't want them to get cold."

Henry's face, which had fallen a little when he learned that Horace had not returned, still looked brighter than before. While Sidney Meeks never let him

4

have the last word, yet he was much better than Sylvia as a safety-valve for pessimism. Meeks was as pessimistic in his way as Henry, although he handled his pessimism, as he did everything else, with diplomacy, and the other man had a secret conviction that when he seemed to be on the opposite side yet he was in reality pulling with the lawyer.

Sidney Meeks was older than Henry, and as unsuccessful as a country lawyer can well be. He lived by himself; he had never married; and the world, although he smiled at it facetiously, was not a pleasant place in his eyes.

Henry, after he had washed himself at the sink in the shop, entered the kitchen, where the table was set, and passed through to the sitting-room, where the lawyer was. Sidney Meeks did not rise. He extended one large, white hand affably. "How are you Henry?" said he, giving the other man's lean, brown fingers a hard shake. "I dropped in here on my way home from the post-office, and your wife tempted me with flapjacks in a lordly dish, and I am about to eat."

"Glad to see you," returned Henry.

"You get home early, or it seems early, now the days are getting so long," said Meeks, as Henry sat down opposite.

"Yes, it's early enough, but I don't get any more pay."

Meeks laughed. "Henry, you are the direct outcome of your day and generation," said he. "Less time, and more pay for less time, is our slogan."

"Well, why not?" returned Henry, surlily, still with a dawn of delighted opposition in his thin, intelligent face. "Why not? Look at the money that's spent all around us on other things that correspond. What's an automobile but less time and more money, eh?"

Meeks laughed. "Give it up until after supper, Henry," he said, as Sylvia's thin, sweet voice was heard from the next room.

"If you men don't stop talking and come right out, these flapjacks will be spoiled!" she cried. The men arose and obeyed her call. "There are compensations for everything," said Meeks, laughing, as he settled down heavily into his chair. He was a large man. "Flapjacks are compensations. Let us eat our compensations and be thankful. That's my way of saying grace. You ought always to say grace, Henry, when you have such a good cook as your wife is to get meals for you. If you had to shift for yourself, the way I do, you'd feel that it was a simple act of decency."

"I don't see much to say grace for," said Henry, with a disagreeable sneer.

"Oh, Henry!" said Sylvia.

"For compensations in the form of flapjacks, with plenty of butter and sugar

5

and nutmeg," said Meeks. "These are fine, Mrs. Whitman."

"A good thick beefsteak at twenty-eight cents a pound, regulated by the beef trust, would be more to my liking after a hard day's work," said Henry.

Sylvia exclaimed again, but she was not in reality disturbed. She was quite well aware that her husband was enjoying himself after his own peculiar fashion, and that, if he spoke the truth, the flapjacks were more to his New England taste for supper than thick beefsteak.

"Well, wait until after supper, and maybe you will change your mind about having something to say grace for," Meeks said, mysteriously.

The husband and wife stared at him. "What do you mean, Mr. Meeks?" asked Sylvia, a little nervously. Something in the lawyer's manner agitated her. She was not accustomed to mysteries. Life had not held many for her, especially of late years.

Henry took another mouthful of flapjacks. "Well, if you can give me any good reason for saying grace you will do more than the parson ever has," he said.

"Oh, Henry!" said Sylvia.

"It's the truth," said Henry. "I've gone to meeting and heard how thankful I ought to be for things I haven't got, and things I have got that other folks haven't, and for forgiveness for breaking commandments, when, so far as I can tell, commandments are about the only things I've been able to keep without taxes—till I'm tired of it."

"Wait till after supper," repeated the lawyer again, with smiling mystery. He had a large, smooth face, with gray hair on the sides of his head and none on top. He had good, placid features, and an easy expression. He ate two platefuls of the flapjacks, then two pieces of cake, and a large slice of custard pie! He was very fond of sweets.

After supper was over Henry and Meeks returned to the sitting-room, and sat down beside the two front windows. It was a small, square room furnished with Sylvia's chief household treasures. There was a hair-cloth sofa, which she and Henry had always regarded as an extravagance and had always viewed with awe. There were two rockers, besides one easy-chair, covered with old-gold plush—also an extravagance. There was a really beautiful old mahogany table with carved base, of which neither Henry nor Sylvia thought much. Sylvia meditated selling enough Calkin's soap to buy a new one, and stow that away in Mr. Allen's room. Mr. Allen professed great admiration for it, to her wonderment. There was also a fine, old, gold-framed mirror, and some china vases on the mantel-shelf. Sylvia was rather ashamed of them. Mrs. Jim Jones had a mirror which she had earned by selling Calkin's soap, which Sylvia considered much handsomer. She would have had ambitions in that direction also, but Henry was firm in his resolve not to have the mirror displaced, nor the vases, although Sylvia descanted upon the superior merits of some vases with gilded pedestals which Mrs. Sam Elliot had in her parlor.

Meeks regarded the superb old table with appreciation as he sat in the sitting-room after supper. "Fine old piece," he said.

Henry looked at it doubtfully. It had been in a woodshed of his grandfather's house, when he was a boy, and he was not as confident about that as he was about the mirror and vases, which had always maintained their parlor estate.

"Sylvia don't think much of it," he said. "She's crazy to have one of carved oak like one Mrs. Jim Jones has."

"Carved oak fiddlestick!" said Sidney Meeks. "It's a queer thing that so much virtue and real fineness of character can exist in a woman without the slightest trace of taste for art."

Henry looked resentful. "Sylvia has taste, as much taste as most women," he said. "She simply doesn't like to see the same old things around all the time, and I don't know as I blame her. The world has grown since that table was made, there's no doubt about that. It stands to reason furniture has improved, too."

"Glad there's something you see in a bright light, Henry."

"I must say that I like this new mission furniture, myself, pretty well," said Henry, somewhat importantly.

"That's as old as the everlasting hills; but the old that's new is the newest thing in all creation," said Meeks. "Sylvia is a foolish woman if she parts with this magnificent old piece for any reproduction made in job lots."

"Oh, she isn't going to part with it. Mr. Allen will like it in his room. He thinks as much of it as you do."

"He's right, too," said Meeks. "There's carving for you; there's a fine grain of wood."

"It's very hard to keep clean," said Sylvia, as she came in rubbing her moist hands. "Now, that new Flemish oak is nothing at all to take care of, Mrs. Jones says."

"This is worth taking care of," said Meeks. "Now, Sylvia, sit down. I have something to tell you and Henry."

Sylvia sat down. Something in the lawyer's manner aroused hers and her husband's keenest attention. They looked at him and waited. Both were slightly pale. Sylvia was a delicate little woman, and Henry was large-framed and tall, but a similar experience had worn similar lines in both faces. They

7

looked singularly alike.

Sidney Meeks had the dramatic instinct. He waited for the silence to gather to its utmost intensity before he spoke. "I had something to tell you when I came in," he said, "but I thought I had better wait till after supper."

He paused. There was another silence. Henry's and Sylvia's eyes seemed to wax luminous.

Sidney Meeks spoke again. He was enjoying himself immensely. "What relation is Abrahama White to you?" he said.

"She is second cousin to Sylvia. Her mother was Sylvia's mother's cousin," said Henry. "What of it?"

"Nothing, except—" Meeks waited again. He wished to make a coup. He had an instinct for climaxes. "Abrahama had a shock this morning," he said, suddenly.

"A shock?" said Henry.

Sylvia echoed him. "A shock!" she gasped.

"Yes, I thought you hadn't heard of it."

"I've been in the house all day," said Sylvia. "I hadn't seen a soul before you came in." She rose. "Who's taking care of her?" she asked. "She ain't all alone?"

"Sit down," said Sidney. "She's well cared for. Miss Babcock is there. She happened to be out of a place, and Dr. Wallace got her right away."

"Is she going to get over it?" asked Sylvia, anxiously. "I must go over there, anyway, this evening. I always thought a good deal of Abrahama."

"You might as well go over there," said the lawyer. "It isn't quite the thing for me to tell you, but I'm going to. If Henry here can eat flapjacks like those you make, Sylvia, and not say grace, his state of mind is dangerous. I am going to tell you. Dr. Wallace says Abrahama can't live more than a day or two, and— she has made a will and left you all her property."

Chapter II

There was another silence. The husband and wife were pale, with mouths agape like fishes. So little prosperity had come into their lives that they were rendered almost idiotic by its approach.

"Us?" said Sylvia, at length, with a gasp.

"Us?" said Henry.

"Yes, you," said Sidney Meeks.

"What about Rose Fletcher, Abrahama's sister Susy's daughter?" asked Sylvia, presently. "She is her own niece."

"You know Abrahama never had anything to do with Susy after she married John Fletcher," replied the lawyer. "She made her will soon afterward, and cut her off."

"I remember what they said at the time," returned Sylvia. "They all thought John Fletcher was going to marry Abrahama instead of Susy. She was enough sight more suitable age for him. He was too old for Susy, and Abrahama, even if she wasn't young, was a beautiful woman, and smarter than Susy ever thought of being."

"Susy had the kind of smartness that catches men," said the lawyer, with a slight laugh.

"I always wondered if John Fletcher hadn't really done a good deal to make Abrahama think he did want her," said Sylvia. "He was just that kind of man. I never did think much of him. He was handsome and glib, but he was all surface. I guess poor Abrahama had some reason to cut off Susy. I guess there was some double-dealing. I thought so at the time, and now this will makes me think so even more."

Again there was a silence, and again that expression of bewilderment, almost amounting to idiocy, reigned in the faces of the husband and wife.

"I never thought old Abraham White should have made the will he did," said Henry, articulating with difficulty. "Susy had just as much right to the property, and there she was cut off with five hundred dollars, to be paid when she came of age."

"I guess she spent that five hundred on her wedding fix," said Sylvia.

"It was a queer will," stammered Henry.

"I think the old man always looked at Abrahama as his son and heir," said the lawyer. "She was named for him, and his father before him, you know. I always thought the poor old girl deserved the lion's share for being saddled with such a name, anyhow."

"It was a dreadful name, and she was such a beautiful girl and woman," said Sylvia. She already spoke of Abrahama in the past tense. "I wonder where the niece is," she added.

"The last I heard of her she was living with some rich people in New York," replied Meeks. "I think they took her in some capacity after her father and mother died."

9

"I hope she didn't go out to work as hired girl," said Sylvia. "It would have been awful for a granddaughter of Abraham White's to do that. I wonder if Abrahama never wrote to her, nor did anything for her."

"I don't think she ever had the slightest communication with Susy after she married, or her husband, or the daughter," replied Meeks. "In fact, I practically know she did not."

"If the poor girl didn't do well, Abrahama had a good deal to answer for," said Sylvia, thoughtfully. She looked worried. Then again that expression of almost idiotic joy overspread her face. "That old White homestead is beautiful —the best house in town," she said.

"There's fifty acres of land with it, too," said Meeks.

Sylvia and Henry looked at each other. Both hesitated. Then Henry spoke, stammeringly:

"I—never knew—just how much of an income Abrahama had," he said.

"Well," replied the lawyer, "I must say not much—not as much as I wish, for your sakes. You see, old Abraham had a lot of that railroad stock that went to smash ten years ago, and Abrahama lost a good deal. She was a smart woman; she could work and save; but she didn't know any more about business than other women. There's an income of about—well, about six hundred dollars and some odd cents after the taxes and insurance are paid. And she has enough extra in the Alford Bank to pay for her last expenses without touching the principal. And the house is in good repair. She has kept it up well. There won't be any need to spend a cent on repairs for some years."

"Six hundred a year after the taxes and insurance are paid!" said Sylvia. She gaped horribly. Her expression of delight was at once mean and infantile.

"Six hundred a year after the taxes and insurance are paid, and all that land, and that great house!" repeated Henry, with precisely the same expression.

"Not much, but enough to keep things going if you're careful," said Meeks. He spoke deprecatingly, but in reality the sum seemed large to him also. "You know there's an income besides from that fine grass-land," said he. "There's more than enough hay for a cow and horse, if you keep one. You can count on something besides in good hay-years."

Henry looked reflective. Then his face seemed to expand with an enormous idea. "I wonder—" he began.

"You wonder what?" asked Sylvia.

"I wonder—if it wouldn't be cheaper in the end to keep an—automobile and sell all the hay."

Sylvia gasped, and Meeks burst into a roar of laughter.

"I rather guess you don't get me into one of those things, butting into stone walls, and running over children, and scaring horses, with you underneath most of the time, either getting blown up with gasolene or covering your clothes with mud and grease for me to clean off," said Sylvia.

"I thought automobiles were against your principles," said Meeks, still chuckling.

"So they be, the way other folks run 'em," said Henry; "but not the way I'd run 'em."

"We'll have a good, steady horse that won't shy at one, if we have anything," said Sylvia, and her voice had weight.

"There's a good buggy in Abrahama's barn," said Meeks.

Sylvia made an unexpected start. "I think we are wicked as we can be!" she declared, violently. "Here we are talking about that poor woman's things before she's done with them. I'm going right over there to see if I can't be of some use."

"Sit down, Sylvia," said Henry, soothingly, but he, too, looked both angry and ashamed.

"You had better keep still where you are to-night," said Meeks. "Miss Babcock is doing all that anybody can. There isn't much to be done, Dr. Wallace says. To-morrow you can go over there and sit with her, and let Miss Babcock take a nap." Meeks rose as he spoke. "I must be going," he said. "I needn't charge you again not to let anybody know what I've told you before the will is read. It is irregular, but I thought I'd cheer up Henry here a bit."

"No, we won't speak of it," declared the husband and wife, almost in unison.

After Meeks had gone they looked at each other. Both looked disagreeable to the other. Both felt an unworthy suspicion of the other.

"I hope she will get well," Sylvia said, defiantly. "Maybe she will. This is her first shock."

"God knows I hope she will," returned Henry, with equal defiance.

Each of the two was perfectly good and ungrasping, but each accused themselves and each other unjustly because of the possibilities of wrong feeling which they realized. Sylvia did not understand how, in the face of such prosperity, she could wish Abrahama to get well, and she did not understand how her husband could, and Henry's mental attitude was the same.

Sylvia sat down and took some mending. Henry seated himself opposite, and stared at her with gloomy eyes, which yet held latent sparks of joy. "I wish

11

Meeks hadn't told us," he said, angrily.

"So do I," said Sylvia. "I keep telling myself I don't want that poor old woman to die, and I keep telling myself that you don't; but I'm dreadful suspicious of us both. It means so much."

"Just the way I feel," said Henry. "I wish he'd kept his news to himself. It wasn't legal, anyhow."

"You don't suppose it will make the will not stand!" cried Sylvia, with involuntary eagerness. Then she quailed before her husband's stern gaze. "Of course I know it won't make any difference," she said, feebly, and drew her darning-needle through the sock she was mending.

Henry took up a copy of the East Westland *Gazette*. The first thing he saw was the list of deaths, and he seemed to see, quite plainly, Abrahama White's among them, although she was still quick, and he loathed himself. He turned the paper with a rattling jerk to an account of a crime in New York, and the difficulty the police had experienced in taking the guilty man in safety to the police station. He read the account aloud.

"Seems to me the principal thing the New York police protect is the criminals," he said, bitterly. "If they would turn a little of their attention to protecting the helpless women and children, seems to me it would be more to the purpose. They're awful careful of the criminals."

Sylvia did not hear. She assented absently. She thought, in spite of herself, of the good-fortune which was to befall them. She imagined herself mistress of the old White homestead. They would, of course, rent their own little cottage and go to live in the big house. She imagined herself looking through the treasures which Abrahama would leave behind her—then a monstrous loathing of herself seized her. She resolved that the very next morning she would go over and help Miss Babcock, that she would put all consideration of material benefits from her mind. She brought her thoughts with an effort to the article which Henry had just read. She could recall his last words.

"Yes, I think you are right," said she. "I think criminals ought not to be protected. You are right, Henry. I think myself we ought to have a doctor called from Alford to-morrow, if she is no better, and have a consultation. Dr. Wallace is good, but he is only one, and sometimes another doctor has different ideas, and she may get help."

"Yes, I think there ought to be a consultation," said Henry. "I will see about it to-morrow. I will go over there with you myself to-morrow morning. I think the police ought not to protect the criminals, but the people who are injured by them."

"Then there would be no criminals. They would have no chance," said Sylvia,

12

sagely. "Yes, I agree with you, Henry, there ought to be a consultation."

She looked at Henry and he at her, and each saw in the other's face that same ignoble joy, and that same resentment and denial of it.

Neither slept that night. They were up early the next morning. Sylvia was getting breakfast and Henry was splitting wood out in the yard. Presently he came stumbling in. "Come out here," he said. Sylvia followed him to the door. They stepped out in the dewy yard and stood listening. Beneath their feet was soft, green grass strewn with tiny spheres which reflected rainbows. Over their heads was a wonderful sky of the clearest angelic blue. This sky seemed to sing with bell-notes.

"The bell is tolling," whispered Henry. They counted from that instant. When the bell stopped they looked at each other.

"That's her age," said Sylvia.

"Yes," said Henry.

Chapter III

The weather was wonderful on Abrahama White's funeral day. The air had at once the keen zest of winter and the languor of summer. One moment one perceived warm breaths of softly undulating pines, the next it was as if the wind blew over snow. The air at once stimulated and soothed. One breathing it realized youth and an endless vista of dreams ahead, and also the peace of age, and of work well done and deserving the reward of rest. There was something in this air which gave the inhaler the certainty of victory, the courage of battle and of unassailable youth. Even old people, pausing to notice the streamer of crape on Abrahama White's door, felt triumphant and undaunted. It did not seem conceivable, upon such a day, that that streamer would soon flaunt for them.

The streamer was rusty. It had served for many such occasions, and suns and rains had damaged it. People said that Martin Barnes, the undertaker, ought to buy some new crape. Martin was a very old man himself, but he had no imagination for his own funeral. It seemed to him grotesque and impossible that an undertaker should ever be in need of his own ministrations. His solemn wagon stood before the door of the great colonial house, and he and his son-in-law and his daughter, who were his assistants, were engaged at their solemn tasks within.

The daughter, Flora Barnes, was arraying the dead woman in her last robe of state, while her father and brother-in-law waited in the south room across the wide hall. When her task was performed she entered the south room with a

13

gentle pride evident in her thin, florid face.

"She makes a beautiful corpse," she said, in a hissing whisper.

Henry Whitman and his wife were in the room, with Martin Barnes and Simeon Capen, his son-in-law. Barnes and Capen rose at once with pleased interest, Henry and Sylvia more slowly; yet they also had expressions of pleasure, albeit restrained. Both strove to draw their faces down, yet that expression of pleasure reigned triumphant, overcoming the play of the facial muscles. They glanced at each other, and each saw an angry shame in the other's eyes because of this joy.

But when they followed Martin Barnes and his assistants into the parlor, where Abrahama White was laid in state, all the shameful joy passed from their faces. The old woman in her last bed was majestic. The dead face was grand, compelling to other than earthly considerations. Henry and Sylvia forgot the dead woman's little store which she had left behind her. Sylvia leaned over her and wept; Henry's face worked. Nobody except himself had ever known it, but he, although much younger, had had his dreams about the beautiful Abrahama White. He remembered them as he looked at her, old and dead and majestic, with something like the light of her lost beauty in her still face. It was like a rose which has fallen in such a windless atmosphere that its petals retain the places which they have held around its heart.

Henry loved his wife, but this before him was associated with something beyond love, which tended to increase rather than diminish it. When at last they left the room he did what was very unusual with him. He was reticent, like the ordinary middle-aged New-Englander. He took his wife's little, thin, veinous hand and clasped it tenderly. Her bony fingers clung gratefully to his.

When they were all out in the south room Flora Barnes spoke again. "I have never seen a more beautiful corpse," said she, in exactly the same voice which she had used before. She began taking off her large, white apron. Something peculiar in her motion arrested Sylvia's attention. She made a wiry spring at her.

"Let me see that apron," said she, in a voice which corresponded with her action.

Flora recoiled. She turned pale, then she flushed. "What for?"

"Because I want to."

"It's just my apron. I—"

But Sylvia had the apron. Out of its folds dropped a thin roll of black silk. Flora stood before Sylvia. Beads of sweat showed on her flat forehead. She twitched like one about to have convulsions. She was very tall, but Sylvia seemed to fairly loom over her. She held the black silk out stiffly, like a bayonet.

"What is this?" she demanded, in her tense voice.

Flora twitched.

"What is it? I want to know."

"The back breadth," replied Flora in a small, scared voice, like the squeak of a mouse.

"Whose back breadth?"

"Her back breadth."

"*Her* back breadth?"

"Yes."

"Robbing the dead!" said Sylvia, pitilessly. Her tense voice was terrible.

Flora tried to make a stand. "She hadn't any use for it," she squeaked, plaintively.

"Robbing the dead! Its bad enough to rob the living."

"She couldn't have worn that dress without any back breadth while she was living," argued Flora, "but now it don't make any odds. It don't show."

"What were you going to do with it?"

Flora was scared into a storm of injured confession. "You 'ain't any call to talk to me so, Mrs. Whitman," she said. "I've worked hard, and I 'ain't had a decent black silk dress for ten years."

"How can you have a dress made out of a back breadth, I'd like to know?"

"It's just the same quality that Mrs. Hiram Adams's was, and—" Flora hesitated.

"Flora Barnes, you don't mean to say that you're robbing the dead of back breadths till you get enough to make you a whole dress?"

Flora whimpered. "Business has been awful poor lately," she said. "It's been so healthy here we've hardly been able to earn the salt to our porridge. Father won't join the trust, either, and lots of times the undertaker from Alford has got our jobs."

"Business!" cried Sylvia, in horror.

"I can't help it if you do look at it that way," Flora replied, and now she was almost defiant. "Our business is to get our living out of folks' dying. There's no use mincing matters. It's our business, just as working in a shoe-shop is your husband's business. Folks have to have shoes and walk when they're alive, and be laid out nice and buried when they're dead. Our business has been poor. Either Dr. Wallace gives awful strong medicine or East Westland is too healthy. We haven't earned but precious little lately, and I need a whole black silk dress and they don't."

Sylvia eyed her in withering scorn. "Need or not," said she, "the one that owns this back breadth is going to have it. I rather think she ain't going to be laid away without a back breadth to her dress."

With that Sylvia crossed the room and the hall, and entered the parlor. She closed the door behind her. When she came out a few minutes later she was pale but triumphant. "There," said she, "it's back with her, and I've got just this much to say, and no more, Flora Barnes. When you get home you gather up all the back breadths you've got, and you do them up in a bundle, and you put them in that barrel the Ladies' Sewing Society is going to send to the missionaries next week, and don't you ever touch a back breadth again, or I'll tell it right and left, and you'll see how much business you'll have left here, I don't care how sickly it gets."

"If father would—only have joined the trust I never would have thought of such a thing, anyway," muttered Flora. She was vanquished.

"You do it, Flora Barnes."

"Yes, I will. Don't speak so, Mrs. Whitman."

"You had better."

The undertaker and his son-in-law and Henry had remained quite silent. Now they moved toward the door, and Flora followed, red and perspiring. Sylvia heard her say something to her father about the trust on the way to the gate, between the tall borders of box, and heard Martin's surly growl in response.

"Laying it onto the trust," Sylvia said to Henry—"such an awful thing as that!"

Henry assented. He looked aghast at the whole affair. He seemed to catch a glimpse of dreadful depths of feminity which daunted his masculine mind. "To think of women caring enough about dress to do such a thing as that!" he said to himself. He glanced at Sylvia, and she, as a woman, seemed entirely beyond his comprehension.

The whole great house was sweet with flowers. Neighbors had sent the early spring flowers from their door-yards, and Henry and Sylvia had bought a magnificent wreath of white roses and carnations and smilax. They had ordered it from a florist in Alford, and it seemed to them something stupendous—as if in some way it must please even the dead woman herself to have her casket so graced.

"When folks know, they won't think we didn't do all we could," Sylvia whispered to Henry, significantly. He nodded. Both were very busy, even with assistance from the neighbors, and a woman who worked out by the day, in preparing the house for the funeral. Everything had to be swept and cleaned and dusted.

When the hour came, and the people began to gather, the house was veritably set in order and burnished. Sylvia, in the parlor with the chief mourners, glanced about, and eyed the smooth lap of her new black gown with a certain complacency which she could not control. After the funeral was over, and the distant relatives and neighbors who had assisted had eaten a cold supper and departed, and she and Henry were alone in the great house, she said, and he agreed, that everything had gone off beautifully. "Just as she would have wished it if she could have been here and ordered it herself," said Sylvia.

They were both hesitating whether to remain in the house that night or go home. Finally they went home. There was an awe and strangeness over them; besides, they began to wonder if people might not think it odd for them to stay there before the will was read, since they could not be supposed to know it all belonged to them.

It was about two weeks before they were regularly established in the great house, and Horace Allen, the high-school teacher, was expected the next day but one. Henry had pottered about the place, and attended to some ploughing on the famous White grass-land, which was supposed to produce more hay than any piece of land of its size in the county. Henry had been fired with ambition to produce more than ever before, but that day his spirit had seemed to fail him. He sat about gloomily all the afternoon; then he went down for the evening mail, and brought home no letters, but the local paper. Sylvia was preparing supper in the large, clean kitchen. She had been looking over her new treasures all day, and she was radiant. She chattered to her husband like a school-girl.

"Oh, Henry," said she, "you don't know what we've got! I never dreamed poor Abrahama had such beautiful things. I have been up in the garret looking over things, and there's one chest up there packed with the most elegant clothes. I never saw such dresses in my life."

Henry looked at his wife with eyes which loved her face, yet saw it as it was, elderly and plain, with all its youthful bloom faded.

"I don't suppose there is anything that will suit you to have made over," he said. "I suppose they are dresses she had when she was young."

Sylvia colored. She tossed her head and threw back her round shoulders.

Feminine vanity dies hard; perhaps it never dies at all.

"I don't know," she said, defiantly. "Three are colors I used to wear. I have had to wear black of late years, because it was more economical, but you know how much I used to wear pink. It was real becoming to me."

Henry continued to regard his wife's face with perfect love and a perfect cognizance of facts. "You couldn't wear it now," he said.

"I don't know," retorted Sylvia. "I dare say I don't look now as if I could. I have been working hard all day, and my hair is all out of crimp. I ain't so sure but if I did up my hair nice, and wasn't all tuckered out, that I couldn't wear a pink silk dress that's there if I tone it down with black."

"I don't believe you would feel that you could go to meeting dressed in pink silk at your time of life," said Henry.

"Lots of women older than I be wear bright colors," retorted Sylvia, "in places where they are dressy. You don't know anything about dress, Henry."

"I suppose I don't," replied Henry, indifferently.

"I think that pink silk would be perfectly suitable and real becoming if I crimped my hair and had a black lace bonnet to wear with it."

"I dare say."

Henry took his place at the supper-table. It was set in the kitchen. Sylvia was saving herself all the steps possible until Horace Allen returned.

Henry did not seem to have much appetite that night. His face was overcast. Along with his scarcely confessed exultation over his good-fortune he was conscious of an odd indignation. For years he had cherished a sense of injury at his treatment at the hands of Providence; now he felt like a child who, pushing hard against opposition to his desires, has that opposition suddenly removed, and tumbles over backward. Henry had an odd sensation of having ignominiously tumbled over backward, and he missed, with ridiculous rancor, his sense of injury which he had cherished for so many years. After kicking against the pricks for so long, he had come to feel a certain self-righteous pleasure in it which he was now forced to forego.

Sylvia regarded her husband uneasily. Her state of mind had formerly been the female complement of his, but the sense of possession swerved her more easily. "What on earth ails you, Henry Whitman?" she said. "You look awful down-in-the-mouth. Only to think of our having enough to be comfortable for life. I should think you'd be real thankful and pleased."

"I don't know whether I'm thankful and pleased or not," rejoined Henry, morosely.

"Why, Henry Whitman!"

"If it had only come earlier, when we had time and strength to enjoy it," said Henry, with sudden relish. He felt that he had discovered a new and legitimate ground of injury which might console him for the loss of the old.

"We may live a good many years to enjoy it now," said Sylvia.

"I sha'n't; maybe you will," returned Henry, with malignant joy.

Sylvia regarded him with swift anxiety. "Why, Henry, don't you feel well?" she gasped.

"No, I don't, and I haven't for some time."

"Oh, Henry, and you never told me! What is the matter? Hadn't you better see the doctor?"

"Doctor!" retorted Henry, scornfully.

"Maybe he could give you something to help you. Whereabouts do you feel bad, Henry?"

"All over," replied Henry, comprehensively, and he smiled like a satirical martyr.

"All over?"

"Yes, all over—body and soul and spirit. I know just as well as any doctor can tell me that I haven't many years to enjoy anything. When a man has worked as long as I have in a shoe-shop, and worried as much and as long as I have, good-luck finds him with his earthworks about worn out and his wings hitched on."

"Oh, Henry, maybe Dr. Wallace—"

"Maybe he can unhitch the wings?" inquired Henry, with grotesque irony. "No, Sylvia, no doctor living can give medicine strong enough to cure a man of a lifetime of worry."

"But the worry's all over now, Henry."

"What the worry's done ain't over."

Sylvia began whimpering softly. "Oh, Henry, if you talk that way it will take away all my comfort! What do you suppose the property would mean to me without you?"

Then Henry felt ashamed. "Lord, don't worry," he said, roughly. "A man can't say anything to you without upsetting you. I can't tell how long I'll live. Sometimes a man lives through everything. All I meant was, sometimes when good-luck comes to a man it comes so darned late it might just as well not come at all."

"Henry, you don't mean to be wicked and ungrateful?"

"If I am I can't help it. I ain't a hypocrite, anyway. We've got some good-fortune, and I'm glad of it, but I'd been enough sight gladder if it had come sooner, before bad fortune had taken away my rightful taste for it."

"You won't have to work in the shop any longer, Henry."

"I don't know whether I shall or not. What in creation do you suppose I'm going to do all day—sit still and suck my thumbs?"

"You can work around the place."

"Of course I can; but there'll be lots of time when there won't be any work to be done—then what? To tell you the truth of it, Sylvia, I've had my nose held to the grindstone so long I don't know as it's in me to keep away from it and live, now."

Henry had not been at work since Abrahama White's death. He had been often in Sidney Meeks's office; only Sidney Meeks saw through Henry Whitman. One day he laughed in his face, as the two men sat in his office, and Henry had been complaining of the lateness of his good-fortune.

"If your property has come too late, Henry," said he, "what's the use in keeping it? What's the sense of keeping property that only aggravates you because it didn't come in your time instead of the Lord's? I'll draw up a deed of gift on the spot, and Sylvia can sign it when you go home, and you can give the whole biling thing to foreign missions. The Lord knows there's no need for any mortal man to keep anything he doesn't want—unless it's taxes, or a quick consumption, or a wife and children. And as for those last, there doesn't seem to be much need of that lately. I have never seen the time since I came into the world when it was quite so hard to get things, or quite so easy to get rid of them, as it is now. Say the word, Henry, and I'll draw up the deed of gift."

Henry looked confused. His eyes fell before the lawyer's sarcastic glance. "You are talking tomfool nonsense," he said, scowling. "The property isn't mine; it's my wife's."

"Sylvia never crossed you in anything. She'd give it up fast enough if she got it through her head how downright miserable it was making you," returned the lawyer, maliciously. Then Sidney relented. There was something pathetic, even tragic, about Henry Whitman's sheer inability to enjoy as he might once have done the good things of life, and his desperate clutch of them in flat contradiction to his words. "Let's drop it," said the lawyer. "I'm glad you have the property and can have a little ease, even if it doesn't mean to you what it once would. Let's have a glass of that grape wine."

Sidney Meeks had his own small amusement in the world. He was one of those who cannot exist without one, and in lieu of anything else he had turned early in life toward making wines from many things which his native soil produced. He had become reasonably sure, at an early age, that he should achieve no great success in his profession. Indeed, he was lazily conscious that he had no fierce ambition to do so. Sidney Meeks was not an ambitious man in large matters. But he had taken immense comfort in toiling in a little vineyard behind his house, and also in making curious wines and cordials from many unusual ingredients. Sidney had stored in his cellar wines from elder flowers, from elderberries, from daisies, from rhubarb, from clover, and currants, and many other fruits and flowers, besides grapes. He was wont to dispense these curious brews to his callers with great pride. But he took especial pride in a grape wine which he had made from selected grapes thirty years ago. This wine had a peculiar bouquet due to something which Sidney had added to the grape-juice, the secret of which he would never divulge.

It was some of this golden wine which Sidney now produced. Henry drank two glasses, and the tense muscles around his mouth relaxed. Sidney smiled. "Don't know what gives it that scent and taste, do you?" asked Sidney. "Well, I know. It's simple enough, but nobody except Sidney Meeks has ever found it out. I tell you, Henry, if a man hasn't set the river on fire, realized his youthful dreams, and all that, it is something to have found out something that nobody else has, no matter how little it is, if you have got nerve enough to keep it to yourself."

Henry fairly laughed. His long, hollow cheeks were slightly flushed. When he got home that night he looked pleasantly at Sylvia, preparing supper. But Sylvia did not look as radiant as she had done since her good-fortune. She said nothing ailed her, in response to his inquiry as to whether she felt well or not, but she continued gloomy and taciturn, which was most unusual with her, especially of late.

"What in the world is the matter with you, Sylvia?" Henry asked. The influence of Sidney Meeks's wine had not yet departed from him. His cheeks were still flushed, his eyes brilliant.

Then Sylvia roused herself. "Nothing is the matter," she replied, irritably, and immediately she became so gay that had Henry himself been in his usual mood he would have been as much astonished as by her depression. Sylvia began talking and laughing, relating long stories of new discoveries which she had made in the house, planning for Horace Allen's return.

"He's going to have that big southwest room and the little one out of it," Sylvia said. "To-morrow you must get the bed moved into the little one, and I'll get the big room fixed up for a study. He'll be tickled to pieces. There's beautiful furniture in the room now. I suppose he'll think it's beautiful. It's terrible old-fashioned. I'd rather have a nice new set of bird's-eye maple to my taste, and a brass bedstead, but I know he'll like this better. It's solid old mahogany."

"Yes, he'll be sure to like it," assented Henry.

After supper, although Sylvia did not relapse into her taciturn mood, Henry went and sat by himself on the square colonial porch on the west side of the house. He sat gazing at the sky and the broad acres of grass-land. Presently he heard feminine voices in the house, and knew that two of the neighbors, Mrs. Jim Jones and Mrs. Sam Elliot, had called to see Sylvia. He resolved that he would stay where he was until they were gone. He loved Sylvia, but women in the aggregate disturbed and irritated him; and for him three women were sufficient to constitute an aggregate.

Henry sat on the fine old porch with its symmetrical pillars. He had an arm-chair which he tilted back against the house wall, and he was exceedingly comfortable. The air was neither warm nor cold. There was a clear red in the west and only one rose-tinged cloud the shape of a bird's wing. He could hear the sunset calls of birds and the laughter of children. Once a cow lowed. A moist sense of growing things, the breath of spring, came into his nostrils. Henry realized that he was very happy. He realized for the first time, with peaceful content, not with joy so turbulent that it was painful and rebellious, that he and his wife owned this grand old house and all those fair acres. He was filled with that great peace of possession which causes a man to feel that he is safe from the ills of life. Henry felt fenced in and guarded. Then suddenly the sense of possession upon earth filled his whole soul with the hope of possession after death. Henry felt, for the first time in his life, as if he had a firm standing-ground for faith. For the first time he looked at the sunset sky, he listened to the birds and children, he smelled the perfume of the earth, and there was no bitterness in his soul. He smiled a smile of utter peace which harmonized with it all, and the conviction of endless happiness and a hereafter seemed to expand all his consciousness.

Chapter IV

The dining-room in the White homestead was a large, low room whose southward windows were shaded at this season with a cloud of gold-green young grape leaves. The paper was a nondescript pattern, a large satin scroll on white. The room was wainscoted in white, and the panel-work around the great chimney was beautiful. A Franklin stove with a pattern of grape-vines was built into the chimney under the high mantel. Sylvia regarded this dubiously.

"I don't think much of that old-fashioned Franklin stove," she told Henry. "Why Abrahama had it left in, after she had her nice furnace, beats me. Seems to me we had better have it taken out, and have a nice board, covered with paper to match this on the room, put there instead. There's a big roll of the paper up garret, and it ain't faded a mite."

"Mr. Allen will like it just the way it is," said Henry, regarding the old stove with a sneaking admiration of which he was ashamed. It had always seemed to him that Sylvia's taste must be better than his. He had always thought vaguely of women as creatures of taste.

"I think maybe he'll like a fire in it sometimes," he said, timidly.

"A fire, when there's a furnace?"

"I mean chilly days in the fall, before we start the furnace."

"Then we could have that nice air-tight that we had in the other house put up. If we had a fire in this old thing the heat would all go up chimney."

"But it would look kind of pretty."

"I was brought up to think a fire was for warmth, not for looks," said Sylvia, tartly. She had lost the odd expression which Henry had dimly perceived several days before, or she was able to successfully keep it in abeyance; still, there was no doubt that a strange and subtle change had occurred within the woman. Henry was constantly looking at her when she spoke, because he vaguely detected unwonted tones in her familiar voice; that voice which had come to seem almost as his own. He was constantly surprised at a look in the familiar eyes, which had seemed heretofore to gaze at life in entire unison with his own.

He often turned upon Sylvia and asked her abruptly if she did not feel well, and what was the matter; and when she replied, as she always did, that nothing whatever was the matter, continued to regard her with a frown of perplexity, from which she turned with a switch of her skirts and a hitch of her slender shoulders. Sylvia, while she still evinced exultation over her new possessions, seemed to do so fiercely and defiantly.

When Horace Allen arrived she greeted him, and ushered him into her new domain with a pride which had in it something almost repellent. At supper-time she led him into the dining-room and glanced around, then at him.

"Well," said she, "don't you think it was about time we had something nice like this, after we had pulled and tugged for nothing all our lives? Don't you think we deserve it if anybody does?"

"I certainly do," replied Horace Allen, warmly; yet he regarded her with somewhat the same look of astonishment as Henry. It did not seem to him that

23

it could be Sylvia Whitman who was speaking. The thought crossed his mind, as he took his place at the table, that possibly coming late in life, after so many deprivations, good-fortune had disturbed temporarily the even balance of her good New England sense.

Then he looked about him with delight. "I say, this is great!" he cried, boyishly. There was something incurably boyish about Horace Allen, although he was long past thirty. "By George, that Chippendale sideboard is a beauty," he said, gazing across at a fine old piece full of dull high lights across its graceful surfaces.

Sylvia colored with pleasure, but she had been brought up to disclaim her possessions to others than her own family. "Mrs. Jim Jones has got a beautiful one she bought selling Calkin's soap," she said. "She thinks it's prettier than this, and I must say it's real handsome. It's solid oak and has a looking-glass on it. This hasn't got any glass."

Horace laughed. He gazed at a corner-closet with diamond-paned doors.

"That is a perfectly jolly closet, too," he said; "and those are perfect treasures of old dishes."

"I think they are rather pretty," said Henry. He was conscious of an admiration for the old blue-and-white ware with its graceful shapes and quaint decorations savoring of mystery and the Far East, but he realized that his view was directly opposed to his wife's. This time Sylvia spoke quite in earnest. As far as the Indian china was concerned, she had her convictions. She was a cheap realist to the bone.

She sniffed. "I suppose there's those that likes it," said she, "but as for me, I can't see how anybody with eyes in their heads can look twice at old, cloudy, blue stuff like that when they can have nice, clear, white ware, with flowers on it that *are* flowers, like this Calkin's soap set. There ain't a thing on the china in that closet that's natural. Whoever saw a prospect all in blue, the trees and plants, and heathen houses, and the heathen, all blue? I like things to be natural, myself."

Horace laughed, and extended his plate for another piece of pie.

"It's an acquired taste," he said.

"I never had any time to acquire tastes. I kept what the Lord gave me," said Sylvia, but she smiled. She was delighted because Horace had taken a second piece of pie.

"I didn't know as you'd relish our fare after living in a Boston hotel all your vacation," said she.

"People can talk about hotel tables all they want to," declared Horace. "Give me home cooking like yours every time. I haven't eaten a blessed thing that tasted good since I went away."

Henry and Sylvia looked lovingly at Horace. He was a large man, blond, with a thick shock of fair hair, and he wore gray tweeds rather loose for him, which had always distressed Sylvia. She had often told Henry that it seemed to her if he would wear a nice suit of black broadcloth it would be more in keeping with his position as high-school principal. He wore a red tie, too, and Sylvia had an inborn conviction that red was not to be worn by fair people, male or female.

However, she loved and admired Horace in spite of these minor drawbacks, and had a fiercely maternal impulse of protection towards him. She was convinced that every mother in East Westland, with a marriageable daughter, and every daughter, had matrimonial designs upon him; and she considered that none of them were good enough for him. She did not wish him to marry in any case. She had suspicions about young women whom he might have met while on his vacation.

After supper, when the dishes had been cleared away, and they sat in the large south room, and Horace had admired that and its furnishings, Sylvia led up to the subject.

"I suppose you know a good many people in Boston," she remarked.

"Yes," replied Horace. "You know, I was born and brought up and educated there, and lived there until my people died."

"I suppose you know a good many young ladies."

"Thousands," said Horace; "but none of them will look at me."

"You didn't ask them?"

"Not all, only a few, but they wouldn't."

"I'd like to know why not?"

Then Henry spoke. "Sylvia," he said, "Mr. Allen is only joking."

"I hope he is," Sylvia said, severely. "He's too young to think of getting married. It makes me sick, though, to see the way girls chase any man, and their mothers, too, for that matter. Mrs. Jim Jones and Mrs. Sam Elliot both came while you were gone, Mr. Allen. They said they thought maybe we wouldn't take a boarder now we have come into property, and maybe you would like to go there, and I knew just as well as if they had spoken what they had in their minds. There's Minnie Jones as homely as a broom, and there's Carrie Elliot getting older, and—"

"Sylvia!" said Henry.

25

"I don't care. Mr. Allen knows what's going on just as well as I do. Neither of those women can cook fit for a cat to eat, let alone anything else. Lucy Ayres came here twice on errands, too, and—"

But Horace colored, and spoke suddenly. "I didn't know that you would take me back," he said. "I was afraid—"

"We don't need to, as far as money goes," said Sylvia, "but Mr. Whitman and I like to have the company, and you never make a mite of trouble. That's what I told Mrs. Jim Jones and Mrs. Sam Elliot."

"I'm glad he's got back," Henry said, after Horace had gone up-stairs for the night and the couple were in their own room, a large one out of the sitting-room.

"So am I," assented Sylvia. "It seems real good to have him here again, and he's dreadful tickled with his new rooms. I guess he's glad he wasn't shoved off onto Mrs. Jim Jones or Mrs. Sam Elliot. I don't believe he has an idea of getting married to any girl alive. He ain't a mite silly over the girls, if they are all setting their caps at him. I'm sort of sorry for Lucy Ayres. She's a pretty girl, and real ladylike, and I believe she'd give all her old shoes to get him."

"Look out, he'll hear you," charged Henry. Their room was directly under the one occupied by Horace.

Presently the odor of a cigar floated into their open window.

"I should know he'd got home. Smoking is an awful habit," Sylvia said, with a happy chuckle.

"He'd do better if he smoked a pipe," said Henry. Henry smoked a pipe.

"If a man is going to smoke at all, I think he had better smoke something besides a smelly old pipe," said Sylvia. "It seems to me, with all our means, you might smoke cigars now, Henry. I saw real nice ones advertised two for five cents the other day, and you needn't smoke more than two a day."

Henry sniffed slightly.

"I suppose you think women don't know anything about cigars," said Sylvia; "but I can smell, anyhow, and I know Mr. Allen is smoking a real good cigar."

"Yes, he is," assented Henry.

"And I don't believe he pays more than a cent apiece. His cigars have gilt papers around them, and I know as well as I want to they're cheap; I know a cent apiece is a much as he pays. He smokes so many he can't pay more than that."

Henry sniffed again, but Sylvia did not hear. She had one deaf ear, and she was lying on her sound one. Then they fell asleep, and it was some time before both woke suddenly. A sound had wakened Henry, an odor Sylvia. Henry had heard a door open, forcing him into wakefulness; Sylvia had smelled the cigar again. She nudged her husband. Just then the tall clock in the sitting-room struck ten deliberately.

"It's late, and he's awake, smoking, now," whispered Sylvia.

Henry said nothing. He only grunted.

"Don't you think it's queer?"

"Oh no. I guess he's only reading," replied Henry. He had a strong masculine loyalty towards Horace, as another man. He waited until he heard Sylvia's heavy, regular breathing again. Then he slipped out of bed and stole to the window. It was a strange night, very foggy, but the fog was shot through with shafts of full moonlight. The air was heavy and damp and sweet. Henry listened a moment at the bedroom window, then he tiptoed out into the sitting-room. He stole across the hall into the best parlor. He raised a window in there noiselessly, looked out, and listened. There was a grove of pines and spruces on that side of the house. There was a bench under a pine. Upon this bench Henry gradually perceived a whiteness more opaque than that of the fog. He heard a voice, then a responsive murmur. Then the fragrant smoke of a cigar came directly in his face. Henry shook his head. He remained motionless a moment. Then he left the room, and going into the hall stole up-stairs. The door of the southwest chamber stood wide open. Henry entered. He was trembling like a woman. He loved the young man, and suspicions, like dreadful, misshapen monsters, filled his fancy. He peeped into the little room which he and Sylvia had fitted up as a bedroom for Horace, and it was vacant.

Henry went noiselessly back down-stairs and into his own room. He lay down without disturbing his wife, but he did not fall asleep. After what seemed to him a long time he heard a stealthy footstep on the stair, and again smelled the aroma of a cigar which floated down from overhead.

That awoke Sylvia. "I declare, he's smoking again," she murmured, sleepily. "It's a dreadful habit."

27

Henry made no reply. He breathed evenly, pretending to be asleep.

Chapter V

Although it was easy for a man, especially for a young marriageable man, to obtain board in East Westland, it was not so easy for a woman; and the facts of her youth and good looks, and presumably marriageable estate, rendered it still more difficult. There was in the little village a hotel, so-called, which had formerly been the tavern. It was now the East Westland House. Once it had been the Sign of the Horse. The old sign-board upon which a steed in flaming red, rampant upon a crude green field against a crude blue sky, had been painted by some local artist, all unknown to fame, and long since at rest in the village graveyard, still remained in the hotel attic, tilted under the dusty eaves.

The Sign of the Horse had been in former days a flourishing hostelry, before which, twice a day, the Boston and the Alford stages had drawn up with mighty flourishes of horns and gallant rearings of jaded steeds. Scarcely a night but it had been crowded by travellers who stayed overnight for the sake of the good beds and the good table and good bar. Now there was no bar. East Westland was a strictly temperance village, and all the liquor to be obtained was exceedingly bad, and some declared diluted by the waters of the village pond.

There was a very small stock of rum, gin, and whiskey, and very young and morbid California wines, kept at the village drug store, and dispensed by Albion Bennet. Albion required a deal of red-tape before he would sell even these doubtful beverages for strictly medicinal purposes. He was in mortal terror of being arrested and taken to the county-seat at Newholm for violation of the liquor law. Albion, although a young and sturdy man not past his youth, was exceedingly afraid of everything. He was unmarried, and boarded at the hotel. There he was divided between fear of burglars, if he slept on the first floor, and of fire if he slept on the second. He compromised by sleeping on the second, with a sufficient length of stout, knotted muslin stowed away in his trunk, to be attached to the bed-post and reach the ground in case of a conflagration.

There was no bank in East Westland, none nearer than Alford, six miles away, and poor Albion was at his wit's end to keep his daily receipts with safety to them and himself. He had finally hit upon the expedient of leaving them every night with Sidney Meeks, who was afraid of nothing. "If anything happens to your money, Albion," said Sidney, "I'll make it good, even if I have to sell my wine-cellar." Albion was afraid even to keep a revolver. His state of terror was pitiable, and the more so because he had a fear of betraying it, which was to some extent the most cruel fear of all. Sidney Meeks was probably the only person in East Westland who understood how it was with him, and he kept his knowledge to himself. Sidney was astute on a diagnosis of his fellow-men's mentalities, and he had an almost womanly compassion even for those weaknesses of which he himself was incapable.

"Good; I'll keep what you have in your till every night for you, and welcome, Albion," he had said. "I understand how you feel, living in the hotel the way you do."

"Nobody knows who is coming and going," said Albion, blinking violently.

"Of course one doesn't, and nobody would dream of coming to my house. Everybody knows I am as poor as Job's off ox. You might get a revolver, but I wouldn't recommend it. You look to me as if you might sleep too sound to make it altogether safe."

"I do sleep pretty sound," admitted Albion, although he did not quite see the force of the other man's argument.

"Just so. Any man who sleeps very sound has no right to keep a loaded revolver by him. He seldom, if ever, wakes up thoroughly if he hears a noise, and he's mighty apt to blaze away at the first one he sees, even if it's his best friend. No, it is not safe."

"I don't think it's very safe myself," said Albion, in a relieved tone. "Miss Hart is always prowling around the house. She doesn't sleep very well, and she's always smelling smoke or hearing burglars. She's timid, like most women. I might shoot her if I was only half awake and she came opposite my door."

"Exactly," said Sidney Meeks. When Albion went away he stared after his bulky, retreating back with a puzzled expression. He shook his head. Fear was the hardest thing in the world for him to understand. "That great, able-bodied man must feel mighty queer," he muttered, as he stowed away the pile of greasy bank-notes and the nickels collected at the soda-fountain in a pile of disordered linen in a bureau drawer. He chuckled to himself at the eagerness with which Albion had seized upon the fancy of his shooting Miss Hart.

Lucinda Hart kept the hotel. She had succeeded to its proprietorship when her father died. She was a middle-aged woman who had been pretty in a tense, nervous fashion. Now the prettiness had disappeared under the strain of her daily life. It was a hard struggle to keep the East Westland House and make both ends meet. She had very few regular boarders, and transients were not as numerous as they had been in the days of the stage-coaches. Now commercial travellers and business men went to Alford overnight instead of remaining at

29

East Westland. Miss Hart used the same feather-beds which had once been esteemed so luxurious. She kept them clean, well aired, and shaken, and she would not have a spring-bed or a hair mattress in the house. She was conservatism itself. She could no more change and be correct to her own understanding than the multiplication table.

"Feather-beds are good enough for anybody who stays in this hotel, I don't care who it is," she said. She would not make an exception, even for Miss Eliza Farrel, the assistant teacher in the high school, although she had, with a distrust of the teacher's personality, a great respect for her position. She was inexorable even when the teacher proposed furnishing a spring-bed and mattress at her own expense. "I'd be willing to accommodate, and buy them myself, but it is a bad example," she said, firmly. "Things that were good enough for our fathers and mothers are good enough for us. Good land! people ain't any different from what they used to be. We haven't any different flesh nor any different bones."

Miss Hart had a theory that many of the modern diseases might be traced directly to the eschewing of feather-beds. "Never heard of appendicitis in my father's time, when folks slept on good, soft feather-beds, and got their bones and in'ards rested," she said.

Miss Hart was as timid in her way as Albion Bennet. She never got enough control of her nervous fears to secure many hours of sound sleep. She never was able to wholly rid herself of the conviction that her own wakefulness and watchfulness was essential to the right running of all the wheels of the universe, although she would have been shocked had she fairly known her own attitude. She patrolled the house by night, moving about the low, uneven corridors with a flickering candle—for she was afraid to carry a kerosene lamp—like a wandering spirit.

She was suspicious, too. She never lodged a stranger overnight but she had grave doubts of his moral status. She imagined him a murderer escaped from justice, and compared his face with the pictures of criminals in the newspapers, or she was reasonably sure that he was dishonest, although she had little to tempt him. She employed one chambermaid and a stable-boy, and did the cooking herself. Miss Hart was not a good cook. She used her thin, tense hands too quickly. She was prone to over-measures of saleratus, to under-measures of sugar and coffee. She erred both from economy and from the haste which makes waste. Miss Eliza Farrel often turned from the scanty, poorly cooked food which was place before her with disgust, but she never seemed to lose an ounce of her firm, fair flesh, nor a shade of her sweet color.

Miss Eliza Farrel was an anomaly. She was so beautiful that her beauty detracted from her charm for both sexes. It was so perfect as to awaken suspicion in a world where nothing is perfect from the hand of nature. Then, too, she was manifestly, in spite of her beauty, not in the first flush of youth, and had, it seemed, no right to such perfection of body. Also her beauty was of a type which people invariably associate with things which are undesirable to the rigidly particular, and East Westland was largely inhabited by the rigidly particular.

East Westland was not ignorant. It read of the crimes and follies of the times, but it read of them with a distinct and complacent sense of superiority. It was as if East Westland said: "It is desirable to read of these things, of these doings among the vicious and the worldly, that we may understand what *we* are." East Westland looked upon itself in its day and generation as a lot among the cities of the plain.

It seemed inconceivable that East Westland people should have recognized the fact that Miss Farrel's beauty was of a suspicious type, but they must have had an instinctive knowledge of it. From the moment that Miss Farrel appeared in the village, although she had the best of references, not a woman would admit her into her house as a boarder, and the hotel, with its feather-beds and poor table, was her only resource. Women said of her that she was made up, that no woman of her age ever looked as she did and had a perfectly irreproachable moral character.

As for the men, they admired her timidly, sheepishly, and also a trifle contemptuously. They did not admit openly the same opinion as the women with regard to the legitimacy of her charms, but they did maintain it secretly. It did not seem possible to many of them that a woman could look just as Eliza Farrel did and be altogether natural. As for her character, they also agreed with the feminine element secretly, although they openly declared the women were jealous of such beauty. It did not seem that such a type could be anything except a dangerous one.

Miss Eliza Farrel was a pure blonde, as blond as a baby. There was not a line nor blemish in her pure, fine skin. The flush on her rounded cheeks and her full lips was like a baby's. Her dimples were like a baby's. Her blond hair was thick and soft with a pristine softness and thickness which is always associated with the hair of a child. Her eyebrows were pencilled by nature, as if nature had been art. Her smile was as fixedly radiant as a painted cherub's. Her figure had that exuberance and slenderness at various portions which no woman really believes in. She looked like a beautiful doll, with an unvarying loveliness of manner and disposition under all vicissitudes of life, but she was undoubtedly something more than a doll.

Even the women listened dubiously and incredulously when she talked. They had never heard a woman talk about such things in the way she did. She had a fine education, being a graduate of one of the women's colleges. She was an accomplished musician and a very successful teacher. Her pupils undoubtedly progressed, although they did not have the blind love and admiration which pupils usually have for a beautiful teacher. To this there was one exception.

Miss Farrel always smiled, never frowned or reprimanded. It was said that Miss Farrel had better government than Miss Florence Dean, the other assistant. Miss Dean was plain and saturnine, and had no difficulty in obtaining a good boarding-place, even with the mother of a marriageable daughter, who had taken her in with far-sighted alacrity. She dreamed of business calls concerning school matters, which Mr. Horace Allen, the principal, might be obliged to make, and she planned to have her daughter, who was a very pretty girl, in evidence. But poor Miss Farrel was thrown back upon the mercies of Miss Hart and the feather-beds and the hotel.

There were other considerations besides the feather-beds and the poor fare which conspired to render the hotel an undesirable boarding-place. Miss Farrel might as well have been under the espionage of a private detective as with Miss Hart. If Miss Hart was suspicious of dire mischief in the cases of her other boarders, she was certain in the case of Eliza Farrel. She would not have admitted her under her roof at all had she not been forced thereto by the necessity for money. Miss Hart herself took care of Miss Farrel's room sometimes. She had no hesitation whatever in looking through her bureau drawers; indeed, she considered it a duty which she owed herself and the character of her house. She had taken away the keys on purpose, and had told miss Farrel, without the slightest compunction, that they were lost. The trunks were locked, and she had never been able to possess herself of the keys, but she felt sure that they contained, if not entire skeletons, at least scattered bones.

She discovered once, quite in open evidence on Miss Farrel's wash-stand, a little porcelain box of pink-tinted salve, and she did not hesitate about telling Hannah, her chambermaid, the daughter of a farmer in the vicinity, and a girl who was quite in her confidence. She called Hannah into the room and displayed the box. "This is what she uses," she said, solemnly.

Hannah, who was young, but had a thick, colorless skin, nodded with an inscrutable expression.

"I have always thought she used something on her face," said Miss Hart. "You can't cheat *me*."

Hannah took up a little, ivory-backed nail-polisher which was also on the wash-stand. "What do you suppose this is?" she asked, timidly, in an awed whisper.

"How do I know? I never use such things myself, and I never knew women who did before," said Miss Hart, severely. "I dare say, after she puts the paint on, she has to use something to smooth it down where the natural color of the skin begins. How do I know?"

Hannah laid the nail-polisher beside the box of salve. She was very much in love with the son of the farmer who lived next to her father's. The next Thursday afternoon was her afternoon off. She watched her chance, and stole into Miss Farrel's room, applied with trembling fingers a little of the nail-salve to her cheeks, then carefully rubbed it all off with the polisher. She then went to her own room, put on a hat and thick veil, and succeeded in getting out of the hotel without meeting Miss Hart. She was firmly convinced that she was painted, and that her cheeks had the lovely peach-bloom of Miss Farrel's.

It seems sometimes as if one's own conviction concerning one's self goes a long way towards establishing that of other people. Hannah, that evening, when she met the young man whom she loved, felt that she was a beauty like Miss Eliza Farrel, and before she went home he had told her how pretty she was and asked her to marry him, and Hannah had consented, reserving the right to work enough longer to earn a little more money. She wished to be married in a white lace gown like one in Miss Farrel's closet. Miss Hart had called Hannah in to look at it one morning when Miss Farrel was at school.

"What do you suppose a school-teacher can want of a dress like this here in East Westland?" Miss Hart had asked, severely. "She can't wear it to meeting, or a Sunday-school picnic, or a church sociable, or even to a wedding in this place. Look at it. It's cut low-neck."

Hannah had looked. That night she had, in the secrecy of her own room, examined her own shoulders, and decided that although they might not be as white as Miss Farrel's, they were presumably as well shaped. She had resolved then and there to be married in a dress like that. Along with her love-raptures came the fairy dream of the lace gown. For once in her life she would be dressed like a princess.

When she told Miss Hart she was going to be married, her mistress sniffed. "You can do just as you like, and you will do just as you like, whether or no," she said; "but you are a poor fool. Here you are getting good wages, and having it all to spend on yourself; and you ain't overworked, and you'll find out you'll be overworked and have a whole raft of young ones, and not a cent of wages, except enough to keep soul and body together, and just enough to wear so you won't be took up for going round indecent. I've seen enough of such kind of work."

"Amos will make a real good husband; everybody says he's the best match anywhere around," replied Hannah, crimson with blushes and halfcrying.

Miss Hart sniffed again. "Jump into the fire if you want to," said she. "I hope you ain't going before fall, and leave me in the lurch in hot weather, and preserves to be put up."

Hannah said she would not think of getting married before November. She did not say a word about the white lace gown, but that evening the desire to look at it again waxed so strong within her that she could not resist it. She was sitting in her own room, after lighting the kerosene lamp in the corridor opposite Miss Farrel's room, which was No. 20, and she was thinking hard about the lace gown, and wondering how much it cost, when she started suddenly. As she sat beside her window, her own lamp not yet lit, she had seen a figure flit past in the misty moonlight, and she was sure it was Miss Farrel. She reflected quickly that it was Thursday evening, when Miss Hart always went to prayer-meeting. Hannah had a cold and had stayed at home, although it was her day off. Miss Hart cherished the belief that her voice was necessary to sustain the singing at any church meeting. She had, in her youth, possessed a fine contralto voice. She possessed only the remnant of one now, but she still sang in the choir, because nobody had the strength of mind to request her to resign. Sunday after Sunday she stood in her place and raised her voice, which was horribly hoarse and hollow, in the sacred tunes, and people shivered and endured. Miss Hart never missed a Sunday service, a choir rehearsal, or a Thursday prayer-meeting, and she did not on that Thursday evening.

Hannah went to her door and listened. She heard laughter down in the room which had been the bar but was now the office. A cloud of tobacco smoke floated from there through the corridor. Hannah drew it in with a sense of delicious peace. Her lover smoked, and somehow the odor seemed to typify to her domestic happiness and mystery. She listened long, looking often at the clock on the wall. "She must be gone," she thought, meaning Miss Hart. She was almost sure that the figure which she had seen flitting under her window in the moonlight was that of the school-teacher. Finally she could not resist the temptation any longer. She hurried down the corridor until she reached No. 20. She tapped and waited, then she tapped and waited again. There was no response. Hannah tried the door. It was locked. She took her chambermaid's key and unlocked the door, looking around her fearfully. Then she opened the door and slid in. She locked the door behind her. Then straight to the closet she went, and that beautiful lace robe seemed to float out towards her. Hannah slipped off her own gown, and in a few moments she stood before the looking-glass, transformed.

She was so radiant, so pleased, that a flush came out on her thick skin; her

34

eyes gleamed blue. The lace gown fitted her very well. She turned this way and that. After all, her neck was not bad, not as white, perhaps, as Miss Farrel's, but quite lovely in shape. She walked glidingly across the room, looking over her shoulder at the trail of lace. She was unspeakably happy. She had a lover, and she was a woman in a fine gown for the first time in her life. The gown was not her own, but she would have one like it. She did not realize that this gown was not hers. She was fairly radiant with the possession of her woman's birthright, this poor farmer's daughter, in whom the instincts of her kind were strong. She glided across the room many times. She surveyed herself in the glass. Every time she looked she seemed to herself more beautiful, and there was something good and touching in this estimation of herself, for she seemed to see herself with her lover's eyes as well as her own.

Finally she sat down in Miss Farrel's rocker; she crossed her knees and viewed with delight the fleecy fall of lace to the floor. Then she fell to dreaming, and her dreams were good. In that gown of fashion she dreamed the dreams of the life to which the women of her race were born. She dreamed of her good housewifery; she dreamed of the butter she would make; she dreamed of her husband coming home to meals all ready and well cooked. She dreamed, underneath the other dreams, of children coming home. She had no realization of the time she sat there. At last she started and turned white. She had heard a key turn in the lock. Then Miss Farrel entered the room— Miss Eliza Farrel, magnificent in pale gray, with a hat trimmed with roses crowning her blond head. Hannah cowered. She tried to speak, but only succeeded in making a sound as if she were deaf and dumb.

Then Miss Farrel spoke. There was a weary astonishment and amusement in her tone, but nothing whatever disturbed or harsh. "Oh, is it you, Hannah?" she said.

Hannah murmured something unintelligible.

Miss Farrel went on, sweetly: "So you thought you would try on my lace gown, Hannah?" she said. "It fits you very well. I see your hands are clean. I am glad of that. Now please take it off and put on your own dress."

Hannah stood up. She was abject.

"There is nothing for you to be afraid of," said Miss Farrel. "Only take off the gown and put on your own, or I am afraid Miss Hart—"

Miss Hart's name acted like a terrible stimulus. Hannah unfastened the lace gown with fingers trembling with haste. She stepped out of the shimmering circle which it made; she was in her own costume in an incredibly short space of time, and the lace gown was in its accustomed place in the closet. Then suddenly Miss Hart opened the door.

35

"I thought I saw a light," said she. She looked from one to the other. "It is after eleven o'clock," she said, further.

"Yes," said Miss Farrel, sweetly. "I have been working. I had to look over some exercises. I think I am not quite well. Have you any digitalis in the house, Miss Hart? Hannah here does not know. I was sorry to disturb her, and she does not know. I have an irritable heart, and digitalis helps it."

"No, I have not got any digitalis," replied Miss Hart, shortly. She gave the hard sound to the *g*, and she looked suspiciously at both women. However, Miss Farrel was undoubtedly pale, and Miss Hart's face relaxed.

"Go back to your room," she said to Hannah. "You won't be fit for a thing to-morrow." Then she said to Miss Farrel: "I don't know what you mean by digitalis. I haven't got any, but I'll mix you up some hot essence of peppermint, and that's the best thing I know of for anything."

"Thank you," said Miss Farrel. She had sank into a chair, and had her hand over her heart.

"I'll have it here in a minute," said Miss Hart. She went out, and Hannah followed her, but not before she and Miss Eliza Farrel had exchanged looks which meant that each had a secret of the other to keep as a precious stolen jewel.

Chapter VI

The next morning Henry was very quiet at the breakfast-table. He said good-morning to Horace in almost a surly manner, and Sylvia glanced from one to the other of the two men. After Horace had gone to school she went out in the front yard to interview Henry, who was pottering about the shrubs which grew on either side of the gravel walk.

"What on earth ailed you and Mr. Allen this morning?" she began, abruptly.

Henry continued digging around the roots of a peony. "I don't know as anything ailed us. I don't know what you are driving at," he replied, lying unhesitatingly.

"Something did ail you. You can't cheat me."

"I don't know what you are driving at."

"Something did ail you. You'll spoil that peony. You've got all the weeds out. What on earth are you digging round it that way for? What ailed you?"

"I don't know what you are driving at."

"You can't cheat me. Something is to pay. For the land's sake, leave that peony alone, and get the weeds out from around that syringa bush. You act as if you were possessed. What ailed you and Mr. Allen this morning? I want to know."

"I don't know what you are driving at," Henry said again, but he obediently turned his attention to the syringa bush. He always obeyed a woman in small matters, and reserved his masculine prerogatives for large ones.

Sylvia returned to the house. Her mouth was set hard. Nobody knew how on occasions Sylvia longed for another woman to whom to speak her mind. She loved her husband, but no man was capable of entirely satisfying all her moods. She started to go to the attic on another exploring expedition; then she stopped suddenly, reflecting. The end of her reflection was that she took off her gingham apron, tied on a nice white one trimmed with knitted lace, and went down the street to Mrs. Thomas P. Ayres's. Thomas P. Ayres had been dead for the last ten years, but everybody called his widow Mrs. T. P. Ayres. Mrs. Ayres kept no maid. She had barely enough income to support herself and her daughter. She came to the door herself. She was a small, delicate, pretty woman, and her little thin hands were red with dish-water.

"Good-morning," she said, in a weary, gentle fashion. "Come in, Mrs. Whitman, won't you?" As she spoke she wrinkled her forehead between her curves of gray hair. She had always wrinkled her forehead, but in some inscrutable fashion the wrinkles had always smoothed out. Her forehead was smooth as a girl's. She smiled, and the smile was exactly in accord with her voice; it was weary and gentle. There was not the slightest joy in it, only a submission and patience which might evince a slight hope of joy to come.

"I've got so much to do I ought not to stop long," said Sylvia, "but I thought I'd run in a minute."

"Walk right in," said Mrs. Ayres, and Sylvia followed her into the sitting-room, which was quite charming, with a delicate flowered paper and a net-work of green vines growing in bracket-pots, which stood all about. There were also palms and ferns. The small room looked like a bower, although it was very humbly furnished. Sylvia sat down.

"You always look so cool in here," she said, "and it's a warm morning for so early in the season."

"It's the plants and vines, I guess," replied Mrs. Ayres, sitting down opposite Mrs. Whitman. "Lucy has real good luck with them."

"How is Lucy this morning?"

Mrs. Ayres wrinkled her forehead again. "She's in bed with a sick headache," she said. "She has an awful lot of them lately. I'm afraid she's kind of run down."

"Why don't you get a tonic?"

"Well, I have been thinking of it, but Dr. Wallace gives such dreadful strong medicines, and Lucy is so delicate, that I have hesitated. I don't know but I ought to take her to Alford to Dr. Gilbert, but she doesn't want to go. She says it is too expensive, and she says there's nothing the matter with her; but she has these terrible headaches almost every other day, and she doesn't eat enough to keep a sparrow alive, and I can't help being worried about her."

"It doesn't seem right," agreed Mrs. Whitman. "Last time I was here I thought she didn't look real well. She's got color, a real pretty color, but it isn't the right kind."

"That's just it," said Mrs. Ayres, wrinkling her forehead. "The color's pretty, but you can see too plain where the red leaves off and where the white begins."

"Speaking about color," said Mrs. Whitman, "I am going to ask you something."

"What?"

"Do you really think Miss Farrel's color is natural?"

"I don't know. It looks so."

"I know it does, but I had it real straight that she keeps some pink stuff that she uses in a box as bold as can be, right in sight on her wash-stand."

"I don't know anything about it," said Mrs. Ayres, in her weary, gentle fashion. "I have heard, of course, that some women do use such things, but none of my folks ever did, and I never knew anybody else who did."

Then Sylvia opened upon the subject which had brought her there. She had reached it by a process as natural as nature itself.

"I know one thing," said she: "I have no opinion of that woman. I can't have. When I hear a woman saying such things as I have heard of her saying about a girl, when I know it isn't true, I make up my mind those things are true about the woman herself, and she's talking about herself, because she's got to let it out, and she makes believe it's somebody else."

Mrs. Ayres's face took on a strange expression. Her sweet eyes hardened and narrowed. "What do you mean?" she asked, sharply.

"I guess I had better not tell you what I mean. Miss Farrel gives herself clean away just by her looks. No living woman was ever made so there wasn't a flaw in her face but that there was a flaw in her soul. We're none of us perfect. If there ain't a flaw outside, there's a flaw inside; you mark my words."

"What was it she said?" asked Mrs. Ayres.

"I don't mean to make trouble. I never did, and I ain't going to begin now," said Sylvia. Her face took on a sweet, hypocritical expression.

"What did she say?"

Sylvia fidgeted. She was in reality afraid to speak, and yet her very soul itched to do so. She answered, evasively. "When a woman talks about a girl running after a man, I think myself she lives in a glass house and can't afford to throw stones," said she. She nodded her head unpleasantly.

Mrs. Ayres reddened. "I suppose you mean she has been talking about my Lucy," said she. "Well, I can tell you one thing, and I can tell Miss Farrel, too. Lucy has never run after Mr. Allen or any man. When she went on those errands to your house I had to fairly make her go. She said that folks would think she was running after Mr. Allen, even if he wasn't there, and she has never been, to my knowledge, more than three times when he was there, and then I made her. I told her folks wouldn't be so silly as to think such things of a girl like her."

"Folks are silly enough for anything. Of course, I knew better; you know that, Mrs. Ayres."

"I don't know what I know," replied Mrs. Ayres, with that forceful indignation of which a gentle nature is capable when aroused.

Mrs. Whitman looked frightened. She opened her lips to speak, when a boy came running into the yard. "Why, who is that?" she cried, nervously.

"It's Tommy Smith from Gray & Snow's with some groceries I ordered," said Mrs. Ayres, tersely. She left the room to admit the boy at the side door. Then Sylvia Whitman heard voices in excited conversation. At the same time she began to notice that the road was filled with children running and exclaiming. She herself hurried to the kitchen door, and Mrs. Ayres turned an ashy face in her direction. At the same time Lucy Ayres, with her fair hair dishevelled, appeared at the top of the back stairs listening. "Oh, it is awful!" gasped Mrs. Ayres. "It is awful! Miss Eliza Farrel is dead, and—"

Sylvia grasped the other woman nervously by the arm. "And what?" she cried.

Lucy gave an hysterical sob and sank down in a slender huddle on the stairs. The grocer's boy looked at them. He had a happy, important expression.

39

"They say—" he began, but Mrs. Ayres forestalled him.

"They say Lucinda Hart murdered her," she screamed out.

"Good land!" said Sylvia. Lucy sobbed again.

The boy gazed at them with intense relish. He realized the joy of a coup. He had never been very important in his own estimation nor that of others. Now he knew what it was to be important. "Yes," he said, gayly; "they say she give her rat poison. They've sent for the sheriff from Alford."

"She never did it in the world. Why, I went to school with her," gasped Mrs. Ayres.

Sylvia had the same conviction, but she backed it with logic. "What should she do it for?" she demanded. "Miss Farrel was a steady boarder, and Lucinda ain't had many steady boarders lately, and she needed the money. Folks don't commit murder without reason. What reason was there?"

"School ain't going to keep to-day," remarked the boy, with glee.

"Of course it ain't," said Sylvia, angrily. "What reason do they give?"

"I 'ain't heard of none," said the boy. "S'pose that will come out at the trial. Hannah Simmons is going to be arrested, too. They think she knowed something about it."

"Hannah Simmons wouldn't hurt a fly," said Sylvia. "What makes them think she knew anything about it?"

"Johnny Soule, that works at the hotel stable, says she did," said the boy. "They think he knows a good deal."

Sylvia sniffed contemptuously. "That Johnny Soule!" said she. "He's half Canadian. Father was French. I wouldn't take any stock in what he said."

"Lucinda never did it," said Mrs. Ayres. "I went to school with her."

Lucy sobbed again wildly, then she laughed loudly. Her mother turned and looked at her. "Lucy," said she, "you go straight back up-stairs and put this out of your mind, or you'll be down sick. Go straight up-stairs and lie down, and I'll bring you up some of that nerve medicine Dr. Wallace put up for you. Maybe you can get to sleep."

Lucy sobbed and laughed again. "Stop right where you are," said her mother, with a wonderful, firm gentleness—"right where you are. Put this thing right out of your mind. It's nothing you can help."

Lucy sobbed and laughed again, and this time her laugh rang so wildly that the grocer's boy looked at her with rising alarm. He admired Lucy. "I say," he said. "Maybe she ain't dead, after all. I heard all this, but you never can tell anything by what folks say. You had better mind your ma and put it all out of your head." The grocer's boy and Lucy had been in the same class at school. She had never noticed him, but he had loved her as from an immeasurable distance. Both were very young.

Lucy lifted a beautiful, frightened face, and stared at him. "Isn't it so?" she cried.

"I dare say it ain't. You had better mind your ma."

"I dare say it's all a rumor," said Sylvia, soothingly.

Mrs. Ayres echoed her. "All a made-up story, I think," said she. "Go right up-stairs, Lucy, and put it out of your head."

Lucy crept up-stairs with soft sobs, and they heard a door close. Then the boy spoke again. "It's so, fast enough," he said, in a whisper, "but there ain't any need for her to know it yet."

"No, there isn't, poor child," said Sylvia.

"She's dreadful nervous," said Mrs. Ayres, "and she thought a lot of Miss Farrel—more, I guess, than most. The poor woman never was a favorite here. I never knew why, and I guess nobody else ever did. I don't care what she may have intimated—I mean what you were talking about, Sylvia. That's all over. Lucy always seemed to like her, and the poor child is so sensitive and nervous."

"Yes, she is dreadful nervous," said Sylvia.

"And I think she ate too much candy yesterday, too," said Mrs. Ayres. "She made some candy from a recipe she found in the paper. I think her stomach is sort of upset, too. I mean to make her think it's all talk about Miss Farrel until she's more herself."

"I would," said Sylvia. "Poor child."

The grocer's boy made a motion to go. "I wonder if they'll hang her," he said, cheerfully.

"Hang her!" gasped Mrs. Ayres. "She never did it any more than I did. I went to school with Lucinda Hart."

"Why should she kill a steady boarder, when the hotel has run down so and she's been so hard up for money?" demanded Sylvia. "Hang her! You'd better run along, sonny; the other customers will be waiting; and you had better not talk too much till you are sure what you are talking about."

The boy went out and closed the door, and they heard his merry whistle as he

41

raced out of the yard.

Chapter VII

Sylvia Whitman, walking home along the familiar village street, felt like a stranger exploring it for the first time. She had never before seen it under the glare of tragedy which her own consciousness threw before her eyes. No tragedy had ever been known in East Westland since she could remember. It had been a peaceful little community, with every day much like the one before and after, except for the happenings of birth and death, which are the most common happenings of nature.

But now came death by violence, and even the wayside weeds seemed to wave in a lurid light. Now and then Sylvia unconsciously brushed her eyes, as if to sweep away a cobweb which obstructed her vision. When she reached home, that also looked strange to her, and even her husband's face in the window had an expression which she had never seen before. So also had Horace Allen's. Both men were in the south room. There was in their faces no expression which seemed to denote a cessation of conversation. In fact, nothing had passed between the two men except the simple statement to each other of the news which both had heard. Henry had made no comment, neither had Horace. Both had set, with gloomy, shocked faces, entirely still. But Sylvia, when she entered, forced the situation.

"Why should she kill a steady boarder, much as she needed one?" she queried.

And Horace responded at once. "There is no possible motive," he said. "The arrest is a mere farce. It will surely prove so."

Then Henry spoke. "I don't understand, for my part, why she is arrested at all," he said, grimly.

Horace laughed as grimly. "Because there is no one else to arrest, and the situation seems to call for some action," he replied.

"But they must have some reason."

"All the reason was the girl's (Hannah Simmons, I believe her name is) seeming to be keeping something back, and saying that Miss Hart gave Miss Farrel some essence of peppermint last night, and the fact that the stable-boy seems to be in love with Hannah, and jealous and eager to do her mistress some mischief, and has hinted at knowing something, which I don't believe, for my part, he does."

"It is all nonsense," said Sylvia. "Whatever Hannah Simmons is keeping to

42

herself, it isn't killing another woman, or knowing that Lucinda Hart did it. There was no reason for either of those women to kill Miss Farrel, and folks don't do such awful things without reason, unless they're crazy, and it isn't likely that Lucinda and Hannah have both come down crazy together, and I know it ain't in the Hart family, or the Simmons. What if poor Lucinda did give Miss Farrel some essence of peppermint? I gave some to Henry night before last, when he had gas in his stomach, and it didn't kill him."

"What they claim is that arsenic was in the peppermint," said Horace, in an odd, almost indifferent voice.

"Arsenic in the peppermint!" repeated Sylvia. "You needn't tell me Lucinda Hart put arsenic in the peppermint, though I dare say she had some in the house to kill rats. It's likely that old tavern was overrun with them, and I know she lost her cat a few weeks ago. She told me herself. He was shot when he was out hunting. Lucinda thought somebody mistook him for a skunk. She felt real bad about it. I feel kind of guilty myself. I can't help thinking if I'd just looked round then and hunted up a kitten for poor Lucinda, she never would have had any need to keep rat poison, and nobody would have suspected her of such an awful thing. I suppose Albion Bennet right up and told she'd bought it, first thing. I think he might have kept still, as long as he'd boarded with Lucinda, and as many favors as she'd showed him. He knew as well as anybody that she never gave it to Miss Farrel."

"Now, Sylvia, he had to tell if he was asked," Henry said, soothingly, for Sylvia was beginning to show signs of hysterical excitement. "He couldn't do anything else."

"He could have forgot," Sylvia returned, shrilly. "Men ain't so awful conscientious about forgetting. He could have forgot."

"He had to tell," repeated Henry. "Don't get all wrought up over it, Sylvia."

"I can't help it. I begin to feel guilty myself. I know I might have found a kitten. I had a lot on my mind, with moving and everything, but I might have done it. Albion Bennet never had the spunk to do anything but tell all he knew. I suppose he was afraid of his own precious neck."

"Ain't it most time to see about dinner?" asked Henry.

Then Sylvia went out of the room with a little hysterical twitter like a scared bird, and the two men were left alone. Silence came over them again. Both men looked moodily at nothing. Finally Henry spoke.

"One of the worst features of any terrible thing like this is that burdens innumerable are either heaped upon the shoulders of the innocent, or they assume them. There's my poor wife actually trying to make out that she is in

43

some way to blame."

"Women are a queer lot," said Horace, in a miserable tone.

Then the door opened suddenly, and Sylvia's think, excited face appeared.

"You don't suppose they'll send them to prison?" she said.

"They'll both be acquitted," said Horace. "Don't worry, Mrs. Whitman."

"I've got to worry. How can I help worrying? Even if poor Lucinda is acquitted, lots of folks will always believe it, and her boarders will drop away, and as for Hannah Simmons, I shouldn't be a mite surprised if it broke her match off."

"It's a dreadful thing," said Henry; "but don't you fret too much over it, Sylvia. Maybe she killed herself, and if they think that Lucinda won't have any trouble afterwards."

"I think some have that opinion now," said Horace.

Sylvia sniffed. "A woman don't kill herself as long as she's got spirit enough to fix herself up," she said. "I saw her only yesterday in a brand-new dress, and her hair was crimped tight enough to last a week, and her cheeks—"

"Come, Sylvia," said Henry, admonishingly.

"You needn't be afraid. I ain't going to talk about them that's dead and gone, and especially when they've gone in such a dreadful way; and maybe it wasn't true," said Sylvia. "But it's just as I say: when a woman is fixed up the way Miss Eliza Farrel was yesterday, she ain't within a week of making way with herself. Seems as if I might have had forethought enough to have got that kitten for poor Lucinda."

Sylvia went out again. The men heard the rattle of dishes. Horace rose with a heavy sigh, which was almost a sob, and went out by the hall door, and Henry heard his retreating steps on the stair. He frowned deeply as he sat by the window. He, too, was bearing in some measure the burden of which he had spoken. It seemed to him very strange that under the circumstances Horace had not explained his mysterious meeting with the woman in the grove north of the house the night before. Henry had a certainty as to her identity—a certainty which he could not explain to himself, but which was none the less fixed.

No suspicion of Horace, as far as the murder was concerned—if murder it was—was in his mind, but he did entertain a suspicion of another sort: of some possibly guilty secret which might have led to the tragedy. "I couldn't feel worse if he was my own son," he thought. He wished desperately that he had gone out in the grove and interrupted the interview. "I'm old enough to be his father," he told himself, "and I know what young men are. I'm to blame myself."

When he heard Horace's approaching footsteps on the stair he turned his face stiffly towards the window, and did not look up when the young man entered the room. But Horace sat down opposite and began speaking rapidly in a low voice.

"I don't know but I ought to go to Mr. Meeks with this instead of you," he said; "and I don't know that I ought to go to anybody, but, hang it, I can't keep the little I know to myself any longer—that is, I can't keep the whole of it. Some I never will tell. Mr. Whitman, I don't know the exact minute Miss Hart gave her that confounded peppermint, and Miss Hart seems rather misty about it, and if the girl knows she won't tell; but I suspect I may be the last person who saw that poor woman alive. I found a note waiting for me from her when I arrived yesterday, and—well, she wanted to see me alone about something very particular, and she—" Horace paused and reddened. "Well, you know what women are, and of course there was really no place at the hotel where I could have been sure of a private interview with her. I couldn't go to her room, and one might as well talk in a trolley-car as that hotel parlor; and she didn't want to come here to the house and be closeted with me, and she didn't want to linger after school, for those school-girls are the very devil when it comes to seeing anything; and though I will admit it does sound ridiculous and romantic, I don't see myself what else she could have done. She asked me in her note to step out in the grove about ten o'clock, when the house was quiet. She wrote she had something very important to say to me. So I felt like a fool, but I didn't go to bed, and I stole down the front stairs, and she was out there in the grove waiting for me, and we sat down on the bench there and she told me some things."

Henry nodded gravely. He now looked at Horace, and there was relief in his frowning face.

"I can tell you some of the things that she said to me," continued Horace, "and I am going to. You are connected with it—that is, you are through your wife. Miss Farrel wasn't Miss at all. She was a married woman." Henry nodded again. "She had not lived with her husband long, however, and she had been married some twenty years ago. She was older than she looked. For some reason she did not get on with him, and he left her. I don't myself feel that I know what the reason was, although she pretended to tell me. She seemed to have a feeling, poor soul, that, beautiful as she was, she excited repulsion rather than affection in everybody with whom she came in contact. 'I might as well be a snake as a woman.' Those were just her words, and, God help her, I do believe there was something true about them, although for the

45

life of me I don't know why it was."

Henry looked at Horace with the eyes of a philosopher. "Maybe it was because she wanted to charm," he said.

Horace shot a surprised glance at him. He had not expected anything like that from Henry, even though he had long said to himself that there were depths below the commonplace surface.

"Perhaps you are right," he said, reflectively. "I don't know but you are. She was a great beauty, and possibly the knowledge of it made her demand too much, long for too much, so that people dimly realized it and were repelled instead of being attracted. I think she loved her husband for a long time after he left her. I think she loved many others, men and women. I think she loved women better than a woman usually does, and women could not abide her. That I know; even the school-girls fought shy of her."

"I have seen the Ayres girl with her," said Henry.

Horace changed color. "She is not one of the school-girls," he replied, hastily.

"I think I have heard Sylvia say that Mrs. Ayres had asked her there to tea."

"Yes, I believe she has. I think perhaps the Ayres family have paid some attention to her," Horace said, constrainedly.

"I have seen the Ayres girl with her a good deal, I know," said Henry.

"Very possibly, I dare say. Well, Miss Farrel did not think she or any one else cared about her very much. She told me that none of her pupils did, and I could not gainsay her, and then she told me what I feel that I must tell you." Horace paused. Henry waited.

Then Horace resumed. He spoke briefly and to the purpose.

"Miss Abrahama White, who left her property to your wife, had a sister," he said. "The sister went away and married, and there was a daughter. First the father died, then the mother. The daughter, a mere child at the time, was left entirely destitute. Miss Farrel took charge of her. She did not tell her the truth. She wished to establish if possible some claim upon her affection. She considered that to claim a relationship would be the best way to further her purpose. The girl was told that Miss Farrel was her mother's cousin. She was further told that she had inherited a very considerable property from her mother, whereas she had not inherited one cent. Miss Farrel gave up her entire fortune to the child. She then, with the nervous dread of awakening dislike instead of love which filled her very soul, managed to have the child, in her character of an heiress, established in a family moving in the best circles, but sadly in need of money. Then she left her, and began supporting herself by

46

teaching. The girl is now grown to be a young woman, and Miss Farrel has not dared see her more than twice since she heaped such benefits upon her. It has been her dream that some day she might reveal the truth, and that gratitude might induce love, but she has never dared put it to the test. Lately she has not been very well, and the thought has evidently come to her more than once that she might die and never accomplish her purpose. I almost think the poor woman had a premonition. She gave me last night the girl's address, and she made me promise that in case of her death she should be sent for. 'I can't bear to think that nobody will come,' she said. Of course I laughed at her. I thought her very morbid, but—well, I have telegraphed to the girl to come in time for the funeral. She is in New York. She and the people with whom she lives have just returned from the South."

"She must come here," Henry said.

"I could think of no other place," said Horace. "You think Mrs. Whitman—"

"Of course," Henry said. He started up to speak to Sylvia, but Horace stopped him.

"I forgot," he said, quickly. "Miss Farrel asked me to promise that I should not tell the girl, in case of her death before she had an opportunity of doing so, of what she had done for her. 'Let her come just because she thinks I am her relative,' she said, 'and because she may possibly feel kindly towards me. If I can have no comfort from it while I am alive, there is no need for her to know her obligation.'"

"It sounds like a mighty queer story to tell Sylvia," Henry said. Then he opened the door and called, and Mrs. Whitman immediately responded. Her hands were white with flour. She had been making biscuits. She still looked nervous and excited.

"What is to pay now?" said she.

Henry told her in few words.

"You mean that Abrahama's niece was taken care of by Miss Farrel when her mother died, and Miss Farrel got a place for her to live with some New York folks, and you mean Miss Farrel was related to her mother?" said Sylvia. She looked sharply at Henry.

"Yes," he replied, feebly. Horace stood looking out of the window.

"She wa'n't," said Sylvia.

"Now, Sylvia."

"If that poor woman that's gone wanted the girl to think she was her relation enough to lie about it I sha'n't tell her, you can depend on that; but it's a lie," said Sylvia. "Miss Farrel wa'n't no relation at all to Susy White. She couldn't have been unless she was related to me, too, on my mother's side, and she wa'n't. I know all about my mother's family. But I sha'n't tell her. I'm glad Miss Farrel got a home for her. It was awful that the child was left without a cent. Of course she must come here, and stay, too. She ought to live with her folks. We've got enough to take care of her. If we can't do as much as rich folks, I guess it will be full as well for the girl."

Henry opened his lips to speak, but a glance from Horace checked him. Sylvia went on talking nervously. The odd manner and tone which Henry had noticed lately in everything she said and did seemed intensified. She talked about what room she should make ready for the girl. She made plan after plan. She was very pale, then she flushed. She walked aimlessly about gesturing with her floury hands.

Finally Henry took her firmly by the shoulder. "Come, Sylvia," he said, "she won't be here until night. Now you had better get dinner. It's past twelve." Sylvia gave a quick, frightened glance at him. Then she went silently out of the room.

"Mrs. Whitman does not seem well," Horace said, softly.

"I think her nerves are all out of order with what she has gone through with lately," said Henry. "It has been a great change that has come to us both, Mr. Allen. When a man and woman have lived past their youth, and made up their minds to bread and butter, and nothing else, and be thankful if you get that much, it seems more like a slap than a gift of Providence to have mince-pie thrust into their mouths. It has been too much for Sylvia, and now, of course, this awful thing that has happened has upset her, and—"

He stopped, for Sylvia opened the door suddenly. "If she wa'n't dead and gone, I wouldn't believe one word of such a tomfool story," said she, with vicious energy. Then she shut the door again.

At dinner Sylvia ate nothing, and did not talk. Neither Henry nor Horace said much. In the afternoon Horace went out to make some arrangements which he had taken upon himself with regard to the dead woman, and presently Henry followed him. Sylvia worked with feverish energy all the afternoon setting a room in order for her expected guest. It was a pretty room, with an old-fashioned paper—a sprawling rose pattern on a tarnished satin ground. The room overlooked the grove, and green branches pressed close against two windows. There was a pretty, old-fashioned dressing-table between the front windows, and Sylvia picked a bunch of flowers and put them in a china vase, and set it under the glass, and thought of the girl's face which it would presently reflect.

"I wonder if she looks like her mother," she thought. She stood gazing at the glass, and shivered as though with cold. Then she started at a sound of wheels outside. In front of the house was Leander Willard, who kept the livery-stable of East Westland. He was descending in shambling fashion over the front wheels, steadying at the same time a trunk on the front seat; and Horace Allen sprang out of the back of the carriage and assisted a girl in a flutter of dark-blue skirts and veil. "She's come!" said Sylvia.

Chapter VIII

Sylvia gave a hurried glance at her hair in the glass. It shone like satin with a gray-gold lustre, folded back smoothly from her temples. She eyed with a little surprise the red spots of excitement which still remained on her cheeks. The changelessness of her elderly visage had been evident to her so long that she was startled to see anything else. "I look as if I had been pulled through a knot-hole," she muttered.

She took off her gingham apron, thrust it hastily into a bureau drawer in the next room, and tied on a clean white one with a hemstitched border. Then she went down-stairs, the starched white bow of the apron-strings covering her slim back like a Japanese sash. She heard voices in the south room, and entered with a little cough. Horace and the new-comer were standing there talking. The moment Sylvia entered, Horace stepped forward. "I hardly know how to introduce you," he said; "I hardly know the relationship. But, Mrs. Whitman, here is Miss Fletcher—Miss Rose Fletcher."

"Who accepts your hospitality with the utmost gratitude," said Miss Rose Fletcher, extending a little hand in a wonderful loose gray travelling glove. Mrs. Whitman took the offered hand and let it drop. She was rigid and prim. She smiled, but the smile was merely a widening of her thin, pale, compressed lips. She looked at the girl with gray eyes, which had a curious blank sharpness in them. Rose Fletcher was so very well dressed, so very redolent of good breeding and style, that it was difficult at first to comprehend if that was all. Finally one perceived that she was a very pretty girl, of a sweet, childish type, in spite of her finished manners and her very sophisticated clothes. Sylvia at first saw nothing except the clothes, and realized nothing except the finished manner. She immediately called to the front her own manners, which were as finished as the girl's, albeit of a provincial type. Extreme manners in East Westland required a wholly artificial voice and an expression wholly foreign to the usual one. Horace had never before seen Sylvia when all her manners were in evidence, and he gazed at her now in astonishment and some dismay.

"Her mother was own sister to Miss Abrahama White, and Abrahama White's mother and my mother were own cousins on the mother's side. My mother was a White," she said. The voice came like a slender, reedy whistle from between her moveless, widened lips. She stood as if encased in armor. Her apron-strings stood out fiercely and were quite evident over each hip. She held her head very high, and the cords on her long, thin neck stood out.

Poor Rose Fletcher looked a little scared and a little amused. She cast a glance at Horace, as if for help. He did not know what to say, but tried manfully to say it. "I have never fully known, in such a case," he remarked, "whether the relationship is second cousin or first cousin once removed." It really seemed to him that he had never known. He looked up with relief as Henry entered the room, and Sylvia turned to him, still with her manners fully in evidence.

"Mr. Whitman, this is Miss Abrahama White's niece," said she.

She bowed stiffly herself as Henry bowed. He was accustomed to Sylvia's company manners, but still he was not himself. He had never seen a girl like this, and he was secretly both angry and alarmed to note the difference between her and Sylvia, and all women to which he had been used. However, his expression changed directly before the quick look of pretty, childish appeal which the girl gave him. It was Rose's first advance to all men whom she met, her little feeler put out to determine their dispositions towards her. It was quite involuntary. She was unconscious of it, but it was as if she said in so many words, "Do you mean to be kind to me? Don't you like the look of me? I mean entirely well. There is no harm in me. Please don't dislike me."

Sylvia saw the glance and interpreted it. "She looks like her mother," she announced, harshly. It was part of Sylvia's extreme manners to address a guest in the third person. However, in this case, it was in reality the clothes which had occasioned so much formality. She immediately, after she had spoken and Henry had awkwardly murmured his assent to her opinion, noticed how tired the girl looked. She was a slender little thing, and looked delicate in spite of a babyish roundness of face, which was due to bone-formation rather than flesh.

Sylvia gave an impression of shoving the men aside as she approached the girl. "You look tired to death," said she, and there was a sweet tone in her force voice.

Rose brightened, and smiled at her like a pleased child. "Oh, I am very tired!" she cried. "I must confess to being very tired, indeed. The train was so fast. I came on the limited from New York, you know, and the soft-coal smoke made me ill, and I couldn't eat anything, even if there had been anything to eat which wasn't all full of cinders. I shall be so very glad of a bath and an opportunity to change my gown. I shall have to beg you to allow your maid to assist me a little. My own maid got married last week, unexpectedly, and I have not yet replaced her."

"I don't keep a hired girl," said Sylvia. She looked, as Henry had, both angry and abashed. "I will fasten up your dress in the neck if that is what you want," said she.

"Oh, that is all," Rose assured her, and she looked abashed, too. Even sophistication is capable of being daunted before utterly unknown conditions. She followed Sylvia meekly up-stairs, and Henry and Horace carried the trunk, which had been left on the front walk, up after them.

Leander Willard was a man of exceeding dignity. He was never willing to carry a trunk even into a house. "If the folks that the trunk belongs to can't heft it in after I've brought it up from the depot, let it set out," he said. "I drive a carriage to accommodate, but I ain't no porter."

Therefore, Henry and Horace carried up the trunk and unstrapped it. Rose looked around her with delight. "Oh, what a lovely room!" she cried.

"It gets the morning sun," said Sylvia. "The paper is a little mite faded, but otherwise it's just as good as it ever was."

"It is perfectly charming," said Rose. She tugged at the jewelled pins in her hat. Sylvia stood watching her. When she had succeeded in removing the hat, she thrust her slender fingers through her fluff of blond hair and looked in the glass. Her face appeared over the bunch of flowers, as Sylvia had thought of its doing. Rose began to laugh. "Good gracious!" she said. "For all I took such pains to wash my face in the lavatory, there is a great black streak on my left cheek. Sometimes I think the Pullmans are dirtier than the common coaches—that more soft-coal smoke comes in those large windows; don't you think so?"

Sylvia colored, but her honesty was fearless. "I don't know what a Pullman is," she said.

Rose stared for a second. "Oh, a parlor-car," she said. "A great many people always say parlor-car." Rose was almost apologetic.

"Did you come in a parlor-car?" asked Sylvia. Rose wondered why her voice was so amazed, even aggressive.

"Why, of course; I always do," said Rose.

"I've seen them go through here," said Sylvia.

"Do you mind telling me where my bath-room is?" asked Rose, looking vaguely at the doors. She opened one. "Oh, this is a closet!" she cried. "What a lovely large one!"

"There ain't such a thing as a bath-room in this house," replied Sylvia. "Abrahama White, your aunt, had means, but she always thought she had better ways for her money than putting in bath-rooms to freeze up in winter and run up plumbers' bills. There ain't any bath-room, but there's plenty of good, soft rain-water from the cistern in your pitcher on the wash-stand there, and there's a new cake of soap and plenty of clean towels."

Rose reddened. Again sophistication felt abashed before dauntless ignorance. She ran to the wash-stand. "Oh, I beg your pardon!" she cried. "Of course this will do beautifully. What a charming old wash-stand!—and the water is delightfully soft." Rose began splashing water over her face. She had taken off her blue travelling-gown and flung it in a heap over a chair. Sylvia straightened it out carefully, noting with a little awe the rustle of its silk linings; then she hung it in the closet. "I'll hang it here, where it won't get all of a muss," said she. Already she began to feel a pleasure which she had never known—the pleasure of chiding a young creature from the heights of her own experience. She began harshly, but before she had finished her voice had a tender cadence.

"Oh, thank you," said the girl, still bending over the wash-basin. "I know I am careless with my things. You see, I have always been so dependent upon my maid to straighten out everything for me. You will do me good. You will teach me to be careful."

She turned around, wiping her face, and smiling at Sylvia, who felt her very soul melt within her, although she still remained rigidly prim, with her stiff apron-strings standing out at right angles. She looked at the girl's slender arms and thin neck, which was pretty though thin. "You don't weigh much, do you?" she said.

"A little over a hundred, I think."

"You must eat lots of fresh vegetables and eggs, and drink milk, and get more flesh on your bones," said Sylvia, and her voice was full of delight, although now—as always, lately—a vague uneasiness lurked in her eyes. Rose, regarding her, thought, with a simple shrewdness which was inborn, that her new cousin must have something on her mind. She wondered if it was her aunt's death. "I suppose you thought a good deal of my aunt who died," she ventured, timidly.

Sylvia regarded her with quick suspicion. She paled a little. "I thought enough of her," she replied. "She had always lived here. We were distant-related, and we never had any words, but I didn't see much of her. She kept herself to herself, especially of late years. Of course, I thought enough of her, and it makes me feel real bad sometimes—although I own I can't help being glad to have so many nice things—to think she had to go away and leave them."

"I know you must feel so," said Rose. "I suppose you feel sometimes as if they weren't yours at all."

Sylvia turned so pale that Rose started. "Why, what is the matter? Are you ill?" she cried, running to her. "Let me get some water for you. You are so white."

Sylvia pushed her away. "There's nothing the matter with me," she said. "Folks can't always be the same color unless they're painted." She gave her head a shake as if to set herself right, and turned resolutely towards Rose's trunk. "Can you unpack, yourself, or do you want me to help you?" she asked.

Rose eyed the trunk helplessly, then she looked doubtfully at Sylvia. A woman who was a relative of hers, and who lived in a really grand old house, and was presumably well-to-do, and had no maids at command, but volunteered to do the service herself, was an anomaly to her.

"I'm afraid it will be too much trouble," she said, hesitatingly. "Marie always unpacked my trunk, but you have no—"

"I guess if I had a girl I wouldn't set her to unpacking your trunk," said Sylvia, vigorously. "Where is your key?"

"In my bag," replied Rose, and she searched for the key in her dark-blue, gold-trimmed bag. "Mrs. Wilton's maid, Anne, packed my trunk for me," she said. "Anne packs very nicely. Mr. Wilton and her sister, Miss Pamela Mack, did not know whether I ought to put on mourning or not for Cousin Eliza, but they said it would be only proper for me to wear black to the funeral. So I have a ready-made black gown and hat in the trunk. I hardly knew how much to bring. I did not know—" She stopped. She had intended to say—"how long I should stay," but she was afraid.

Sylvia finished for her. "You can stay just as long as you are a mind to," said she. "You can live here all the rest of your life, as far as that is concerned. You are welcome. It would suit me, and it would suit Mr. Whitman."

Rose looked at Sylvia in amazement as she knelt stiffly on the floor unlocking her trunk. "Thank you, you are very kind," she said, feebly. She had a slight sensation of fear at such a wealth of hospitality offered her from a stranger, although she was a distant relative.

"You know this was your own aunt's house and your own aunt's things," said Sylvia, beginning to remove articles from the trunk, "and I want you to feel at home here—just as if you had a right here." The words were cordial, but there was a curious effect as if she were repeating a well-rehearsed lesson.

"Thank you," Rose said again, more feebly than before. She watched Sylvia lifting out gingerly a fluffy white gown, which trailed over her lean arm to the floor. "That is a tea-gown; I think I will put it on now," said Rose. "It will be so comfortable, and you are not formal here, are you?"

"Eh?"

"You are not formal here in East Westland, are you?"

"No," replied Sylvia, "we ain't formal. So you want to put on—this?"

"Yes, I think I will."

Sylvia laid the tea-gown on the bed, and turned to the trunk again.

"You know, of course, that Aunt Abrahama and mamma were estranged for years before mamma died," said Rose. She sat before the white dressing-table watching Sylvia, and the lovely turn of her neck and her blond head were reflected in the glass above the vase of flowers.

"Yes, I knew something about it."

"I never did know much, except that Aunt Abrahama did not approve of mamma's marriage, and we never saw her nor heard of her. Wasn't it strange," she went on, confidentially, "how soon after poor mamma's death all my money came to me?"

Sylvia turned on her. "Have you got money?" said she. "I thought you were poor."

"Yes, I think I have a great deal of money. I don't know how much. My lawyers take care of it, and there is a trustee, who is very kind. He is a lawyer, too. He was a friend of poor Cousin Eliza's. His name is McAllister. He lives in Chicago, but he comes to New York quite often. He is quite an old gentleman, but very nice indeed. Oh yes, I have plenty of money. I always have had ever since mamma died—at least, since a short time after. But we were very poor, I think, after papa died. I think we must have been. I was only a little girl when mamma died, but I seem to remember living in a very little, shabby place in New York—very little and shabby—and I seem to remember a great deal of noise. Sometimes I wonder if we could have lived beside the elevated road. It does not seem possible that we could have been as poor as that, but sometimes I do wonder. And I seem to remember a close smell about our rooms, and that they were very hot, and I remember when poor mamma died, although I was so young. I remember a great many people, who seemed very kind, came in, and after that I was in a place with a good many other little girls. I suppose it was a school. And then—" Rose stopped and turned white, and a look of horror came over her face.

"What then?" asked Sylvia. "Don't you feel well, child?"

"Yes, I feel well—as well as I ever feel when I almost remember something terrible and never quite do. Oh, I hope I never shall quite remember. I think I should die if I did."

Sylvia stared at her. Rose's face was fairly convulsed. Sylvia rose and hesitated a moment, then she stepped close to the girl and pulled the fair head to her lean shoulder. "Don't; you mustn't take on so," she said. "Don't try to remember anything if it makes you feel like that. You'll be down sick."

"I am trying not to remember, and always the awful dread lest I shall comes over me," sobbed the girl. "Mr. McAllister says not to try to remember, too, but I am so horribly afraid that I shall try in spite of me. Mrs. Wilton and Miss Pamela don't know anything about it. I never said anything about it to them. I did once to Mr. McAllister, and I did to Cousin Eliza, and she said not to try, and now I am telling you, I suppose because you are related to me. It came over me all of a sudden."

Rose sobbed again. Sylvia smoothed her hair, then she shook her by the slender, soft shoulders, and again that overpowering delight seized her. "Come, now," she said, "don't you cry another minute. You get up and lay your underclothes away in the bureau drawers. It's almost time to get supper, and I can't spend much more time here."

Rose obeyed. She packed away piles of laced and embroidered things in the bureau drawers, and under Sylvia's directions hung up her gowns in the closet. As she did this she volunteered further information.

"I do remember one thing," she said, with a shudder, "and I always know if I could remember back of that the dreadful thing would come to me." She paused for a moment, then she said, in a shocked voice: "Mrs. Whitman."

"What is it?"

"I really do remember that I was in a hospital once when I was little. I remember the nurses and the little white beds. That was not dreadful at all. Everybody petted me, but that was when the trying not to remember began."

"Don't you think of it another minute," Sylvia said, sternly.

"I won't; I won't, really. I—"

"For goodness' sake, child, don't hang that heavy coat over that lace waist— you'll ruin it!" cried Sylvia.

Rose removed the coat hurriedly, and resumed, as Sylvia took it out of her hand: "It was right after that Cousin Eliza Farrel came, and then all that money was left to me by a cousin of father's, who died. Then I went to live with Mrs. Wilton and Miss Pamela, and I went to school, and I went abroad, and I always had plenty, and never any trouble, except once in a while being afraid I should remember something dreadful. Poor Cousin Eliza Farrel taught school all the time. I never saw her but twice after the first time. When I grew older I tried to have her come and live with me. Mrs. Wilton and Miss Pamela have always been very nice to me, but I have never loved them. I could never seem to get at enough of them to love."

"You had better put on that now," said Sylvia, indicating the fluffy mass on the bed. "I'll help you."

"I don't like to trouble you," Rose said, almost pitifully, but she stood still while Sylvia, again with that odd sensation of delight, slipped over the young head a lace-trimmed petticoat, and fastened it, and then the tea-gown. The older woman dressed the girl with exactly the same sensations that she might have experienced in dressing her own baby for the first time. When the toilet was completed she viewed the result, however, with something that savored

56

of disapproval.

Rose, after looking in the glass at her young beauty in its setting of lace and silk, looked into Sylvia's face for the admiration which she felt sure of seeing there, and shrank. "What is the matter? Don't I look nice?" she faltered.

Sylvia looked critically at the sleeves of the tea-gown, which were mere puffs of snowy lace, streaming with narrow ribbons, reaching to the elbow. "Do they wear sleeves like that now in New York?" asked she.

"Why, yes!" replied Rose. "This tea-gown came home only last week from Madame Felix."

"They wear sleeves puffed at the bottom instead of the top, and a good deal longer, in East Westland," said Sylvia.

"Why, this was made from a Paris model," said Rose, meekly. Again sophistication was abashed before the confidence of conservatism.

"I don't know anything about Paris models," said Sylvia. "Mrs. Greenaway gets all her patterns right from Boston."

"I hardly think madame would have made the sleeves this way unless it was the latest," said Rose.

"I don't know anything about the latest," said Sylvia. "We folks here in East Westland try to get the *best*." Sylvia felt as if she were chiding her own daughter. She spoke sternly, but her eyes beamed with pleasure. The young girl's discomfiture seemed to sweeten her very soul.

"For mercy's sake, hold up your dress going down-stairs," she admonished. "I swept the stairs this morning, but the dust gathers before you can say boo, and that dress won't do up."

Rose gathered up the tail of her gown obediently, and she also experienced a certain odd pleasure. New England blood was in her veins. It was something new and precious to be admonished as a New England girl might be admonished by a fond mother.

When she went into the south room, still clinging timidly to her lace train, Horace rose. Henry sat still. He looked at her with pleased interest, but it did not occur to him to rise. Horace always rose when Sylvia entered a room, and Henry always rather resented it. "Putting on society airs," he thought to himself, with a sneer.

However, he smiled involuntarily; the girl was so very pretty and so very unlike anything which he had ever seen. "Dressed up as if she were going to a ball, in a dress made like a night-gown," he thought, but he smiled. As for Horace, he felt dazzled. He had scarcely realized how pretty Rose was under

57

the dark-blue mist of her veil. He placed a chair for her, and began talking about the journey and the weather while Sylvia got supper. Henry was reading the local paper. Rose's eyes kept wandering to that. Suddenly she sprang to her feet, was across the room in a white swirl, and snatched the paper from Henry's hands.

"What is this, oh, what is this?" she cried out.

She had read before Horace could stop her. She turned upon him, then upon Henry. Her face was very pale and working with emotion.

"Oh," she cried, "you only telegraphed me that poor Cousin Eliza was dead! You did not either of you tell me she was murdered. I loved her, although I had not seen her for years, because I have so few to whom my love seemed to belong. I was sorry because she was dead, but murdered!"

Rose threw herself on a chair, and sobbed and sobbed.

"I loved her; I did love her," she kept repeating, like a distressed child. "I did love her, poor Cousin Eliza, and she was murdered. I did love her."

Chapter IX

Horace was right in his assumption that the case against Lucinda Hart and Hannah Simmons would never be pressed. Although it was proved beyond a doubt that Eliza Farrel had swallowed arsenic in a sufficiently large quantity to cause death, the utter absence of motive was in the favor of the accused, and then the suspicion that the poison might have been self-administered, if not with suicidal intent, with another, steadily gained ground. Many thought Miss Farrel's wonderful complexion might easily have been induced by the use of arsenic.

At all events, the evidence against Lucinda and Hannah, when sifted, was so exceedingly flimsy, and the lack of motive grew so evident, that there was no further question of bringing them to trial. Still the suspicion, once raised, grew like a weed, as suspicion does grow in the ready soil of the human heart. For a month after the tragedy it seemed as if Sylvia Whitman's prophecy concerning the falling off of the hotel guests was destined to fail. The old hostelry was crowded. Newspaper men and women from all parts of the country flocked there, and also many not connected with the press, who were morbidly curious and revelled in the sickly excitement of thinking they might be living in the house of a poisoner. Lucinda Hart sent in her resignation from the church choir. Her experience, the first time she had sung after Eliza Farrel's death, did not exactly daunt her; she was not easily daunted. But she had raised her husky contralto, and lifted her elderly head in its flowered bonnet before that watchful audience of old friends and neighbors, and had gone home and written her stiffly worded note of resignation.

She attended church the following Sunday. She said to herself that her absence might lead people to think there was some ground for the awful charge which had been brought against her. She bought a smart new bonnet and sat among the audience, and heard Lucy Ayres, who had a beautiful contralto, sing in her place. Lucy sang well, and looked very pretty in her lace blouse and white hat, but she was so pale that people commented on it. Sylvia, who showed a fairly antagonistic partisanship for Lucinda, spoke to her as she came out of church, and walked with her until their roads divided. Sylvia left Henry to follow with Rose Fletcher, who was still staying in East Westland, and pressed close to Lucinda.

"How are you?" she said.

"Well enough; why shouldn't I be?" retorted Lucinda.

It was impossible to tell from her manner whether she was grateful for, or resented, friendly advances. She held her head very high. There was a stiff, jetted ornament on her new bonnet, and it stood up like a crest. She shot a suspicious glance at Sylvia. Lucinda in those days entertained that suspicion of suspicion which poisons the very soul.

"I don't know why you shouldn't be," replied Sylvia. She herself cast an angry glance at the people around them, and that angry glance was like honey to Lucinda. "You were a fool to give up your place in the choir," said Sylvia, still with that angry, wandering gaze. "I'd sung. I'd shown 'em; and I'd sung out of tune if I'd wanted to."

"You don't know what it was like last Sunday," said Lucinda then. She did not speak complainingly or piteously. There was proud strength in her voice, but it was emphatic.

"I guess I do know," said Sylvia. "I saw everybody craning their necks, and all them strangers. You've got a lot of strangers at the hotel, haven't you, Lucinda?"

"Yes," said Lucinda, and there was an echo in her monosyllable like an expletive.

Sylvia nodded sympathizingly. "Some of them write for the papers, I suppose?" said she.

"Some of them. I know it's my bread-and-butter to have them, but I never saw such a parcel of folks. Talk about eyes in the backs of heads, they're all eyes and all ears. Sometimes I think they ain't nothing except eyes and ears and tongue. But there's a lot besides who like to think maybe they're eating poison. I know I'm watched every time I stir up a mite of cake, but I stir away."

"You must have your hands full."

"Yes; I had to get Abby Smith to come in and help."

"She ain't good for much."

"No, she ain't. She's thinkin' all the time of how she looks, instead of what she's doing. She waits on table, though, and helps wash dishes. She generally forgets to pass the vegetables till the meat is all et up, and they're lucky if they get any butter; but I can't help it. They only pay five dollars a week, and get a lot of enjoyment out of watching me and Hannah, and they can't expect everything."

The two women walked along the country road. There were many other people besides the church-going throng in their Sunday best, but they seemed isolated, although closely watched. Presently, however, a young man, well dressed in light gray, with a white waistcoat, approached them.

"Why, good-day, Miss Hart!" he said, raising his hat.

Lucinda nodded stiffly and walked on. She did not speak to him, but to Sylvia. "He is staying at the hotel. He writes for a New York paper," she informed Sylvia, distinctly.

The young man laughed. "And Miss Hart is going to write for it, too," he said, pleasantly and insinuatingly. "She is going to write an article upon how it feels to be suspected of a crime when one is innocent, and it will be the leading feature in next Sunday's paper. She is to have her picture appear with it, too, and photographs of her famous hotel and the room in which the murder was said to have been committed, aren't you, Miss Hart?"

"Yes," replied Lucinda, with stolidity.

Sylvia stared with amazement. "Why, Lucinda!" she gasped.

"When I find out folks won't take no, I give 'em yes," said Lucinda, grimly.

"I knew I could finally persuade Miss Hart," said the young man, affably. He was really very much of a gentleman. He touched his hat, striking into a pleasant by-path across a field to a wood beyond.

"He's crazy over the country," remarked Lucinda; and then she was accosted again, by another gentleman. This time he was older and stouter, and somewhat tired in his aspect, but every whit as genially persuasive.

"He writes for a New York paper," said Lucinda to Sylvia, in exactly the same tone which she had used previously. "He wants me to write a piece for his paper on my first twenty-four hours under suspicion of crime."

"And you are going to write it, aren't you, Miss Hart?" asked the gentleman.

"Yes," replied Lucinda, with alacrity.

This time the gentleman looked a trifle suspicious. He pressed his inquiry. "Can you let us have the copy by Wednesday?" he asked.

"Yes," said Lucinda. Her "yes" had the effect of a snap.

The gentleman talked a little more at length with regard to his article, and Lucinda never failed with her ready "yes."

They were almost at the turn of the road, where Sylvia would leave Lucinda, when a woman appeared. She was young, but she looked old, and her expression was one of spiritual hunger.

"This lady writes for a Boston paper," said Lucinda. "She came yesterday. She wants me to write a piece for her paper upon women's unfairness to women."

"Based upon the late unfortunate occurrence at Miss Hart's hotel," said the woman.

"Yes," said Lucinda, "of course; everything is based on that. She wants me to write a piece upon how ready women are to accuse other women of doing things they didn't do."

"And you are going to write it?" said the woman, eagerly.

"Yes," said Lucinda.

"Oh, thank you! you are a perfect dear," said the woman. "I am so much pleased, and so will Mr. Evans be when he hears the news. Now I must ask you to excuse me if I hurry past, for I ought to wire him at once. I can get back to Boston to-night."

The woman had left them, with a swish of a frilled silk petticoat under a tailored skirt, when Sylvia looked at Lucinda. "You ain't goin' to?" said she.

"No."

"But you said so."

"You'd say anything to get rid of them. I've said no till I found out they wouldn't take it, so then I began to say yes. I guess I've said yes, in all, to about seventeen."

"And you don't mean to write a thing?"

"I guess I ain't going to begin writing for the papers at my time of life."

"But what will they do?"

"They won't get the pieces."

"Can't they sue you, or anything?"

"Let them sue if they want to. After what I've been through lately I guess I sha'n't mind that."

"And you are telling every one of them you'll write a piece?"

"Of course I am. It's the only thing they'll let me tell them. I want to get rid of them somehow."

Sylvia looked at Lucinda anxiously. "Is it true that Albion Bennet has left?" she said.

"Yes; he was afraid of getting poisoned. Mrs. Jim Jones has taken him. I reckon I sha'n't have many steady boarders after this has quieted down."

"But how are you going to get along, Lucinda?"

"I shall get along. Everybody gets along. What's heaped on you you have to get along with. I own the hotel, and I shall keep more hens and raise more garden truck, and let Hannah go if I can't pay her. I shall have some business, enough to keep me alive, I guess."

"Is it true that Amos Quimby has jilted Hannah on account of—?"

"Guess so. He hasn't been near her since."

"Ain't it a shame?"

"Hannah's got to live with what's heaped on her shoulders, too," said Lucinda. "Folks had ought to be thankful when the loads come from other people's hands, instead of their own, and make the best of it. Hannah has got a good appetite. It ain't going to kill her. She can go away from East Westland by-and-by if she wants to, and get another beau. Folks didn't suspect her much, anyway. I've got the brunt of it."

"Lucinda," said Sylvia, earnestly. "Folks can't really believe you'd go and do such a thing."

"It's like flies after molasses," said Lucinda. "I never felt I was so sweet before in my life."

"What can they think you'd go and poison a good, steady boarder like that for?"

"She paid a dollar a day," said Lucinda.

62

"I know she did."

"And I liked her," said Lucinda. "I know lots of folks didn't, but I did. I know what folks said, and I'll own I found things in her room, but I don't care what folks do to their outsides as long as their insides are right. Miss Farrel was a real good woman, and she had a kind of hard time, too."

"Why, I thought she had a real good place in the high-school; and teachers earn their money dreadful easy."

"It wasn't that."

"What was it?"

Lucinda hesitated. "Well," she said, finally, "it can't do her any harm, now she's dead and gone, and I don't know as it was anything against her, anyway. She just set her eyes by your boarder."

"Not Mr. Allen? You don't mean Mr. Allen, Lucinda?"

"What other boarder have you had? I've known about it for a long time. Hannah and me both have known, but we never opened our lips, and I don't want it to go any further now."

"How did you find out?"

"By keeping my eyes and ears open. How does anybody find out anything?"

"I don't believe Mr. Allen ever once thought of her," said Sylvia, and there was resentment in her voice.

"Of course he didn't. Maybe he'll take a shine to that girl you've got with you now."

"Neither one of them has even thought of such a thing," declared Sylvia, and her voice was almost violent.

"Well, I don't know," Lucinda said, indifferently. "I have had too much to look out for of my own affairs since the girl came to know anything about that. I only thought of their being in the same house. I always had sort of an idea myself that maybe Lucy Ayres would be the one."

"I hadn't," said Sylvia. "Not but she—well, she looked real sick to-day. She didn't look fit to stand up there and sing. I should think her mother would be worried about her. And she don't sing half as well as you do."

"Yes, she does," replied Lucinda. "She sings enough sight better than I do."

"Well, I don't know much about music," admitted Sylvia. "I can't tell if anybody gets off the key."

"I can," said Lucinda, firmly. "She sings enough sight better than I can, but I sang plenty well enough for them, and if I hadn't been so mad at the way I've been treated I'd kept on. Now they can get on without me. Lucy Ayres does look miserable. There's consumption in her family, too. Well, it's good for her lungs to sing, if she don't overdo it. Good-bye, Sylvia."

"Good-bye," said Sylvia. She hesitated a moment, then she said: "Don't you mind, Lucinda. Henry and I think just the same of you as we've always thought, and there's a good many besides us. You haven't any call to feel bad."

"I don't feel bad," said Lucinda. "I've got spunk enough and grit enough to bear any load that I 'ain't heaped on my own shoulders, and the Lord knows I 'ain't heaped this. Don't you worry about me, Sylvia. Good-bye."

Lucinda went her way. She held her nice black skirt high, but her plodding feet raised quite a cloud of dust. Her shoulders were thrown back, her head was very erect, the jetted ornament on her bonnet shone like a warrior's crest. She stepped evenly out of sight, as evenly as if she had been a soldier walking in line and saying to himself, "Left, right; left, right."

Chapter X

When Sylvia reached home she found Rose Fletcher and Horace Allen sitting on the bench under the oak-trees of the grove north of the house. She marched out there and stood before them, holding her fringed parasol in such a way that it made a concave frame for her stern, elderly face and thin shoulders. "Rose," said she, "you had better go into the house and lay down till dinner-time. You have been walking in the sun, and it is warm, and you look tired."

She spoke at once affectionately and severely. It seemed almost inconceivable that this elderly country woman could speak in such wise to the city-bred girl in her fashionable attire, with her air of self-possession.

But the girl looked up at her as if she loved her, and answered, in just the way in which Sylvia liked her to answer, with a sort of pretty, childish petulance, defiant, yet yielding. "I am not in the least tired," said she, "and it did not hurt me to walk in the sun, and I like to sit here under the trees."

Rose was charming that morning. Her thick, fair hair was rolled back from her temples, which had at once something noble and childlike about them. Her face was as clear as a cameo. She was dressed in mourning for her aunt, but her black robe was thin and the fine curves of her shoulders and arms were revealed, and the black lace of her wide hat threw her fairness into relief like a setting of onyx.

"You had better go into the house," said Sylvia, her eyes stern, her mouth smiling. A maternal instinct which dominated her had awakened suddenly in the older woman's heart. She adored the girl to such an extent that the adoration fairly pained her. Rose herself might easily have found this exacting affection, this constant watchfulness, irritating, but she found it sweet. She could scarcely remember her mother, but the memory had always been as one of lost love. Now she seemed to have found it again. She fairly coquetted with this older woman who loved her, and whom she loved, with that charming coquettishness sometimes seen in a daughter towards her mother. She presumed upon this affection which she felt to be so staple. She affronted Sylvia with a delicious sense of her own power over her and an underlying affection, which had in it the protective instinct of youth which dovetailed with the protective instinct of age.

It had been planned that she was to return to New York immediately after Miss Farrel's funeral. In fact, her ticket had been bought and her trunk packed, when a telegram arrived rather late at night. Rose had gone to bed when Sylvia brought it up to her room. "Don't be scared," she said, holding the yellow envelope behind her. Rose stared at her, round-eyed, from her white nest. She turned pale.

"What is it?" she said, tremulously.

"There's no need for you to go and think anything has happened until you read it," Sylvia said. "You must be calm."

"Oh, what is it?"

"A telegram," replied Sylvia, solemnly. "You must be calm."

Rose laughed. "Oh, Mrs. Wilton and Miss Pamela are forever sending telegrams," she said. "Very likely it is only to say somebody will meet me at the Grand Central."

Sylvia looked at the girl in amazement, as she coolly opened and read the telegram. Rose's face changed expression. She regarded the yellow paper thoughtfully a moment before she spoke.

"If anything has happened, you must be calm," said Sylvia, looking at her anxiously. "Of course you have lived with those people so many years you have learned to think a good deal of them; that is only natural; but, after all, they ain't your own."

Rose laughed again, but in rather a perplexed fashion. "Nothing has happened," she said—"at least, nothing that you are thinking of—but—"

"But what?"

"Why, Mrs. Wilton and Miss Pamela are going to sail for Genoa to-morrow, and that puts an end to my going to New York to them."

A great brightness overspread Sylvia's face. "Well, you ain't left stranded," she said. "You've got your home here."

Rose looked gratefully at her. "You do make me feel as if I had, and I don't know what I should do if you did not, but"—she frowned perplexedly—"all the same, one would not have thought they would have gone off in this way without giving me a moment's notice," she said, in rather an injured fashion, "after I have lived with them so long. I never thought they really cared much about me. Mrs. Wilton and Miss Pamela look too hard at their own tracks to get much interest in anybody or anything outside; but starting off in this way! They might have thought that I would like to go—at least they might have told me."

Suddenly her frown of perplexity cleared away. "I know what has happened," she said, with a nod to Sylvia. "I know exactly what has happened."

"What?"

"Mrs. Wilton's and Miss Pamela's aunt Susan has died, and they've got the money. They have been waiting for it ever since I have been with them. Their aunt was over ninety, and it did begin to seem as if she would never die."

"Was she very rich?"

"Oh, very; millions; and she never gave a cent to Mrs. Wilton and Miss Pamela. She has died, and they have just made up their minds to go away. They have always said they should live abroad as soon as they were able." Rose looked a little troubled for a moment, then she laughed. "They kept me as long as they needed me," said she, with a pleasant cynicism, "and I don't know but I had lived with them long enough to suit myself. Mrs. Wilton and Miss Pamela were always nice to me, but sometimes—well, sometimes I felt so outside them that I was awfully lonesome. And Mrs. Wilton always did just what you knew she would, and so did Miss Pamela, and it was a little like living with machines that were wound up to do the right thing by you, but didn't do it of their own accord. Now they have run down, just like machines. I know as well as I want to that Aunt Susan has died and left them her money. I shall get a letter to-morrow telling me about it. I think myself that Mrs. Wilton and Miss Pamela will get married now. They never gave up, you know. Mrs. Wilton's husband died ages ago, and she was as much of an old maid as Miss Pamela, and neither of them would give up. They will be countesses or duchesses or something within a year."

Rose laughed, and Sylvia beamed upon her. "If you feel that you can stay

66

here," she said, timidly.

"*If* I feel that I can," said Rose. She stretched out her slender arms, from which the lace-trimmed sleeves of her night-gown fell away to the shoulder, and Sylvia let them close around her thin neck and felt the young cheek upon her own with a rapture like a lover's.

"Those folks she lived with in New York are going to Europe to-morrow," she told Henry, when she was down-stairs again, "and they have treated that poor child mean. They have never told her a word about it until now. She says she thinks their rich aunt has died and left them her money, and they have just cleared out and left her."

"Well, she can stay with us as long as she is contented," said Henry.

"I rather guess she can," said Sylvia.

Henry regarded her with the wondering expression which was often on his face nowadays. He had glimpses of the maternal depths of his wife's heart, which, while not understanding, he acquiesced in; but there was something else which baffled him.

But now for Sylvia came a time of contentment, apparently beyond anything which had ever come into her life. She fairly revelled in her possession of Rose, and the girl in her turn seemed to reciprocate. Although the life in East Westland was utterly at variance with the life she had known, she settled down in it, of course with sundry hitches of adjustment. For instance, she could not rid herself at first of the conviction that she must have, as she had always had, a maid.

"I don't know how to go to work," she said to Sylvia one day. "Of course I must have a maid, but I wonder if I had better advertise or write some of my friends. Betty Morrison may know of some one, or Sally Maclean. Betty and Sally always seem to be able to find ways out of difficulties. Perhaps I had better write them. Maybe it would be safer than to advertise."

Sylvia and Rose were sitting together in the south room that afternoon. Sylvia looked pathetically and wistfully at the girl. "What do you want a maid for?" she asked, timidly.

Rose stared. "What for? Why, what I always want a maid for: to attend to my wardrobe and assist me in dressing, to brush my hair, and—everything," ended Rose, comprehensively.

Sylvia continued to regard her with that wistful, pathetic look.

"I can sew braid on your dresses, and darn your stockings, and button up your dresses, and brush your hair, too, just as well as anybody," she said.

Rose ran over to her and went down on her knees beside her. "You dear," she said, "as if you didn't have enough to do now!"

"This is a very convenient house to do work in," said Sylvia, "and now I have my washing and ironing done, I've got time on my hands. I like to sew braid on and darn stockings, and always did, and it's nothing at all to fasten up your waists in the back; you know that."

"You dear," said Rose again. She nestled her fair head against Sylvia's slim knees. Sylvia thrilled. She touched the soft puff of blond hair timidly with her bony fingers. "But I have always had a maid," Rose persisted, in a somewhat puzzled way. Rose could hardly conceive of continued existence without a maid. She had managed very well for a few days, but to contemplate life without one altogether seemed like contemplating the possibility of living without a comb and hair-brush. Sylvia's face took on a crafty expression.

"Well," said she, "if you must have a maid, write your friends, and I will have another leaf put in the dining-table."

Rose raised her head and stared at her. "Another leaf in the dining-table?" said she, vaguely.

"Yes. I don't think there's room for more than four without another leaf."

"But—my maid would not eat at the table with us."

"Would she be willing to eat in the kitchen—cold victuals—after we had finished?"

Rose looked exceedingly puzzled. "No, she would not; at least, no maid I ever had would have," she admitted.

"Where is she going to eat, then? Would she wait till after we were through and eat in the dining-room?"

"I don't believe she would like that, either."

"Where is she going to eat?" demanded Sylvia, inexorably.

Rose gazed at her.

"She could have a little table in here, or in the parlor," said Sylvia.

Rose laughed. "Oh, that would never do!" said she. "Of course there was a servants' dining-room at Mrs. Wilton's, and there always is in a hotel, you know. I never thought of that."

"She has got to eat somewhere. Where is she going to eat?" asked Sylvia, pressing the question.

Rose got up and kissed her. "Oh, well, I won't bother about it for a while, anyway," said she. "Now I think of it, Betty is sure to be off to Newport by now, and Sally must be about to sail for Paris to buy her trousseau. She is going to marry Dicky van Snyde in the autumn (whatever she sees in him)! So I doubt if either of them could do anything about a maid for me. I won't bother at all now, but I am not going to let you wait upon me. I am going to help you."

Sylvia took one of Rose's little hands and looked at it. "I guess you can't do much with hands like yours," said she, admiringly, and with an odd tone of resentment, as if she were indignant at the mere suggestion of life's demanding service from this dainty little creature, for whom she was ready to immolate herself.

However, Rose had in her a vein of persistency. She insisted upon wiping the dishes and dusting. She did it all very badly, but Sylvia found the oddest amusement in chiding her for her mistakes and in setting them right herself. She would not have been nearly as well pleased had Rose been handy about the house. One evening Henry caught Sylvia wiping over all the dishes which Rose had wiped, and which were still damp, the while she was fairly doubled up with suppressed mirth.

"What in creation ails you, Sylvia?" asked Henry.

She extended towards him a plate on which the water stood in drops. "Just see this plate that dear child thinks she has wiped," she chuckled.

"You women do beat the Dutch," said Henry.

However, Rose did prove herself an adept in one respect. She had never sewed much, but she had an inventive genius in dress, and, when she once took up her needle, used it deftly.

When Sylvia confided to her her aspiration concerning the pink silk which she had found among Abrahama's possessions, Rose did not laugh at all, but she looked at her thoughtfully.

"Don't you think it would be suitable if I had it made with some black lace?" asked Sylvia, wistfully. "Henry thinks it is too young for me, but—"

"Not black," Rose said, decisively. The two were up in the attic beside the old chest of finery. Rose took out an old barege of an ashes-of-roses color. She laid a fold of the barege over the pink silk, then she looked radiantly at Sylvia.

"It will make a perfectly lovely gown for you if you use the pink for a petticoat," said she, "and have the gown made of this delicious old stuff."

"The pink for a petticoat?" gasped Sylvia.

"It is the only way," said Rose; "and you must have gray gloves, and a bonnet

69

of gray with just one pale-pink rose in it. Don't you understand? Then you will harmonize with your dress. Your hair is gray, and there is pink in your cheeks. You will be lovely in it. There must be a very high collar and some soft creamy lace, because there is still some yellow left in your hair."

Rose nodded delightedly at Sylvia, and the dressmaker came and made the gown according to Rose's directions. Sylvia wore it for the first time when she walked from church with Lucinda Hart and found Rose and Horace sitting in the grove. After Rose had replied to Sylvia's advice that she should go into the house, she looked at her with the pride of proprietorship. "Doesn't she look simply lovely?" she asked Horace.

"She certainly does," replied the young man. He really gazed admiringly at the older woman, who made, under the glimmering shadows of the oaks, a charming nocturne of elderly womanhood. The faint pink on her cheeks seemed enhanced by the pink seen dimly through the ashen shimmer of her gown; the creamy lace harmonized with her yellow-gray hair. She was in her own way as charming as Rose in hers.

Sylvia actually blushed, and hung her head with a graceful sidewise motion. "I'm too old to be made a fool of," said she, "and I've got a good looking-glass." But she smiled the smile of a pretty woman conscious of her own prettiness. Then all three laughed, although Horace but a moment before had looked very grave, and now he was quite white. Sylvia noticed it. "Why, what ails you, Mr. Allen?" she said. "Don't you feel well?"

"Perfectly well."

"You look pale."

"It is the shadow of the oaks."

Sylvia noticed a dainty little white box in Rose's lap. "What is that?" she asked.

"It is a box of candy that dear, sweet Lucy Ayres who sang to-day made her own self and gave to me," replied Rose. "She came up to me on the way home from church and slipped it into my hand, and I hardly know her at all. I do think it is too dear of her for anything. She is such a lovely girl, and her voice is beautiful." Rose looked defiantly at Horace. "Mr. Allen has been trying to make me promise not to eat this nice candy," she said.

"I don't think candy is good for anybody, and girls eat altogether too much of it," said Horace, with a strange fervor which the occasion hardly seemed to warrant.

"Wouldn't I know he was a school-teacher when I heard him speak like that, even if nobody had ever told me?" said Rose. "Of course I am going to eat this candy that dear Lucy made her own self and gave me. I should be very ungrateful not to, and I love candy, too."

"I will send for some to Boston to-morrow," cried Horace, eagerly.

Rose regarded him with amazement. "Why, Mr. Allen, you just said you did not approve of candy at all, and here you are proposing to send for some for me," she said, "when I have this nice home-made candy, a great deal purer, because one knows exactly what is in it, and you say I must not eat this."

Rose took up a sugared almond daintily and put it to her lips, but Horace was too quick for her. Before she knew what he was about he had dashed it from her hand, and in the tumult the whole box of candy was scattered. Horace trampled on it, it was impossible to say whether purposely or accidentally, in the struggle.

Both Rose and Sylvia regarded him with amazement, mixed with indignation.

"Why, Mr. Allen!" said Rose. Then she added, haughtily: "Mr. Allen, you take altogether too much upon yourself. You have spoiled my candy, and you forget that you have not the least right to dictate to me what I shall or shall not eat."

Sylvia also turned upon Horace. "Home-made candy wouldn't hurt her," she said. "Why, Mr. Allen, what do you mean?"

"Nothing. I am very sorry," said Horace. Then he walked away without another word, and entered the house. The girl and the woman stood looking at each other.

"What did he do such a thing for?" asked Rose.

"Goodness knows," said Sylvia.

Rose was quite pale. She began to look alarmed. "You don't suppose he's taken suddenly insane or anything?" said she.

"My land! no," said Sylvia. "Men do act queer sometimes."

"I should think so, if this is a sample of it," said Rose, eying the trampled candy. "Why, he ground his heel into it! What right had he to tell me I should or should not eat it?" she said, indignantly, again.

"None at all. Men are queer. Even Mr. Whitman is queer sometimes."

"If he is as queer as that, I don't see how you have lived with him so long. Did he ever make you drop a nice box of candy somebody had given you, and trample on it, and then walk off?"

"No, I don't know as he ever did; but men do queer things."

"I don't like Mr. Allen at all," said Rose, walking beside Sylvia towards the house. "Not at all. I don't like him as well as Mr. James Duncan."

Sylvia looked at her with quick alarm. "The man who wrote you last week?"

"Yes, and wanted to know if there was a hotel here so he could come."

"I thought——" began Sylvia.

"Yes, I had begun the letter, telling him the hotel wasn't any good, because I knew he would know what that meant—that there was no use in his asking me to marry him again, because I never would; but now I think I shall tell him the hotel is not so bad, after all," said Rose.

"But you don't mean——"

"I don't know what I do mean," said Rose, nervously. "Yes, I do know what I mean. I always know what I mean, but I don't know what men mean making me drop candy I have had given me, and trampling on it, and men don't know that I know what I mean." Rose was almost crying.

"Go up-stairs and lay down a little while before dinner," said Sylvia, anxiously.

"No," replied Rose; "I am going to help you. Don't, please, think I am crying because I feel badly. It is because I am angry. I am going to set the table."

But Rose did not set the table. She forgot all about it when she had entered the south room and found Henry Whitman sitting there with the Sunday paper. She sat down opposite and looked at him with her clear, blue, childlike eyes. She had come to call him Uncle Henry.

"Uncle Henry?" said she, interrogatively, and waited.

Henry looked across at her and smiled with the somewhat abashed tenderness which he always felt for this girl, whose environment had been so very different from his and his wife's. "Well?" he said.

"Uncle Henry, do you think a man can tell another man's reasons for doing a queer thing better than a woman can?"

"Perhaps."

"I almost know a woman could tell why a woman did a queer thing, better than a man could," said Rose, reflectively. She hesitated a little.

Henry waited, his worn, pleasant face staring at her over a vividly colored page of the paper.

"Suppose," said Rose, "another woman had given Aunt Sylvia a box of candy which she had made herself, real nice candy, and suppose the woman who had given it to her was lovely, and you had knocked a piece of candy from Aunt Sylvia's mouth just as she was going to taste it, and had startled her so you made her drop the whole box, and then set your heel hard on the pieces; what would you have done it for?"

The girl's face wore an expression of the keenest inquiry. Henry looked at her, wrinkling his forehead. "If another woman had given Sylvia a box of candy she had made, and I knocked a piece from her hand just as she was going to taste it, and made her drop the whole box, and had trampled all the rest of the candy underfoot, what should I have done it for?" he repeated.

"Yes."

Henry looked at her. He heard a door shut up-stairs. "I shouldn't have done it," he said.

"But suppose you had done it?"

"I shouldn't have."

Rose shrugged her shoulders. "You are horrid, Uncle Henry," she said.

"But I shouldn't have done it," repeated Henry. He heard Horace's step on the stair. Rose got up and ran out of the room by another door from that which Horace entered. Horace sat down in the chair which Rose had just vacated. He looked pale and worried. The eyes of the two men met. Henry's eyes asked a question. Horace answered it.

"I am in such a devil of a mess as never man was yet, I believe," he said.

Henry nodded gravely.

"The worst of it is I can't tell a living mortal," Horace said, in a whisper. "I am afraid even to think it."

At dinner Rose sat with her face averted from Horace. She never spoke once to him. As they rose from the table she made an announcement. "I am going to run over and see Lucy Ayres," she said. "I am going to tell her an accident happened to my candy, and maybe she will give me some more."

Henry saw Horace's face change. "Candy is not good for girls; it spoils their complexion. I have just been reading about it in the Sunday paper," said Henry. Sylvia unexpectedly proved his ally. Rose had not eaten much dinner, although it had been an especially nice one, and she felt anxious about her.

"I don't think you ought to eat candy when you have so little appetite for good, wholesome meat and vegetables," she said.

73

"I want to see Lucy, too," said Rose. "I am going over there. It is a lovely afternoon. I have nothing I want to read and nothing to do. I am going over there."

Henry's eyes questioned Horace's, which said, plainly, to the other man, "For God's sake, don't let her go; don't let her go!"

Rose had run up-stairs for her parasol. Horace turned away. He understood that Henry would help him. "Don't let her go over there this afternoon," said Henry to Sylvia, who looked at him in the blankest amazement.

"Why not, I'd like to know?" asked Sylvia.

"Don't let her go," repeated Henry.

Sylvia looked suspiciously from one man to the other. The only solution which a woman could put upon such a request immediately occurred to her. She said to herself, "Hm! Mr. Allen wants Rose to stay at home so he can see her himself, and Henry knows it."

She stiffened her neck. Down deep in her heart was a feeling more seldom in women's hearts than in men's. She would not have owned that she did not wish to part with this new darling of her heart—who had awakened within it emotions of whose strength the childless woman had never dreamed. There was also another reason, which she would not admit even to herself. Had Rose been, indeed, her daughter, and she had possessed her from the cradle to womanhood, she would probably have been as other mothers, but now Rose was to her as the infant she had never borne. She felt the intense jealousy of ownership which the mother feels over the baby in her arms. She wished to snatch Rose from every clasp except her own.

She decided at once that it was easy to see through the plans of Horace and her husband, and she determined to thwart them. "I don't see why she shouldn't go," she said. "It is a lovely afternoon. The walk will do her good. Lucy Ayres is a real nice girl, and of course Rose wants to see girls of her own age now and then."

"It is Sunday," said Henry. He felt and looked like a hypocrite as he spoke, but the distress in Horace's gaze was too much for him.

Sylvia sniffed. "Sunday," said she. "Good land! what has come over you, Henry Whitman? It has been as much as I could do to get you to go to meeting the last ten years, and now all of a sudden you turn around and think it's wicked for a young girl to run in and see another young girl Sunday afternoon." Sylvia sniffed again very distinctly, and then Rose entered the room.

Her clear, fair face looked from one to another from under her black hat. "What is the matter?" she asked.

Sylvia patted her on the shoulder. "Nothing is the matter," said she. "Run along and have a good time, but you had better be home by five o'clock. There is a praise meeting to-night, and I guess we'll all want to go, and I am going to have supper early."

After Rose had gone and Sylvia had left the room, the two men looked at each other. Horace was ashy pale. Henry's face showed alarm and astonishment. "What is it?" he whispered.

"Come out in the grove and have a smoke," said Horace, with a look towards the door through which Sylvia had gone.

Henry nodded. He gathered up his pipe and tobacco from the table, and the two men sauntered out of the house into the grove. But even there not much was said. Both smoked in silence, sitting on the bench, before Horace opened his lips in response to Henry's inquiry.

"I don't know what it is, and I don't know that it is anything, and that is the worst of it," he said, gloomily; "and I can't see my way to telling any mortal what little I do know that leads me to fear that it is something, although I would if I were sure and actually knew beyond doubt that there was—" He stopped abruptly and blew a ring of smoke from his cigar.

"Something is queer about my wife lately," said Henry, in a low voice.

"What?"

"That's just it. I feel something as you do. It may be nothing at all. I tell you what, young man, when women talk, as women are intended by an overruling Providence to talk, men know where they are at, but when a woman doesn't talk men know where they ain't."

"In my case there has been so much talk that I seem to be in a fog of it, and can't see a blessed thing sufficiently straight to know whether it is big enough to bother about or little enough to let alone; but I can't repeat the talk—no man could," said Horace.

"In my case there ain't talk enough," said Henry. "I ain't in a fog; I'm in pitch darkness."

Chapter XI

The two men sat for some time out in the grove. It was very pleasant there. The air was unusually still, and only the tops of the trees whitened

75

occasionally in a light puff of wind like a sigh. Now and then a carriage or an automobile passed on the road beyond, but not many of them. It was not a main thoroughfare. The calls and quick carols of the birds, punctuated with sharp trills of insects, were almost the only sounds heard. Now and then Sylvia's face glanced at them from a house window, but it was quickly withdrawn. She never liked men to be in close conclave without a woman to superintend, yet she could not have told why. She had a hazy impression, as she might have had if they had been children, that some mischief was afoot.

"Sitting out there all this time, and smoking, and never seeming to speak a word," she said to herself, as she returned to her seat beside a front window in the south room and took up her book. She was reading with a mild and patronizing interest a book in which the heroine did nothing which she would possibly have done under given circumstances, and said nothing which she would have said, and was, moreover, a distinctly different personality from one chapter to another, yet the whole had a charm for the average woman reader. Henry had flung it aside in contempt. Sylvia thought it beautiful, possibly for the reason that her own hard sense was sometimes a strenuous burden, and in reading this she was forced to put it behind her. However, the book did not prevent her from returning every now and then to her own life and the happenings in it. Hence her stealthy journeys across the house and peeps at the men in the grove. If they were nettled by a sense of feminine mystery, she reciprocated. "What on earth did they want to stop Rose from going to see Lucy for?" seemed to stare at her in blacker type than the characters of the book.

Presently, when she saw Horace pass the window and disappear down the road, she laid the book on the table, with a slip of paper to keep the place, and hurried out to the grove. She found Henry leisurely coming towards the house. "Where has he gone?" she inquired, with a jerk of her shoulder towards the road.

"Mr. Allen?"

"Yes."

"How should I know?"

"Don't you know?"

"Maybe I do," said Henry, smiling at Sylvia with his smile of affection and remembrance that she was a woman.

"Why don't you tell?"

"Now, Sylvia," said Henry, "you must remember that Mr. Allen is not a child. He is a grown man, and if he takes it into his head to go anywhere you can't say anything."

Sylvia looked at Henry with a baffled expression. "I think he might spend his time a good deal more profitably Sunday afternoon than sitting under the trees and smoking, or going walking," said she, rashly and inconsequentially. "If he would only sit down and read some good book."

"You can't dictate to Mr. Allen what he shall or shall not do," Henry repeated.

"Why didn't you want Rose to go to Lucy's?" asked Sylvia, making a charge in an entirely different quarter.

Henry scorned to lie. "I don't know," he replied, which was the perfect truth as far as it went. It did not go quite far enough, for he did not add that he did not know why Horace Allen did not want her to go, and that was his own reason.

However, Sylvia could not possibly fathom that. She sniffed with her delicate nostrils, as if she actually smelled some questionable odor of character. "You men have mighty queer streaks, that's all I've got to say," she returned.

When they were in the house again she resumed her book, reading every word carefully, and Henry took up the Sunday paper, which he had not finished. The thoughts of both, however, turned from time to time towards Horace. Sylvia did not know where he had gone. She did not suspect. Henry knew, but he did not know why. Horace had sprung suddenly to his feet and caught up his hat as the two men had been sitting under the trees. Henry had emitted a long puff of tobacco smoke and looked inquiringly at him through the filmy blue of it.

"I can't stand it another minute," said Horace, almost with violence. "I've got to know what is going on. I am going to the Ayres's myself. I don't care what they think. I don't care what she thinks. I don't care what anybody thinks." With that he was gone.

Henry took another puff at his pipe. It showed the difference between the masculine and the feminine point of view that Henry did not for one moment attach a sentimental reason to Horace's going. He realized Rose's attractions. The very probable supposition that she and Horace might fall in love with and marry each other had occurred to him, but this he knew at once had nothing to do with that. He turned the whole over and over in his mind, with no result. He lacked enough premises to arrive at conclusions. He had started for the house and his Sunday paper when he met Sylvia, and had resolved to put it all out of his mind. But he was not quite able. There is a masculine curiosity as well as a feminine, and one is about as persistent as the other.

Meantime Horace was walking down the road towards the Ayres house. It was a pretty, much-ornamented white cottage, with a carefully kept lawn and shade trees. At one side was an old-fashioned garden with an arbor. In this arbor, as Horace drew near, he saw the sweep of feminine draperies. It seemed to him that the arbor was full of women. In reality there were only three—Lucy, her mother, and Rose.

When Rose had rung the door-bell she had been surprised by what sounded like a mad rush to answer her ring. Mrs. Ayres opened the door. She looked white and perturbed, and behind her showed Lucy's face, flushed and angry.

"I knew it was Miss Fletcher; I told you so, mother," said Lucy, and her low, sweet voice rang out like an angry bird's with a sudden break for the high notes.

Mrs. Ayres kept her self-possession of manner, although her face showed not only nervousness but something like terror. "Good-afternoon, Miss Fletcher," she said. "Please walk in."

"She said for me to call her Rose," cried Lucy. "Please come in, Rose. I am glad to see you."

In spite of the cordial words the girl's voice was strange. Rose stared from daughter to mother and back again. "If you were engaged," she said, rather coldly, "if you would prefer that I come some other time—"

"No, indeed," cried Lucy, "no other time. Yes, every other time. What am I saying? But I want you now, too. Come right up to my room, Rose. I know you will excuse my wrapper and my bed's being tumbled. I have been lying down. Come right up."

Rose followed Lucy, and to her astonishment became aware that Lucy's mother was following her. Mrs. Ayres entered the room with the two girls. Lucy looked impatiently at her, and spoke as Rose wondered any daughter could speak. "Rose and I have some things to talk over, mother," she said.

"Nothing, I guess, that your mother cannot hear," returned Mrs. Ayres, with forced pleasantry. She sat down, and Lucy flung herself petulantly upon the bed, where she had evidently been lying, but seemingly not reposing, for it was much rumpled, and the pillows gave evidence of the restless tossing of a weary head. Lucy herself had a curiously rumpled aspect, though she was not exactly untidy. Her soft, white, lace-trimmed wrapper carelessly tied with blue ribbons was wrinkled, her little slippers were unbuttoned. Her mass of soft hair was half over her shoulders. There were red spots on the cheeks which had been so white in the morning, and her eyes shone. She kept tying and untying two blue ribbons at the neck of her wrapper as she lay on the bed and talked rapidly.

"I look like a fright, I know," she said. "I was tired after church, and slipped off my dress and lay down. My hair is all in a muss."

"It is such lovely hair that it looks pretty anyway," said Rose.

Lucy drew a strand of her hair violently over her shoulder. It almost seemed as if she meant to tear it out by the roots.

"Lucy!" said her mother.

"Oh, mother, do let me alone!" cried the girl. Then she said, looking angrily at her tress of hair, then at Rose: "It is not nearly as pretty as yours. You know it isn't. All men are simply crazy over hair your color. I hate my hair. I just hate it."

"Lucy!" said her mother again, in the same startled but admonitory tone.

Lucy made an impatient face at her. She threw back the tress of hair. "I hate it," said she.

Rose began to feel awkward. She noticed Mrs. Ayres's anxious regard of her daughter, and she thought with disgust that Lucy Ayres was not so sweet a girl as she had seemed. However, she felt an odd kind of sympathy and pity for her. Lucy's pretty face and her white wrapper seemed alike awry with nervous suffering, which the other girl dimly understood, although it was the understanding of a normal character with regard to an abnormal one.

Rose resolved to change the subject. "I did enjoy your singing so much this morning," she said.

"Thank you," replied Lucy, but a look of alarm instead of pleasure appeared upon her face, which Rose was astonished to see in the mother's likewise.

"I feel so sorry for poor Miss Hart, because I cannot think for a moment that she was guilty of what they accused her of," said Rose, "that I don't like to say anything about her singing. But I will say this much: I did enjoy yours."

"Thank you," said Lucy again. Her look of mortal terror deepened. From being aggressively nervous, she looked on the verge of a collapse.

Mrs. Ayres rose, went to Lucy's closet, and returned with a bottle of wine and a glass. "Here," she said, as she poured out the red liquor. "You had better drink this, dear. You know Dr. Wallace said you must drink port wine, and you are all tired out with your singing this morning."

Lucy seized the glass and drank the wine eagerly.

"It must be a nervous strain," said Rose, "to stand up there, before such a crowded audience as there was this morning, and sing."

"Yes, it is," agreed Mrs. Ayres, in a harsh voice, "and especially when anybody isn't used to it. Lucy is not at all strong."

"I hope it won't be too much for her," said Rose; "but it is such a delight to listen to her after—"

"Oh, I am tired and sick of hearing Miss Hart's name!" cried Lucy, unpleasantly.

"Lucy!" said Mrs. Ayres.

"Well, I am," said Lucy, defiantly. "It has been nothing but Miss Hart, Miss Hart, from morning until night lately. Nobody thinks she poisoned Miss Farrel, of course. It was perfect nonsense to accuse her of it, and when that is said, I think myself that is enough. I see no need of this eternal harping upon it. I have heard nothing except 'poor Miss Hart' until I am nearly wild. Come, Rose, I'll get dressed and we'll go out in the arbor. It is too pleasant to stay indoors. This room is awfully close."

"I think perhaps I had better not stay," Rose replied, doubtfully. It seemed to her that she was having a very strange call, and she began to be indignant as well as astonished.

"Of course you are going to stay," Lucy said, and her voice was sweet again. "We'll let Miss Hart alone and I'll get dressed, and we'll go in the arbor. It is lovely out there to-day."

With that Lucy sprang from the bed and let her wrapper slip from her shoulders. She stood before her old-fashioned black-walnut bureau and began brushing her hair. Her white arms and shoulders gleamed through it as she brushed with what seemed a cruel violence.

Rose laughed in a forced way. "Why, dear, you brush your hair as if it had offended you," she said.

"Don't brush so hard, Lucy," said Mrs. Ayres.

"I just hate my old hair, anyway," said Lucy, with a vicious stroke of the brush. She bent her head over, and swept the whole dark mass downward until it concealed her face and nearly touched her knees. Then she gave it a deft twist, righted herself, and pinned the coil in place.

"How beautifully you do up your hair," said Rose.

Lucy cast an appreciative glance at herself in the glass. The wine had deepened the glow on her cheeks. Her eyes were more brilliant. She pulled her hair a little over one temple, and looked at herself with entire satisfaction. Lucy had beautiful neck and arms, unexpectedly plump for a girl so apparently slender. Her skin was full of rosy color, too. She gazed at the superb curve of her shoulders rising above the dainty lace of her corset-cover, and smiled undisguisedly.

"I wish my neck was as plump as yours," said Rose.

"Yes, she has a nice, plump neck," said Mrs. Ayres. While the words showed maternal pride, the tone never relaxed from its nervous anxiety.

Lucy's smile vanished suddenly. "Well, what if it is plump?" said she. "What is the use of it? A girl living here in East Westland can never wear a dress to show her neck. People would think she had gone out of her mind."

Rose laughed. "I have some low-neck gowns," said she, "but I can't wear them, either. Maybe that is fortunate for me, my neck is so thin."

"You will wear them in other places," said Lucy. "You won't stay here all your days. You will have plenty of chances to wear your low-neck gowns." She spoke again in her unnaturally high voice. She turned towards her closet to get her dress.

"Lucy!" said Mrs. Ayres.

"Well, it is the truth," said Lucy. "Don't preach, mother. If you were a girl, and somebody told you your neck was pretty, and you knew other girls had chances to wear low-neck dresses, you wouldn't be above feeling it a little."

"My neck was as pretty as yours when I was a girl, and I never wore a low-neck dress in my life," said Mrs. Ayres.

"Oh, well, you got married when you were eighteen," said Lucy. There was something almost coarse in her remark. Rose felt herself flush. She was sophisticated, and had seen the world, although she had been closely if not lovingly guarded; but she shrank from some things as though she had never come from under a country mother's wing in her life.

Lucy got a pale-blue muslin gown from the closet and slipped it over her shoulders. Then she stood for her mother to fasten it in the back. Lucy was lovely in this cloud of blue, with edgings of lace on the ruffles and knots of black velvet. She fastened her black velvet girdle, and turned herself sidewise with a charming feminine motion, to get the effect of her slender waist between the curves of her small hips and bust. Again she looked pleased.

"You are dear in that blue gown," said Rose.

Lucy smiled. Then she scowled as suddenly. She could see Rose over her shoulder in the glass. "It is awful countrified," said she. "Look at the sleeves and look at yours. Where was yours made?"

"My dressmaker in New York made it," faltered Rose. She felt guilty because her gown was undeniably in better style.

"There's no use trying to have anything in East Westland," said Lucy.

While she was fastening a little gold brooch at her throat, Rose again tried to change the subject. "That candy of yours looked perfectly delicious," said she. "You must teach me how you make it."

Mrs. Ayres went dead white in a moment. She looked at Lucy with a look of horror which the girl did not meet. She went on fastening her brooch. "Did you like it?" she asked, carelessly.

"An accident happened to it, I am sorry to say," explained Rose. "Mr. Allen and I were out in the grove, and somehow he jostled me, and the candy got scattered on the ground, and he stepped on it."

"Were you and he alone out there?" asked Lucy, in a very quiet voice.

Rose looked at her amazedly. "Why, no, not when that happened!" she replied. "Aunt Sylvia was there, too." She spoke a little resentfully. "What if Mr. Allen and I had been alone; what is that to her?" she thought.

"There is some more candy," said Lucy, calmly. "I will get it, and then we will go out in the arbor. I will teach you to make the candy any day. It is very simple. Come, Rose dear. Mother, we are going out in the arbor."

Mrs. Ayres rose immediately. She preceded the two girls down-stairs, and came through the sitting-room door with a dish of candy in her hand just as they reached it. "Here is the candy, dear," she said to Lucy, and there was something commanding in her voice.

Lucy took the dish, a pretty little decorated affair, with what seemed to Rose an air of suspicion and a grudging "thank you, mother."

"Come, Rose," she said. She led the way and Rose followed. Mrs. Ayres returned to the sitting-room. The girls went through the old-fashioned garden with its flower-beds outlined with box, in which the earlier flowers were at their prime, to the arbor. It was a pretty old structure, covered with the shaggy arms of an old grape-vine whose gold-green leaves were just uncurling. Lucy placed the bowl of candy on the end of the bench which ran round the interior, and, to Rose's surprise, seated herself at a distance from it, and motioned Rose to sit beside her, without offering her any candy. Lucy leaned against

Rose and looked up at her. She looked young and piteous and confiding. Rose felt again that she was sweet and that she loved her. She put her arm around Lucy.

"You are a dear," said she.

Lucy nestled closer. "I know you must have thought me perfectly horrid to speak as I did to mother," said she, "but you don't understand."

Lucy hesitated. Rose waited.

"You see, the trouble is," Lucy went on, "I love mother dearly, of course. She is the best mother that ever a girl had, but she is always so anxious about me, and she follows me about so, and I get nervous, and I know I don't always speak as I should. I am often ashamed of myself. You see—"

Lucy hesitated again for a longer period. Rose waited.

"Mother has times of being very nervous," Lucy said, in a whisper. "I sometimes think, when she follows me about so, that she is not for the time being quite herself."

Rose started and looked at the other girl in horror. "Why don't you have a doctor?" said she.

"Oh, I don't mean that she—I don't mean that there is anything serious, only she has always been over-anxious about me, and at times I fancy she is nervous, and then the anxiety grows beyond limit. She always gets over it. I don't mean that—"

"Oh, I didn't know," said Rose.

"I never mean to be impatient," Lucy went on, "but to-day I was very tired, and I wanted to see you especially. I wanted to ask you something."

"What?"

Lucy looked away from Rose. She seemed to shrink within herself. The color faded from her face. "I heard something," she said, faintly, "but I said I wouldn't believe it until I had asked you."

"What is it?"

"I heard that you were engaged to marry Mr. Allen."

Rose flushed and moved away a little from Lucy. "You can contradict the rumor whenever you hear it again," said she.

"Then it isn't true?"

"No, it isn't."

Lucy nestled against Rose, in spite of a sudden coldness which had come over the other girl. "You are so dear," said she.

Rose looked straight ahead, and sat stiffly.

"I am thoroughly angry at such rumors, merely because a girl happens to be living in the same house with a marriageable man," said she.

"Yes, that is so," said Lucy. She remained quiet for a few moments, leaning against Rose, her blue-clad shoulder pressing lovingly the black-clad one. Then she moved away a little, and reared her pretty back with a curious, snakelike motion. Rose watched her. Lucy's eyes fastened themselves upon her, and something strange happened. Either Lucy Ayres was a born actress, or she had become actually so imbued, through abnormal emotion and love, with the very spirit of the man that she was capable of projecting his own emotions and feelings into her own soul and thence upon her face. At all events, she looked at Rose, and slowly Rose became bewildered. It seemed to her that Horace Allen was looking at her through the eyes of this girl, with a look which she had often seen since their very first meeting. She felt herself glowing from head to foot. She was conscious of a deep crimson stealing all over her face and neck. Her eyes fell before the other girl's. Then suddenly it was all over. Lucy rose with a little laugh. "You sweet, funny creature," she said. "I can make you blush, looking at you, as if I were a man. Well, maybe I love you as well as one." Lucy took the bowl of candy from the bench and extended it to Rose. "Do have some candy," said she.

"Thank you," said Rose. She looked bewildered, and felt so. She took a sugared almond and began nibbling at it. "Aren't you going to eat any candy yourself?" said she.

"I have eaten so much already that it has made my head ache," replied Lucy. "Is it good?"

"Simply delicious. You must teach me how you make such candy."

"Lucy will be glad to teach you any day," said Mrs. Ayres's voice. She had come swiftly upon them, and entered the arbor with a religious newspaper in her hand. Lucy no longer seemed annoyed by her mother's following her. She only set the candy behind her with a quick movement which puzzled Rose.

"Aren't you going to offer your mother some?" she asked, laughing.

"Mother can't eat candy. Dr. Wallace has forbidden it," Lucy said, quickly.

"Yes, that is quite true," assented Mrs. Ayres. She began reading her paper. Lucy offered the bowl again to Rose, who took a bonbon. She was just swallowing it when Horace Allen appeared. He made a motion which did not escape Mrs. Ayres. She rose and confronted him with perfect calmness and dignity. "Good-afternoon, Mr. Allen," she said.

Lucy had sprung up quickly. She was very white. Horace said good-afternoon perfunctorily, and looked at Rose.

Mrs. Ayres caught up the bowl of candy. "Let me offer you some, Mr. Allen," she said. "It is home-made candy, and quite harmless, I assure you."

Her fair, elderly face confronted him smilingly, her voice was calm.

"Thank you," said Horace, and took a sugared almond.

Lucy made a movement as if to stop him, but her mother laid her hand with gentle firmness on her arm. "Sit down, Lucy," she said, and Lucy sat down.

Chapter XII

Henry Whitman and his wife Sylvia remained, the one reading his Sunday paper, the other her book, while Horace and Rose were away. Henry's paper rustled, Sylvia turned pages gently. Occasionally she smiled the self-satisfied smile of the reader who thinks she understands the author, to her own credit. Henry scowled over his paper the scowl of one who reads to disapprove, to his own credit.

Both were quite engrossed. Sylvia had reached an extremely interesting portion of her book, and Henry was reading a section of his paper which made him fairly warlike. However, the clock striking four aroused both of them.

"I think it is very funny that they have not come home," said Sylvia.

"I dare say they will be along pretty soon," said Henry.

Sylvia looked keenly at him. "Henry Whitman, did he go to the Ayres's?" said she.

Henry, cornered, told the truth. "Well, I shouldn't wonder," he admitted.

"I think it is pretty work," said Sylvia, angry red spots coming in her cheeks.

Henry said nothing.

"The idea that a young man can't be in the house with a girl any longer than this without his fairly chasing her," said Sylvia.

"Who knows that he is?"

"Do you think he is interested in the Ayres girl?"

"No, I don't."

"Then it is Rose," said Sylvia. "Pretty work, I call it. Here she is with her own folks in this nice home, with everything she needs."

Henry looked at Sylvia with astonishment. "Why," he said, "girls get married! You got married yourself."

"I know I did," said Sylvia, "but that hasn't got anything to do with it. Of course he has to chase her the minute she comes within gunshot."

"Still, there's one thing certain, if she doesn't want him he can take it out in chasing, if he is chasing, and I don't think he is," said Henry. "Nobody is going to make Rose marry any man."

"She don't act a mite in love with him," said Sylvia, ruminatingly. "She seemed real mad with him this noon about that candy. Henry, that was a funny thing for him to do."

"What?" asked Henry, who had so far only gotten Rose's rather vague account of the candy episode.

Sylvia explained. "He actually knocked that candy out of her hand, and made her spill the whole box, and then trampled on it. I saw him."

Henry stared at Sylvia. "It must have been an accident," said he.

"It looked like an accident on purpose," said Sylvia. "Well, I guess I'll go out and make some of that salad they like so much for supper."

After Sylvia had gone Henry sat for a while reflecting, then he went noiselessly out of the front door and round to the grove. He found the scattered pieces of candy and the broken box quickly enough. He cast a wary glance around, and gathered the whole mass up and thrust it into the pocket of his Sunday coat. Then he stole back to the house and got his hat and went out again. He was hurrying along the road, when he met Horace and Rose returning. Rose was talking, seemingly, with a cold earnestness to her companion. Horace seemed to be listening passively. Henry thought he looked pale and anxious. When he saw Henry he smiled. "I have an errand, a business errand," explained Henry. "Please tell Mrs. Whitman I shall be home in time for supper. I don't think she knew when I went out. She was in the kitchen."

"All right," replied Horace.

After he had passed them Henry caught the words, "I think you owe me an explanation," in Rose's voice.

"It is about this blamed candy," thought Henry, feeling the crumpled mass in his pocket. He had a distrust of candy, and it occurred to him that he would have an awkward explanation to make if the candy should by any possibility melt and stick to the pocket of his Sunday coat. He therefore took out the broken box and carried it in his hand, keeping the paper wrapper firmly around it. "What in creation is it all about?" he thought, irritably. He felt a sense of personal injury. Henry enjoyed calm, and it seemed to him that he was being decidedly disturbed, as by mysterious noises breaking in upon the even tenor of his life.

"Sylvia is keeping something to herself that is worrying her to death, in spite of her being so tickled to have the girl with us, and now here is this candy," he said to himself. He understood that for some reason Horace had not wanted Rose to eat the candy, that he had resorted to fairly desperate measures to prevent it, but he could not imagine why. He had no imagination for sensation or melodrama, and the candy affair was touching that line. He had been calmly prosaic with regard to Miss Farrel's death. "They can talk all they want to about murder and suicide," he had said to Sylvia. "I don't believe a word of it."

"But the doctors found—" began Sylvia.

"Found nothing," interposed Henry. "What do doctors know? She et something that hurt her. How do doctors know but what anybody might eat something that folks think is wholesome, that, if the person ain't jest right for it, acts like poison? Doctors don't know much. She et something that hurt her."

"Poor Lucinda's cooking is enough to hurt 'most anybody," admitted Sylvia; "but they say they found—"

"Don't talk such stuff," said Henry, fiercely. "She et something. I don't know what you women like best to suck at, candy or horrors."

Now Henry was forced to admit that he himself was confronted by something mysterious. Why had Horace fairly flung that candy on the ground, and trampled on it, unless he had suddenly gone mad, or—? There Henry brought himself up with a jolt. He absolutely refused to suspect. "I'd jest as soon eat all that's left of the truck myself," he thought, "only I couldn't bear candy since I was a child, and I ain't going to eat it for anybody."

Henry had to pass the Ayres house. Just as he came abreast of it he heard a hysterical sob, then another, from behind the open windows of a room on the second floor, whose blinds were closed. Henry made a grimace and went his way. He was bound for Sidney Meeks's. He found the lawyer in his office in an arm-chair, which whirled like a top at the slightest motion of its occupant. Around him were strewn Sunday papers, all that could be bought. On the desk before him stood a bottle of clear yellow wine, half-emptied.

Sidney looked up and smiled as Henry entered. "Here I am in a vortex of crime and misrule," he said, "and I should have been out of my wits if it had not been for that wine. There's another glass over there, Henry; get it and help yourself."

"Guess I won't take any now, thank you," said Henry. "It's just before supper."

"Maybe you are wise," admitted the lawyer. He slouched before Henry in untidy and unmended, but clean, Sunday attire. Sidney Meeks was as clean as a gentleman should be, but there was never a crease except of ease in his clothes, and he was so buttonless that women feared to look at him closely. "It might go to your head," said Sidney. "It went to mine a little, but that was unavoidable. After one of those papers there my head was mighty near being a vacuum."

"What do you read the papers for?" asked Henry.

"Because," said Sidney, "I feel it incumbent upon me to be well informed concerning two things, although I verily believe it to be true that I have precious little of either, and they cannot directly concern me. I want to know about the stock market, although I don't own a blessed share in anything except an old mine out West on a map; and I want to know what evil is fermenting in the hearts of men, though I am pretty sure, in spite of the original sin part of it, that precious little is fermenting in mine. About three o'clock this afternoon I came to the conclusion that we were in hell or Sodom, or else the newspaper men got saved from the general destruction along with Lot. So I got a bottle of this blessed wine, and now I am fully convinced that I am on a planet which is the work of the Lord Almighty, and only created for an end of redemption and eternal bliss, and that the newspaper men are enough sight better than Lot ever thought of being, and are spending Sunday as they should, peacefully in the bosoms of their own families. In fact, Henry, my mental and spiritual outlook has cleared. What in creation is that wad of broken box you are carrying as if it would go off any minute?"

Henry told him the story in a few words.

"Gee whiz!" said Meeks. "I thought I had finished the Sunday papers and here you are with another sensation. Let's see the stuff."

Henry gave the crumpled box with the mass of candy to Meeks, who examined it closely. He smelled of it. He even tasted a bit. "It's all beyond me," he said, finally. "I am loath to admit that a sensation has lit upon us here in East Westland. Leave it with me, and I'll see what is the matter with it, if there's anything. I don't think myself there's anything, but I'll take it to Wallace. He's an analytical chemist, and holds his tongue, which is worth more than the chemistry."

"You will not say a word—" began Henry, but Meeks interrupted him.

"Don't you know me well enough by this time?" he demanded, and Henry admitted that he did.

"Do you suppose I want all this blessed little town in a tumult, and the devil to pay?" said Meeks. "It is near time for me to start some daisy wine, too. I shouldn't have a minute free. There'd be suits for damages, and murder trials, and the Lord knows what. I'd rather make my daisy wine. Leave this damned sticky mess with me, and I'll see to it. What in creation any young woman in her senses wants to spend her time in making such stuff for, anyway, beats me. Women are all more or less fools, anyhow. I suppose they can't help it, but we ought to have it in mind."

"I suppose there's something in it," said Henry, rather doubtfully.

Meeks laughed. "Oh, I don't expect any man with a wife to agree with me," he said. "You might as well try to lift yourself by your boot-straps; but I've got standing-ground outside the situation and you haven't. Good-night, Henry. Don't fret yourself over this. I'll let you know as soon as I know myself."

Henry, passing the Ayres house on his way home, fancied he heard again a sob, but this time it was so stifled that he was not sure. "It's mighty queer work, anyway," he thought. He thought also that though he should have liked a son, he was very glad that he and Sylvia had not owned a daughter. He was fond of Rose, but, although she was a normal girl, she often gave him a sense of mystery which irritated him.

Had Henry Whitman dreamed of what was really going on in the Ayres house, he would have been devoutly thankful that he had no daughter. He had in reality heard the sob which he had not been sure of. It had come from Lucy's room. Her mother was there with her. The two had been closeted together ever since Rose had gone. Lucy had rushed up-stairs and pulled off her pretty gown with a hysterical fury. She had torn it at the neck, because the hooks would not unfasten easily, before her mother, who moved more slowly, had entered the room.

"What are you doing, Lucy?" Mrs. Ayres asked, in a voice which was at once tender and stern.

"Getting out of this old dress," replied Lucy, fiercely.

"Stand round here by the light," said her mother, calmly. Lucy obeyed. She stood, although her shoulders twitched nervously, while her mother unfastened her gown. Then she began almost tearing off her other garments.

"Lucy," said Mrs. Ayres, "you are over twenty years old, and a woman grown, but you are not as strong as I am, and I used to take you over my knee and spank you when you were a child and didn't behave, and I'll do it now if you are not careful. You unfasten that corset-cover properly. You are tearing the lace."

Lucy gazed at her mother a moment in a frenzy of rage, then suddenly her face began to work piteously. She flung herself face downward upon her bed, and sobbed long, hysterical sobs. Then Mrs. Ayres waxed tender. She bent over the girl, and gently untied ribbons and unfastened buttons, and slipped a night-gown over her head. Then she rolled her over in the bed, as if she had been a baby, and laid her own cheek against the hot, throbbing one of the girl. "Mother's lamb," she said, softly. "There, there, dear, mother knows all about it."

"You don't," gasped the girl. "What do you know? You—you were married when you were years younger than I am." There was something violently accusing in her tone. She thrust her mother away and sat up in bed, and looked at her with fierce eyes blazing like lamps in her soft, flushed face.

"I know it," said Mrs. Ayres. "I know it, and I know what you mean, Lucy; but there is something else which I know and you do not."

"I'd like to know what!"

"How a mother reads the heart of her child."

Lucy stared at her mother. Her face softened. Then it grew burning red and angrier. "You taunt me with that," she said, in a whisper—"with that and everything." She buried her face in her crushed pillow again and burst into long wails.

Mrs. Ayres smoothed her hair. "Lucy," said she, "listen. I know what is going on within you as you don't know it yourself. I know the agony of it as you don't know it yourself."

"I'd like to know how."

"Because you are my child; because I can hardly sleep for thinking of you; because every one of my waking moments is filled with you. Lucy, because I am your mother and you are yourself. I am not taunting you. I understand."

"You can't."

"I do. I know just how you felt about that young man from the city who boarded at the hotel six years ago. I know how you felt about Tom Merrill, who called here a few times, and then stopped, and married a girl from Boston. I have known exactly how you have felt about all the others, and—I know about this last." Her voice sank to a whisper.

"I have had some reason," Lucy said, with a terrible eagerness of self-defence. "I have, mother."

"What?"

"One day, the first year he came, I was standing at the gate beside that flowering-almond bush, and it was all in flower, and he came past and he looked at the bush and at me, then at the bush again, and he said, 'How beautiful that is!' But, mother, he meant me."

"What else?"

"You remember he called here once."

"Yes, Lucy, to ask you to sing at the school entertainment."

"Mother, it was for more than that. You did not hear him speak at the door. He said, 'I shall count on you; you cannot disappoint me.' You did not hear his voice, mother."

"What else, Lucy?"

"Once, one night last winter, when I was coming home from the post-office, it was after dark, and he walked way to the house with me, and he told me a lot about himself. He told me how all alone in the world he was, and how hard it was for a man to have nobody who really belonged to him in the wide world, and when he said good-night at the gate he held my hand—quite a while; he did, mother."

"What else, Lucy?"

"You remember that picnic, the trolley picnic to Alford. He sat next to me coming home, and—"

"And what?"

"There were only—four on the seat, and he—he sat very close, and told me some more about himself: how he had been alone ever since he was a little boy, and—how hard it had been. Then he asked how long ago father died, and if I remembered, and if I missed him still."

"I don't quite understand, dear, how that—"

"You didn't hear the way he spoke, mother."

"What else, Lucy?"

"He has always looked at me very much across the church, and whenever I have met him it has not been so much what—he said as—his manner. You have not known what his manner was, and you have not heard how he spoke, nor seen his eyes when—he looked at me—"

"Yes, dear, you are right. I have not. Then you have thought he was in love with you?"

"Sometimes he has made me think so, mother," Lucy sobbed.

Mrs. Ayres gazed pitifully at the girl. "Then when you thought perhaps he was not you felt badly."

"Oh, mother!"

"You were not yourself."

"Oh, mother!"

Mrs. Ayres took the girl by her two slender shoulders; she bent her merciful, loving face close to the younger one, distraught, and full of longing, primeval passion. "Lucy," she whispered, "your mother never lost sight of—anything."

Lucy turned deadly white. She stared back at her mother.

"You thought perhaps he was in love with Miss Farrel, didn't you?" Mrs. Ayres said, in a very low whisper.

Lucy nodded, still staring with eyes of horrified inquiry at her mother.

"You had seen him with her?"

"Ever so many times, walking, and he took her to ride, and I saw him coming out of the hotel. I thought—"

"Listen, Lucy." Mrs. Ayres's whisper was hardly audible. "Mother made some candy and sent it to Miss Farrel. She—never had any that anybody else made. It—was candy that would not hurt anybody that she had."

Lucy's face lightened as if with some veritable illumination.

"Mother perhaps ought not to have let you think—as you did, so long," said Mrs. Ayres, "but she thought perhaps it was best, and, Lucy, mother has begun to realize that it was. Now you think, perhaps, he is in love with this other girl, don't you?"

"They are living in the same house," returned Lucy, in a stifled shriek, "and—and—I found out this afternoon that she—she is in love with him. And she is so pretty, and—" Lucy sobbed wildly.

"Mother has been watching every minute," said Mrs. Ayres.

"Mother, I haven't killed him?"

"No, dear. Mother made the candy."

Lucy sobbed and trembled convulsively. Mrs. Ayres stroked her hair until she was a little quieter, then she spoke. "Lucy," she said, "the time has come for you to listen to mother, and you must listen."

Lucy looked up at her with her soft, terrible eyes.

"You are not in love with this last man," said Mrs. Ayres, quietly. "You were not in love with any of the others. It is all because you are a woman, and the natural longings of a woman are upon you. The time has come for you to listen and understand. It is right that you should have what you want, but if the will of God is otherwise you must make the best of it. There are other things in life, or it would be monstrous. It will be no worse for you than for thousands of other women who go through life unmarried. You have no excuse to—commit crime or to become a wreck. I tell you there are other things besides that which has taken hold of you, soul and body. There are spiritual things. There is the will of God, which is above the will of the flesh and the will of the fleshly heart. It is for you to behave yourself and take what comes. You are still young, and if you were not there is always room in life for a gift of God. You may yet have what you are crying out for. In the mean time—"

Lucy interrupted with a wild cry. "Oh, mother, you will take care of me, you will watch me!"

"You need not be afraid, Lucy," said Mrs. Ayres, grimly and tenderly. "I will watch you, and—" She hesitated a moment, then she continued, "If I ever catch you buying that again—"

But Lucy interrupted.

"Oh, mother," she said, "this last time it was not—it really was not—*that!* It was only something that would have made her sick a little. It would not have —It was not *that!*"

"If I ever do catch you buying that again," said Mrs. Ayres, "you will know what a whipping is." Her tone was almost whimsical, but it had a terrible emphasis.

Lucy shrank. "I didn't put enough of *that* in to—to do much harm," she murmured, "but I never will again."

"No, you had better not," assented Mrs. Ayres. "Now slip on your wrapper and come down-stairs with me. I am going to warm up some of that chicken on toast the way you like it, for supper, and then I am coming back up-stairs with you, and you are going to lie down, and I'll read that interesting book we got out of the library."

Lucy obeyed like a child. Her mother helped her slip the wrapper over her head, and the two went down-stairs.

After supper that night Sidney Meeks called at the Whitmans'. He did not stay long. He had brought a bottle of elder-flower wine for Sylvia. As he left he looked at Henry, who followed him out of the house into the street. They paused just outside the gate.

"Well?" said Henry, interrogatively.

"All right," responded Meeks. "What it is all about beats me. The stuff wouldn't hurt a babe in arms, unless it gave it indigestion. Your boarder hasn't insanity in his family, has he?"

"Not that I know of," replied Henry. Then he repeated Meeks's comment. "It beats me," he said.

When Henry re-entered the house Sylvia looked at him. "What were you and Mr. Meeks talking about out in the street?" she asked.

"Nothing," replied Henry, lying as a man may to a woman or a child.

"He's in there with her," whispered Sylvia. "They went in there the minute Mr. Meeks and you went out." Sylvia pointed to the best parlor and looked miserably jealous.

"Well," said Henry, tentatively.

"If they've got anything to say I don't see why they can't say it here," said Sylvia.

"The door is open," said Henry.

"I ain't going to listen, if it is, and you know I can't hear with one ear," said Sylvia. "Of course I don't care, but I don't see why they went in there. What were you and Mr. Meeks talking about, Henry?"

"Nothing," answered Henry, cheerfully, again.

Chapter XIII

Rose Fletcher had had a peculiar training. She had in one sense belonged to the ranks of the fully sophisticated, who are supposed to swim on the surface of things and catch all the high lights of existence, like bubbles, and in another sense it had been very much the reverse. She might, so far as one side of her character was concerned, have been born and brought up in East Westland, as her mother had been before her. She had a perfect village simplicity and wonder at life, as to a part of her innermost self, which was only veneered by her contact with the world. In part she was entirely different from all the girls in the place, and the difference was really in the grain. That had come from her assimilation at a very tender age with the people who had had the care of her. They had belonged by right of birth with the most brilliant social lights, but lack of money had hampered them. They blazed, as it were, under ground glass with very small candle-powers, although they were on the same shelf with the brilliant incandescents. Rose's money had been the main factor which enabled them to blaze at all. Otherwise they might have still remained on the shelf, it is true, but as dark stars.

Rose had not been sent away to school for two reasons. One reason was Miss Farrel's, the other originated with her caretakers. Miss Farrel had a jealous dread of the girl's forming one of those erotic friendships, which are really diseased love-affairs, with another girl or a teacher, and the Wiltons' reason was a pecuniary one. Among the Wiltons' few assets was a distant female relative of pronounced accomplishments and educational attainments, who was even worse off financially than they. It had become with her a question of bread-and-butter and the simplest necessaries of life, whereas Mrs. Wilton and her sister, Miss Pamela, still owned the old family mansion, which, although reduced from its former heights of fashion, was grand, with a subdued and dim grandeur, it is true, but still grand; and there was also a fine old country-house in a fashionable summer resort. There were also old servants and jewels and laces and all that had been. The difficulty was in retaining it with the addition of repairs, and additions which are as essential to the mere existence of inanimate objects as food is to the animate, these being as their law of growth. Rose Fletcher's advent, although her fortune was, after all, only a moderate one, permitted such homely but necessary things as shingles to be kept intact upon roofs of old family homes; it enabled servants to be paid and fuel and food to be provided. Still, after all, had poor Eliza Farrel, that morbid victim of her own hunger for love, known what economies were practised at her expense, in order that all this should be maintained, she would have rebelled. She knew that the impecunious female relative was a person fully adequate to educate Rose, but she did not know that her only stipend therefor was her bread-and-butter and the cast-off raiment of Mrs. Wilton and Miss Pamela. She did not know that when Rose came out her stock of party gowns was so limited that she had to refuse many invitations or appear always as the same flower, as far as garments were concerned. She did not know that during Rose's two trips abroad the expenses had been so carefully calculated that the girl had not received those advantages usually supposed to be derived from foreign travel.

While Mrs. Wilton and Miss Pamela would have scorned the imputation of deceit or dishonesty, their moral sense in those two directions was blunted by their keen scent for the conventionalities of life, which to them had almost become a religion. They had never owned to their inmost consciousness that Rose had not derived the fullest benefit from Miss Farrel's money; it is doubtful if they really were capable of knowing it. When a party gown for Rose was weighed in the balance with some essential for maintaining their position upon the society shelf, it had not the value of a feather. Mrs. Wilton and Miss Pamela gave regular dinner-parties and receptions through the season, but they invited people of undoubted social standing whom Miss Farrel would have neglected for others on Rose's account. By a tacit agreement, never voiced in words, young men or old who might have made too heavy drains upon wines and viands were seldom invited. The preference was for dyspeptic clergymen and elderly and genteel females with slender appetites, or stout people upon diets. It was almost inconceivable how Mrs. Wilton and Miss Pamela, with no actual consultations to that end, practised economies and maintained luxuries. They seemed to move with a spiritual unity like the physical one of the Siamese twins. Meagre meals served magnificently, the most splendid conservatism with the smallest possible amount of comfort, moved them as one.

Rose, having been so young when she went to live with them, had never realized the true state of affairs. Mrs. Wilton and Miss Pamela had not encouraged her making visits in houses where her eyes might have been opened. Then, too, she was naturally generous, and not sharp-eyed concerning her own needs. When there were no guests at dinner, and she rose from the table rather unsatisfied after her half-plate of watery soup, her delicate little befrilled chop and dab of French pease, her tiny salad and spoonful of dessert, she never imagined that she was defrauded. Rose had a singularly sweet, ungrasping disposition, and an almost childlike trait of accepting that which was offered her as the one and only thing which she deserved. When there was a dinner-party, she sat between an elderly clergyman and a stout judge, who was dieting on account of the danger of apoplexy, with the same graceful agreeableness with which she would have sat between two young men.

Rose had not developed early as to her temperament. She had played with dolls until Miss Pamela had felt it her duty to remonstrate. She had charmed the young men whom she had seen, and had not thought about them when once they were out of sight. Her pulses did not quicken easily. She had imagination, but she did not make herself the heroine of her dreams. She was sincerely puzzled at the expression which she saw on the faces of some girls when talking with young men. She felt a vague shame and anger because of it, but she did not know what it meant. She had read novels, but the love interest in them was like a musical theme which she, hearing, did not fully understand. She was not in the least a boylike girl; she was wholly feminine, but the feminine element was held in delicate and gentle restraint. Without doubt Mrs. Wilton's old-fashioned gentility, and Miss Pamela's, and her governess's, who belonged to the same epoch, had served to mould her character not altogether undesirably. She was, on the whole, a pleasant and surprising contrast to girls of her age, with her pretty, shy respect for her elders, and lack of self-assertion, along with entire self-possession and good breeding. However, she had missed many things which poor Miss Farrel had considered desirable for her, and which her hostesses with their self-sanctified evasion had led her to think had been done.

Miss Farrel, teaching in her country school, had had visions of the girl riding a thoroughbred in Central Park, with a groom in attendance; whereas the reality was the old man who served both as coachman and butler, in carefully kept livery, guiding two horses apt to stumble from extreme age through the shopping district, and the pretty face of the girl looking out of the window of an ancient coupé which, nevertheless, had a coat of arms upon its door. Miss Farrel imagined Rose in a brilliant house-party at Wiltmere, Mrs. Wilton's and Miss Pamela's country home; whereas in reality she was roaming about the fields and woods with an old bull-terrier for guard and companion. Rose generally carried a book on these occasions, and generally not a modern book. Her governess had a terror of modern books, especially of novels. She had looked into a few and shuddered. Rose's taste in literature was almost Elizabethan. She was not allowed, of course, to glance at early English novels, which her governess classed with late English and American in point of morality, but no poetry except Byron was prohibited.

Rose loved to sit under a tree with the dog in a white coil beside her, and hold her book open on her lap and read a word now and then, and amuse herself with fancies the rest of the time. She grew in those days of her early girlhood to have firm belief in those things which she never saw nor heard, and the belief had not wholly deserted her. She never saw a wood-nymph stretch out a white arm from a tree, but she believed in the possibility of it, and the belief gave her a curious delight. When she returned to the house for her scanty, elegantly served dinner with the three elder ladies, her eyes would be misty with these fancies and her mouth would wear the inscrutable smile of a baby's at the charm of them.

When she first came to East Westland she was a profound mystery to Horace, who had only known well two distinct types of girls—the purely provincial and her reverse. Rose, with her mixture of the two, puzzled him. While she was not in the least shy, she had a reserve which caused her to remain a secret to him for some time. Rose's inner life was to her something sacred, not to be lightly revealed. At last, through occasional remarks and opinions, light began to shine through. He had begun to understand her the Sunday he had followed her to Lucy Ayres's. He had, also, more than begun to love her. Horace Allen would not have loved her so soon had she been more visible as to her inner self. Things on the surface rarely interested him very much. He had not an easily aroused temperament, and a veil which stimulated his imagination and aroused his searching instinct was really essential if he were to fall in love. He had fallen in love before, he had supposed, although he had never asked one of the fair ones to marry him. Now he began to call up various faces and wonder if this were not the first time. All the faces seemed to dim before this present one. He realized something in her very dear and precious, and for the first time he felt as if he could not forego possession. Hitherto it had been easy enough to bear the slight wrench of leaving temptation and moving his tent. Here it was different. Still, the old objection remained. How could he marry upon his slight salary?

The high-school in East Westland was an endowed institution. The principal received twelve hundred a year. People in the village considered that a prodigious income. Horace, of course, knew better. He did not think that sum sufficient to risk matrimony. Here, too, he was hampered by another consideration. It was intolerable for him to think of Rose's wealth and his paltry twelve hundred per year. An ambition which had always slumbered within his mind awoke to full strength and activity. He began to sit up late at night and write articles for the papers and magazines. He had got one accepted, and received a check which to his inexperience seemed promisingly large. In spite of all his anxiety he was exalted. He began to wonder if circumstances would not soon justify him in reaching out for the sweet he coveted. He made up his mind not to be precipitate, to wait until he was sure, but his impatience had waxed during the last few hours, ever since that delicious note of stilted, even cold, praise and that check had arrived. When Rose had started to go up-stairs he had not been able to avoid following her into the hall. The door of the parlor stood open, and the whole room was full of the soft shimmer of moonlight. It looked like a bower of romance. It seemed full of soft and holy and alluring mysteries. Horace looked down at Rose, Rose looked up at him. Her eyes fell; she trembled deliciously.

"It is very early," he said, in a whispering voice which would not have been known for his. It had in it the male cadences of wooing music.

Rose stood still.

"Let us go in there a little while," whispered Horace. Rose followed him into the room; he gave the door a little push. It did not quite close, but nearly. Horace placed a chair for Rose beside a window into which the moon was shining; then he drew up one beside it, but not very close. He neither dared nor was sure that he desired. Alone with the girl in this moonlit room, an awe crept over him. She looked away from him out of the window, and he saw that this same awe was over her also. All their young pulses were thrilling, but this awe which was of the spirit held them in check. Rose, with the full white moonlight shining upon her face, gained an ethereal beauty which gave her an adorable aloofness. The young man seemed to see her through the vista of all his young dreams. She was the goddess before which his soul knelt at a distance. He thought he had never seen anything half so lovely as she was in that white light, which seemed to crown her with a frosty radiance like a nimbus. Her very expression was changed. She was smiling, but there was something a little grave and stern about her smile. Her eyes, fixed upon the clear crystal of the moon sailing through the night blue, were full of visions. It did not seem possible to him that she could be thinking of him at all, this beautiful creature with her pure regard of the holy mystery of the nightly sky; but in reality Rose, being the more emotional of the two, and also, since she was not the one to advance, the more daring, began to tremble with impatience for his closer contact, for the touch of his hand upon hers.

She would have died before she would have made the first advance, but it filled her as with secret fire. Finally a sort of anger possessed her, anger at herself and at Horace. She became horribly ashamed of herself, and angry at him because of the shame. She gazed out at the wonderful masses of shadows which the trees made, and she gazed up again at the sky and that floating crystal, and it seemed impossible that it was within her as it was. Her clear face was as calm as marble, her expression as immovable, her gaze as direct. It seemed as if a man must be a part of the wonderful mystery of the moonlit night to come within her scope of vision at all.

Rose chilled, when she did not mean to do so, by sheer maidenliness. Horace, gazing at her calm face, felt in some way rebuked. He had led a decent sort of life, but after all he was a man, and what right had he to even think of a creature like that? He leaned back in his chair, removing himself farther from her, and he also gazed at the moon. That mysterious thing of silver light and shadows, which had illumined all the ages of creation by their own reflected light, until it had come to be a mirror of creation itself, seemed to give him a sort of chill of the flesh. After all, what was everything in life but a repetition of that which had been and a certainty of death? Rose looked like a ghost to his fancy. He seemed like a ghost to himself, and felt reproached for the hot ardor surging in his fleshly heart.

"That same moon lit the world for the builders of the Pyramids," he said, tritely enough.

"Yes," murmured Rose, in a faint voice. The Pyramids chilled her. So they were what he had been thinking about, and not herself.

Horace went on. "It shone upon all those ancient battle-fields of the Old Testament, and the children of Israel in their exile," he said.

Rose looked at him. "It shone upon the Garden of Eden after Adam had so longed for Eve that she grew out of his longing and became something separate from himself, so that he could see her without seeing himself all the time; and it shone upon the garden in Solomon's Song, and the roses of Sharon, and the lilies of the valley, and the land flowing with milk and honey," said she, in a childish tone of levity which had an undercurrent of earnestness in it. All her emotional nature and her pride arose against Pyramids and Old Testament battle-fields, when she had only been conscious that the moon shone upon Horace and herself. She was shamed and angry as she had never been shamed and angry before.

Horace leaned forward and gazed eagerly at her. After all, was he mistaken? He was shrewd enough, although he did not understand the moods of women very well, and it did seem to him that there was something distinctly encouraging in her tone. Just then the night wind came in strongly at the window beside which they were sitting. An ardent fragrance of dewy earth and plants smote them in the face.

"Do you feel the draught?" asked Horace.

"I like it."

"I am afraid you will catch cold."

"I don't catch cold at all easily."

"The wind is very damp," argued Horace, with increasing confidence. He grew very bold. He seized upon one of her little white hands. "I won't believe it unless I can feel for myself that your hands are not cold," said he. He felt the little soft fingers curl around his hand with the involuntary, pristine force of a baby's. His heart beat tumultuously.

"Oh—" he began. Then he stopped suddenly as Rose snatched her hand away and again gazed at the moon.

"It is a beautiful night," she remarked, and the harmless deceit of woman, which is her natural weapon, was in her voice and manner.

Horace was more obtuse. He remained leaning eagerly towards the girl. He extended his hand again, but she repeated, in her soft, deceitful voice, "Yes, a perfectly beautiful night."

Then he observed Sylvia Whitman standing beside them. "It is a nice night enough," said she, "but you'll both catch your deaths of cold at this open window. The wind is blowing right in on you."

She made a motion to close it, stepping between Rose and Horace, but the young man sprang to his feet. "Let me close it, Mrs. Whitman," said he, and did so.

"It ain't late enough in the season to set right beside an open window and let the wind blow in on you," said Sylvia, severely. She drew up a rocking-chair and sat down. She formed the stern apex of a triangle of which Horace and Rose were the base. She leaned back and rocked.

"It is a pleasant night," said she, as if answering Rose's remark, "but to me there's always something sort of sad about moonlight nights. They make you think of times and people that's gone. I dare say it is different with you young folks. I guess I used to feel different about moonlight nights years ago. I remember when Mr. Whitman and I were first married, we used to like to set out on the front door-step and look at the moon, and make plans."

"Don't you ever now?" asked Rose.

"Now we go to bed and to sleep," replied Sylvia, decisively. There was a silence. "I guess it's pretty late," said Sylvia, in a meaning tone. "What time is it, Mr. Allen?"

Horace consulted his watch. "It is not very late," said he. It did not seem to him that Mrs. Whitman could stay.

"It can't be very late," said Rose.

"What time is it?" asked Sylvia, relentlessly.

"About half-past ten," replied Horace, with reluctance.

"I call that very late," said Sylvia. "It is late for Rose, anyway."

"I don't feel at all tired," said Rose.

"You must be," said Sylvia. "You can't always go by feelings."

She swayed pitilessly back and forth in her rocking-chair. Horace waited in an agony of impatience for her to leave them, but she had no intention of doing so. She rocked. Now and then she made some maddening little remark which had nothing whatever to do with the situation. Then she rocked again. Finally she triumphed. Rose stood up. "I think it is getting rather late," said she.

"It is very late," agreed Sylvia, also rising. Horace rose. There was a slight pause. It seemed even then that Sylvia might take pity upon them and leave them. But she stood like a rock. It was quite evident that she would settle again into her rocking-chair at the slightest indication which the two young people made of a disposition to remain.

Rose gave a fluttering little sigh. She extended her hand to Horace. "Good-night, Mr. Allen," she said.

"Good-night," returned Horace. "Good-night, Mrs. Whitman."

"It is time you went to bed, too," said Sylvia.

"I think I'll go in and have a smoke with Mr. Whitman first," said Horace.

"He's going to bed, too," said Sylvia. "He's tired. Good-night, Mr. Allen. If you open that window again, you'll be sure and shut it down before you go up-stairs, won't you?"

Horace promised that he would. Sylvia went with Rose into her room to unfasten her gown. A lamp was burning on the dressing-table. Rose kept her back turned towards the light. Her pretty face was flushed and she was almost in tears. Sylvia hung the girl's gown up carefully, then she looked at her lovingly. Unless Rose made the first advance, when Sylvia would submit with inward rapture but outward stiffness, there never were good-night kisses exchanged between the two.

"You look all tired out," said Sylvia.

"I am not at all tired," said Rose. She was all quivering with impatience, but her voice was sweet and docile. She put up her face for Sylvia to kiss. "Good-night, dear Aunt Sylvia," said she.

"Good-night," said Sylvia. Rose felt merely a soft touch of thin, tightly closed lips. Sylvia did not know how to kiss, but she was glowing with delight.

When she joined Henry in their bedroom down-stairs he looked at her in some disapproval. "I don't think you'd ought to have gone in there," he said.

"Why not?"

"Why, you must expect young folks to be young folks, and it was only natural for them to want to set there in the moonlight."

"They can set in there in the moonlight if they want to," said Sylvia. "I didn't hinder them."

"I think they wanted to be alone."

"When they set in the moonlight, I'm going to set, too," said Sylvia. She slipped off her gown carefully over her head. When the head emerged Henry saw that it was carried high with the same rigidity which had lately puzzled him, and that her face had that same expression of stern isolation.

"Sylvia," said Henry.

"Well?"

"Does anything worry you lately?"

Sylvia looked at him with sharp suspicion. "I'd like to know why you should think anything worries me," she said, "as comfortable as we are off now."

"Sylvia, have you got anything on your mind?"

"I don't want to see young folks making fools of themselves," said Sylvia, shortly, and her voice had the same tone of deceit which Rose had used when she spoke of the beautiful night.

"That ain't it," said Henry, quietly.

"Well, if you want to know," said Sylvia, "she's been pestering me with wanting to pay board if she stays along here, and I've put my foot down; she sha'n't pay a cent."

"Of course we can't let her," agreed Henry. Then he added, "This was all her own aunt's property, anyway, and if there hadn't been a will it would have come to her."

"There was a will," said Sylvia, fastening her cotton night-gown tightly around her skinny throat.

"Of course she's going to stay as long as she's contented, and she ain't going to pay board," said Henry; "but that ain't the trouble. Have you got anything on your mind, Sylvia?"

"I hope so," replied Sylvia, sharply. "I hope I've got a little something on my mind. I ain't a fool."

Henry said no more. Neither he nor Sylvia went to sleep at once. The moon's pale influence lit their room and seemed disturbing in itself. Presently they both smelled cigar smoke.

"He's smoking," said Sylvia. "Well, nothing makes much difference to you men, as long as you can smoke. I'd like to know what you'd do in my place."

"Have you got anything on your mind, Sylvia?"

"Didn't I say I hoped I had? Everybody has something on her mind, unless she's a tarnation fool, and I ain't never set up for one."

Henry did not speak again.

Chapter XIV

The next morning at breakfast Rose announced her intention of going to see if

Lucy Ayres would not go to drive with her.

"There's one very nice little horse at the livery-stable," said she, "and I can drive. It is a beautiful morning, and poor Lucy did not look very well yesterday, and I think it will do her good."

Horace turned white. Henry noticed it. Sylvia, who was serving something, did not. Henry had thought he had arrived at a knowledge of Horace's suspicions, which in themselves seemed to him perfectly groundless, and now that he had, as he supposed, proved them to be so, he was profoundly puzzled. Before he had gone to Horace's assistance. Now he did not see his way clear towards doing so, and saw no necessity for it. He ate his breakfast meditatively. Horace pushed away his plate and rose.

"Why, what's the matter?" asked Sylvia. "Don't you feel well, Mr. Allen?"

"Perfectly well; never felt better."

"You haven't eaten enough to keep a sparrow alive."

"I have eaten fast," said Horace. "I have to make an early start this morning. I have some work to do before school."

Rose apparently paid no attention. She went on with her plans for her drive.

"Are you sure you know how to manage a horse?" said Sylvia, anxiously. "I used to drive, but I can't go with you because the washerwoman is coming."

"Of course I can drive," said Rose. "I love to drive. And I don't believe there's a horse in the stable that would get out of a walk, anyway."

"You won't try to pass by any steam-rollers, and you'll look out for automobiles, won't you?" said Sylvia.

Horace left them talking and set out hurriedly. When he reached the Ayres house he entered the gate, passed between the flowering shrubs which bordered the gravel walk, and rang the bell with vigor. He was desperate. Lucy herself opened the door. When she saw Horace she turned red, then white. She was dressed neatly in a little blue cotton wrapper, and her pretty hair was arranged as usual, with the exception of one tiny curl-paper on her forehead. Lucy's hand went nervously to this curl-paper.

"Oh, good-morning!" she said, breathlessly, as if she had been running.

Horace returned her greeting gravely. "Can I see you a few moments, Miss Lucy?" he said.

A wild light came into the girl's eyes. Her cheeks flushed again. Again she spoke in her nervous, panting voice, and asked him in. She led the way into the parlor and excused herself flutteringly. She was back in a few moments.

Instead of the curl-paper there was a little, soft, dark, curly lock on her forehead. She had also fastened the neck of her wrapper with a gold brooch. The wrapper sloped well from her shoulders and displayed a lovely V of white neck. She sat down opposite Horace, and the simple garment adjusted itself to her slim figure, revealing its tender outlines.

Lucy looked at Horace, and her expression was tragic, foolish, and of almost revolting wistfulness. She was youth and womanhood in its most helpless and pathetic revelation. Poor Lucy could not help herself. She was a thing always devoured and never consumed by a flame of nature, because of the lack of food to satisfy an inborn hunger.

Horace felt all this perfectly in an analytical way. He sympathized in an analytical way, but in other respects he felt that curious resentment and outrage of which a man is capable and which is fiercer than outraged maidenliness. For a man to be beloved when his own heart does not respond is not pleasant. He cannot defend himself, nor even recognize facts, without being lowered in his own self-esteem. Horace had done, as far as he could judge, absolutely nothing whatever to cause this state of mind in Lucy. He was self-exonerated as to that, but the miserable reason for it all, in his mere existence as a male of his species, filled him with shame for himself and her, and also with anger.

He strove to hold to pity, but anger got the better of him. Anger and shame coupled together make a balking team. Now the man was really at a loss what to say. Lucy sat before him with her expression of pitiable self-revelation, and waited, and Horace sat speechless. Now he was there, he wondered what he had been such an ass as to come for. He wondered what he had ever thought he could say, would say. Then Rose's face shone out before his eyes, and his impulse of protection made him firm. He spoke abruptly. "Miss Lucy—" he began. Lucy cast her eyes down and waited, her whole attitude was that of utter passiveness and yielding. "Good Lord! She thinks I have come here at eight o'clock in the morning to propose!" Horace thought, with a sort of fury. But he did not speak again at once. He actually did not know how to begin, what to say. He did not, finally, say anything. He rose. It seemed to him that he must prevent Rose from going to drive with Lucy, but he saw no way of doing so.

When he rose it was as if Lucy's face of foolish anticipation of joy was overclouded. "You are not going so soon?" she stammered.

"I have to get to school early this morning," Horace said, in a harsh voice. He moved towards the door. Lucy also had risen. She now looked altogether tragic. The foolish wistfulness was gone. Instead, claws seemed to bristle all over her tender surface. Suddenly Horace realized that her slender, wiry body was pressed against his own. He was conscious of her soft cheek against his. He felt at once in the grip of a tiger and a woman, and horribly helpless, more helpless than he had ever been in his whole life. What could he say or do? Then suddenly the parlor door opened and Mrs. Ayres, Lucy's mother, stood there. She saw with her stern, melancholy gaze the whole situation.

"Lucy!" she said.

Lucy started away from Horace, and gazed in a sort of fear and wrath at her mother.

"Lucy," said Mrs. Ayres, "go up to your own room."

Lucy obeyed. She slunk out of the door and crept weakly up-stairs. Horace and Mrs. Ayres looked at each other. There was a look of doubt in the woman's face. For the first time she was not altogether sure. Perhaps Lucy had been right, after all, in her surmises. Why had Horace called? She finally went straight to the point.

"What did you come for, Mr. Allen?" said she.

Suddenly Horace thought of the obvious thing to say, the explanation to give. "Miss Fletcher is thinking of coming later to take Miss Lucy for a drive," said he.

"And you called to tell her?" said Mrs. Ayres.

Horace looked at her. Mrs. Ayres understood. "Miss Fletcher must come with a double-seated carriage so that I can go," said she. "My daughter is very nervous about horses. I never allow her to go to drive without me."

She observed, with a sort of bitter sympathy, the look of relief overspread Horace's face. "I will send a telephone message from Mrs. Steele's, next door, so there will be no mistake," she said.

"Thank you," replied Horace. His face was burning.

Mrs. Ayres went on with a melancholy and tragic calm. "I saw what I saw when I came in," said she. "I have only to inform you that—any doubts which you may have entertained, any fears, are altogether groundless. Everything has been as harmless as—the candy you ate last night."

Horace started and stared at her. In truth, he had lain awake until a late hour wondering what might be going to happen to him.

"I made it," said Mrs. Ayres. "I attend to everything. I have attended to everything." She gazed at him with a strange, pathetic dignity. "I have no apologies nor excuses to make to you," she said. "I have only this to say, and you can reflect upon it at your leisure. Sometimes, quite often, it may happen that too heavy a burden, a burden which has been gathering weight since the first of creation, is heaped upon too slender shoulders. This burden may bend innocence into guilt and modesty into shamelessness, but there is no more reason for condemnation than in a case of typhoid fever. Any man of good sense and common Christianity should take that view of it."

"I do," cried Horace, hurriedly. He looked longingly at the door. He had never felt so shamed in his life, and never so angrily sympathetic.

"I will go over to Mrs. Steele's and telephone immediately," said Mrs. Ayres, calmly. "Good-morning, Mr. Allen."

"Good-morning," said Horace. There was something terrible about the face of patient defiance which the woman lifted to his.

"You will not—" she began.

Horace caught her thin hand and pressed it heartily. "Good God, Mrs. Ayres!" he stammered.

She nodded. "Yes, I understand. I can trust you," she said. "I am very glad it happened with you."

Horace was relieved to be out in the open air. He felt as if he had escaped from an atmosphere of some terrible emotional miasma. He reflected that he had heard of such cases as poor Lucy Ayres, but he had been rather incredulous. He walked along wondering whether it was a psychological or physical phenomenon. Pity began to get the better of his shame for himself and the girl. The mother's tragic face came before his eyes. "What that woman must have to put up with!" he thought.

When he had commenced the morning session of school he found himself covertly regarding the young girls. He wondered if such cases were common. If they were, he thought to himself that the man who threw the first stone was the first criminal of the world. He realized the helplessness of the young things before forces of nature of which they were brought up in so much ignorance, and his soul rebelled. He thought to himself that they should be armed from the beginning with wisdom.

He was relieved that at first he saw in none of the girl-faces before him anything which resembled in the slightest degree the expression which he had seen in Lucy Ayres's. These girls, most of them belonging to the village (there were a few from outside, for this was an endowed school, ranking rather higher than an ordinary institution), revealed in their faces one of three interpretations of character. Some were full of young mischief, chafing impatiently at the fetters of school routine. They were bubbling over with innocent animal life; they were longing to be afield at golf or tennis. They hated their books.

Some were frankly coquettish and self-conscious, but in a most healthy and normal fashion. These frequently adjusted stray locks of hair, felt of their belts at their backs to be sure that the fastenings were intact, then straightened themselves with charming little feminine motions. Their flowerlike faces frequently turned towards the teacher, and there was in them a perfect consciousness of the facts of sex and charm, but it was a most innocent, even childlike consciousness.

The last type belonged to those intent upon their books, soberly adjusted to the duties of life already, with little imagination or emotion. This last was in the minority.

"Thank God!" Horace thought, as his eyes met one and another of the girl-faces. "She is not, cannot be, a common type." And then he felt something like a chill of horror as his eyes met those of a new pupil, a girl from Alford, who had only entered the school the day before. She was not well dressed. There was nothing coquettish about her, but in her eyes shone the awful, unreasoning hunger which he had seen before. Upon her shoulders, young as they were, was the same burden, the burden as old as creation, which she was required to bear by a hard destiny, perhaps of heredity. There was something horribly pathetic in the girl's shy, beseeching, foolish gaze at Horace. She was younger and shyer than Lucy and, although not so pretty, immeasurably more pathetic.

"Another," thought Horace. It was a great relief to him when, only a week later, this girl found an admirer in one of the schoolboys, who, led by some strange fascination, followed her instead of one of the prettier, more attractive girls. Then the girl began to look more normal. She dressed more carefully and spent more time in arranging her hair. After all, she was very young, and abnormal instincts may be quieted with a mere sop at the first.

When Horace reached home that day of the drive he found that Rose had returned. Sylvia said that she had been at home half an hour.

"She went to Alford," she said, "and I'm afraid she's all tired out. She came home looking as white as a sheet. She said she didn't want any dinner, but finally said she would come down."

At the dinner-table Rose was very silent. She did not look at Horace at all. She ate almost nothing. After dinner she persisted in assisting Sylvia in clearing away the table and washing the dishes. Rose took a childish delight in polishing the china with her dish-towel. New England traits seemed to awake within her in this New England home. Sylvia was using the willow ware now, Rose was so pleased with it. The Calkin's soap ware was packed away on the top shelf of the pantry.

"It is perfectly impossible, Aunt Sylvia," Rose had declared, and Sylvia had listened. She listened with much more docility than at first to the decrees of sophistication.

"The painting ain't nearly as natural," she had said, feebly, regarding the moss rosebuds on a Calkin's soap plate with fluctuating admiration which caused her pain by its fluctuations.

"Oh, but, Aunt Sylvia, to think of comparing for one minute ware like that with this perfectly wonderful old willow ware!" Rose had said.

"Well, have your own way," said Sylvia, with a sigh. "Maybe I can get used to everything all blue, when it ain't blue, after awhile. I know you have been around more than I have, and you ought to know."

So the gold-and-white ware which had belonged to Sylvia's mother decked the breakfast-table and the willow ware did duty for the rest of the time. "I think it is very much better that you have no maid," Rose said. "I simply would not trust a maid to care for china like this."

Rose took care of her room now, and very daintily. "She'll be real capable after awhile," Sylvia told Henry.

"I didn't know as she'd be contented to stay at all, we live so different from the way she's been used to," said Henry.

"It's the way her mother was brought up, and the way she lived, and what's in the blood will work out," said Sylvia. "Then, too, I guess she didn't care any too much about those folks she lived with. For my part, I think it's the queerest thing I ever heard of that Miss Farrel, if she took such a notion to the child, enough to do so much for her, didn't keep her herself."

"Miss Farrel was a queer woman," said Henry.

"I guess she wasn't any too well balanced," agreed Sylvia.

"What do you suppose tired Rose out so much this morning?" asked Henry. "It isn't such a very long ride to Alford."

"I don't know. She looked like a ghost when she got home. I'm glad she's laying down. I hope she'll get a little nap."

That was after dinner, when the house had been set in order, and Sylvia was at one front window in the cool sitting-room, with a basket of mending, and Henry at another with a library book. Henry was very restless in these days. He pottered about the place and was planning to get in a good hay crop, but this desultory sort of employment did not take the place of his regular routine of toil. He missed it horribly, almost as a man is said to miss a pain of long standing. He knew that he was better off without it, that he ought to be happier, but he knew that he was not.

For years he had said bitterly that he had no opportunity for reading and improving his mind. Now he had opportunity, but it was too late. He could not become as interested in a book as he had been during the few moments he had been able to snatch from his old routine of toil. Some days it seemed to Henry that he must go back to the shop, that he could not live in this way. He had begun to lose all interest in what he had anticipated with much pleasure—the raising of grass on Abrahama White's celebrated land. He felt that he knew nothing about such work, that agriculture was not for him. If only he could stand again at his bench in the shop, and cut leather into regular shapes, he felt that while his hands toiled involuntarily his mind could work. Some days he fairly longed so for the old familiar odor of tanned hides, that odor which he had once thought sickened him, that he would go to the shop and stand by the open door, and inhale the warm rush of leather-scented air with keen relish. But he never told this to Sylvia.

Henry was not happy. At times it seemed to him that he really wished that he and Sylvia had never met with this good-fortune. Once he turned on Sidney Meeks with a fierce rejoinder, when Sidney had repeated the sarcasm which he loved to roll beneath his tongue like a honeyed morsel, that if he did not want his good-fortune it was the easiest thing in the world to relinquish it.

"It ain't," said Henry; "and what's more, you know it ain't. Sylvia don't want to give it up, and I ain't going to ask her. You know I can't get rid of it, but it's true what I say: when good things are so long coming they get sour, like most things that are kept too long. What's the use of a present your hands are too cramped to hold?"

Sidney looked gravely at Henry, who had aged considerably during the last few weeks. "Well, I am ready to admit," he said, "that sometimes the mills of the gods grind so slow and small that the relish is out of things when you get them. I'm willing to admit that if I had to-day what I once thought I couldn't live without, I'd give up beat. Once I thought I'd like to have the biggest law practice of any lawyer in the State. If I had it now I'd be ready to throw it all up. It would come too late. Now I'd think it was more bother than it was worth. How'd I make my wines and get any comfort out of life? Yes, I guess it's true, Henry, when Providence is overlong in giving a man what he wants, it contrives somehow to suck the sweetness out of what he gets, though he may not know it, and when what he thought he wanted does come to him it is like a bee trying to make honey out of a flower that doesn't hold any. Why don't you go back to the shop, Henry, and have done with it?"

"Sylvia—" began Henry.

But Sidney cut in. "If you haven't found out," said he, "that in the long-run doing what is best for yourself is doing what's best for the people who love you best, you haven't found out much."

"I don't know," Henry said, in a puzzled, weary way. "Sometimes it seems to me I can't keep on living the way I am living, and live at all; and then I don't know."

"I know," said Sidney. "Get back to your tracks."

"Sylvia would feel all cut up over it. She wouldn't understand."

"Of course she wouldn't understand, but women always end in settling down to things they don't understand, when they get it through their heads it's got to be, and being just as contented, unless they're the kind who fetch up in lunatic asylums, and Sylvia isn't that kind. The inevitable may be a hard pill for her to swallow, but it will never stick in her throat."

Henry shook his head doubtfully. He had been thinking it over since. He had thought of it a good deal after dinner that day, as he sat with the unread book in his lap. Sylvia's remarks about Rose diverted his attention, then he began thinking again. Sylvia watched him furtively as she sewed. "You ain't reading that book at all," she said. "I have been watching you, and you 'ain't turned a single page since I spoke last."

"I don't see why I should," returned Henry. "I don't see why anybody but a fool should ever open the book, to begin with."

"What is the book?"

Henry looked at the title-page. "It is *Whatever*, by Mrs. Fane Raymond," he said, absently.

"I've heard it was a beautiful book."

"Most women would like it," said Henry. "It seems to be a lot written about a fool woman that didn't know what she wanted, by another fool woman who didn't know, either, and was born cross-eyed as to right and wrong."

"Why, Henry Whitman, it ain't true!"

"I suppose it ain't."

"No book is true—that is, no story."

"If it ain't true, so much the less reason to tell such a pack of stupid lies," said Henry. He closed the book with a snap.

"Why, Henry, ain't you going to finish it?"

"No, I ain't. I'm going back to the shop to work."

"Henry Whitman, you ain't!"

"Yes, I am. As for pottering round here, and trying to get up an interest in things I ought to have begun instead of ended in, and setting round reading books that I can't keep my mind on, and if I do, just get madder and madder, I won't. I'm going back to work with my hands the way I've been working the last forty years, and then I guess I'll get my mind out of leading-strings."

"Henry Whitman, be you crazy?"

"No, but I shall be if I set round this way much longer."

"You don't need to do a mite of work."

"You don't suppose it's the money I'm thinking about! It's the work."

"What will folks say?"

"I don't care what they say."

"Henry Whitman, I thought I knew you, but I declare it seems as if I have never known you at all," Sylvia said. She looked at him with her puzzled, troubled eyes, in which tears were gathering. She was still very pale.

A sudden pity for her came over Henry. After all, he ought to try to make his position clear to her. "Sylvia," he said, "what do you think you would do, after all these years of housekeeping, if you had to stand in a shoe-shop, from morning till night, at a bench cutting leather?"

Sylvia stared at him. "Me?"

"Yes, you."

"Why, you know I couldn't do it, Henry Whitman!"

"Well, no more can I stand such a change in my life. I can't go to farming and setting around after forty years in a shoe-shop, any more than you can work in a shoe-shop after forty years of housekeeping."

"It ain't the same thing at all," said Sylvia.

"Why not?"

"Because it ain't." Sylvia closed her thin lips conclusively. This, to her mind, was reasoning which completely blocked all argument.

Henry looked at her hopelessly. "I didn't suppose you would understand," he said.

"I don't see why you thought so," said Sylvia. "I guess I have a mind capable of understanding as much as a man. There is no earthly sense in your going to work in the shop again, with all our money. What would folks say, and why do you want to do it?"

"I have told you why."

"You haven't told me why at all."

Henry said no more. He looked out of the window with a miserable expression. The beautiful front yard, with its box-bordered flower-beds, did not cheer him with the sense of possession. He heard a bird singing with a flutelike note; he heard bees humming over the flowers, and he longed to hear, instead, the buzz and whir of machines which had become the accompaniment of his song of life. A terrible isolation and homesickness came over him. He thought of the humble little house in which he and Sylvia had lived so many years, and a sort of passion of longing for it seized him. He felt that for the moment he fairly loathed all this comparative splendor with which he was surrounded.

"What do you think she would say if you went back to the shop?" asked Sylvia. She jerked her head with an upward, sidewise movement towards Rose's room.

"She may not be contented to live here very long, anyway. It's likely that when the summer's over she'll begin to think of her fine friends in New York, and want to lead the life she's been used to again," said Henry. "It ain't likely it would make much difference to her."

Sylvia looked at Henry as he had never seen her look before. She spoke with a passion of utterance of which he had never thought her capable. "She is going to stay right here in her aunt Abrahama's house, and have all she would have had if there hadn't been any will," said she, fiercely.

"You would make her stay if she didn't want to?" said Henry, gazing at her wonderingly.

"She's got to want to stay," said Sylvia, still with the same strange passion. "There'll be enough going on; you needn't worry. I'm going to have parties for her, if she wants them. She says she's been used to playing cards, and you know how we were brought up about cards—to think they were wicked. Well, I don't care if they are wicked. If she wants them she's going to have card-parties, and prizes, too, though I 'most know it's as bad as gambling. And if she wants to have dancing-parties (she knows how to dance) she's going to have them, too. I don't think there's six girls in East Westland who know how to dance, but there must be a lot in Alford, and the parlor is big enough for 'most everything. She shall have every mite as much going on as she would have in New York. She sha'n't miss anything. I'm willing to have some dinners with courses, too, if she wants them, and hire Hannah Simmons's little sister to wait on the table, with a white cap on her head and a white apron with a bib. I'm willing Rose shall have everything she wants. And then, you know, Henry, there's the church sociables and suppers all winter, and she'll like to go to them; and they will most likely get up a lecture and concert course. If she can't be every mite as lively here in East Westland as in New York, if I set out to have her, I'll miss my guess. There's lots of beautiful dresses up-stairs that belonged to her aunt, and I'm going to have the dressmaker come here and make some over for her. It's no use talking, she's going to stay."

"Well, I am sure I hope she will," said Henry, still regarding his wife with wonder.

"She is going to, and if she does stay, you know you can't go back to work in the shop, Henry Whitman. I'd like to know how you think you could set down to the table with her, smelling of leather the way you used to."

"There might be worse smells."

"That's just because you are used to it."

"That's just it," cried Henry, pathetically. "Can't you get it through your head, Sylvia? It is because I'm used to it. Can't you see it's kind of dangerous to turn a man out of his tracks after he's been in them so long?"

"There ain't any need for you to work in the shop. We've got plenty of money without," said Sylvia, settling back immovably in her chair, and Henry gave it up.

Sylvia considered that she had won the victory. She began sewing again. Henry continued to look out of the window.

"She is a delicate little thing, and I guess it's mighty lucky for her that she came to live in the country just as she did," Sylvia observed.

"I suppose you know what's bound to happen if she and Mr. Allen stay on in the same house," said Henry. "As far as I am concerned, I think it would be a good arrangement. Mr. Allen has a good salary, and she has enough to make up for what he can't do; and I would like to keep the child here myself, but I somehow thought you didn't like the idea."

Again Sylvia turned white, and stared at her husband almost with horror. "I don't see why you think it is bound to happen," said she.

Henry laughed. "It doesn't take a very long head to think so."

"It sha'n't happen. That child ain't going to marry anybody."

"Sylvia, you don't mean that you want her to be an old maid!"

"It's the best thing for any girl, if she only thought so, to be an old maid," said Sylvia.

Henry laughed a little. "That's a compliment to me."

"I ain't saying anything against you. I've been happy enough, and I suppose I've been better off than if I'd stayed single; but Rose has got enough to live on, and what any girl that's got enough to live on wants to get married for beats me."

Henry laughed again, a little bitterly this time. "Then you wouldn't have married me if you had had enough to live on?" he said.

Sylvia looked at him, and an odd, shamed tenderness came into her elderly face. "There's no use talking about what wasn't, anyway," said she, and Henry understood.

After a little while Sylvia again brought up the subject of Horace and Rose. She was evidently very uneasy about it. "I don't see why you think because a young man and girl are in the same house anything like that is bound to happen," said she.

"Well, perhaps not; maybe it won't," said Henry, soothingly. He saw that it troubled Sylvia, and it had always been an unwritten maxim with him that Sylvia should not be troubled if it could be helped. He knew that he himself was about to trouble her, and why should she be vexed, in addition, about an uncertainty, as possibly this incipient love-affair might be. After all, why should it follow that because a young man and a girl lived in the same house they should immediately fall in love? And why should it not be entirely possible that they might have a little love-making without any serious consequences? Horace had presumably paid a little attention to girls before, and it was very probable that Rose had received attention. Why bother about such a thing as this when poor Sylvia would really be worried over his,

Henry's, return to his old, humble vocation?

For Henry, as he sat beside the window that pleasant afternoon, was becoming more and more convinced it must happen. It seemed to him that his longing was gradually strengthening into a purpose which he could not overcome. It seemed to him that every flutelike note of a bird in the pleasance outside served to make this purpose more unassailable, as if every sweet flower-breath and every bee-hum, every drawing of his wife's shining needle through the white garment which she was mending, all served to render his purpose so settled a thing that any change in it was as impossible as growth in a granite ledge. That very day Henry had been approached by the superintendent of Lawson & Fisher's, where he had worked, and told that his place, which had been temporarily filled, was vacant and ready for him. He had said that he must consider the matter, but he had known in his heart that the matter admitted of no consideration. He looked gloomy as he sat there with his unread book in his hand, yet gradually an eager, happy light crept into his eyes.

After supper he told Sylvia he was going down to the store. He did go, but on his way he stopped at the superintendent's house and told that he would report for work in the morning.

Rose had not come down to supper. Henry had wondered why, and sympathized in part with Sylvia's anxiety. Still, he had a vague feeling that a young girl's not coming down to supper need not be taken very seriously, that young girls had whims and fancies which signified nothing, and that it was better to let them alone until they got over them. He knew that Sylvia, however, would take the greatest comfort in coddling the girl, and he welcomed the fact as conducing to his making his arrangements for the next day. He thought that Sylvia would not have the matter in mind at all, since she had the girl to fuss over, and that she would not ask him any questions. On his way home he stopped at Sidney Meeks's. He found the lawyer in a demoralized dining-room, which had, nevertheless, an air of homely comfort, with its chairs worn into hollows to fit human anatomies, and its sideboard set out with dusty dishes and a noble ham. Meeks was a very good cook, although one could not confidently assert that dust and dirt did not form a part of his ingredients. One of his triumphs was ham cooked in a manner which he claimed to have invented. After having been boiled, it was baked, and frequently basted in a way which Meeks kept as secret as the bouquet of his grape wine. Sidney sat at the table eating bread and ham spread with mustard, and there were also a mysterious pie in reserve and a bottle of wine. "Draw up, Henry," said Sidney.

"I've had supper."

"What?"

"Sylvia had chicken salad and flapjacks and hot biscuits."

Sidney sniffed. "Cut a slice off that ham," he ordered, "and draw a chair up. Not that one; you'll go through. Yes, that's right. Bring over another wineglass while you're about it. This is daisy wine, ten years old. I've got a pie here that I'll be willing to stake your fortune you can't analyze. It's after the pattern of the cold pasties you read about in old English novels. You shall guess what's in it. Draw up."

Henry obeyed. He found himself sitting opposite Sidney, eating and drinking with intense enjoyment. Sidney chuckled. "Good?" said he.

"I don't know when my victuals have tasted right before," said Henry. He received a large wedge of the pie on his plate, and his whole face beamed with the first taste.

Sidney leaned across the table and whispered. "Squabs," said he, "and— robins, big fat ones. I shot 'em night before last. It's all nonsense the fuss folks make about robins, and a lot of other birds, as far as that goes—damned sentiment. Year before last I hadn't a bushel of grapes on my vines because the robins stole them, and not a half-bushel of pears on that big seckel-pear-tree. If they'd eaten them up clean I wouldn't have felt so bad, but there the ground would be covered with pears rotted on account of one little peck. They are enough sight better to be on women's bonnets than eating up folks' substance, though I don't promulgate that doctrine abroad. And one thing I ain't afraid to say: big fat robins ought to be made some use of. This pie is enough sight more wholesome for the bodies of men who have immortal souls dependent a little on what is eaten, in spite of the preaching, than Western tainted beef. I made up my mind that pie was the natural destiny of a robin, and I make squab-and-robin pies every week of my life. The robins are out of mischief in that pie, and they are doing us good. What makes you look so, though, Henry? There's something besides my pie and ham and wine that gives that look to your face."

"I'm going back to the shop to-morrow," said Henry.

Sidney looked at him. "Most folks would say you were an uncommon fool," said he. "I suppose you know that."

"I can't help it," said Henry, happily. Along with the savory pie in his mouth came a subtler relish to his very soul. The hunger of the honest worker who returns to his work was being appeased.

Chapter XV

117

While Henry was at Sidney Meeks's, Horace sat alone smoking and reading the evening paper. He kept looking up from the paper and listening. He was hoping that Rose, in spite of the fact that she had not been able to come down to supper, might yet make her appearance. He speculated on her altered looks and manner at dinner. He could not help being a little anxious, in spite of all Mrs. Ayres's assurances and the really vague nature of his own foreboding. He asked himself if he had had from the beginning anything upon which to base suspicion. Given the premises of an abnormal girl with a passion for himself which humiliated him, an abnormal woman like Miss Farrel with a similar passion, albeit under better control, the melodramatic phases of the candy, and sudden death, and traces of arsenical poison, what should be the conclusion?

He himself had eaten some of presumably the same candy with no ill effects. Mrs. Ayres had assured him of her constant watchfulness over her daughter, who was no doubt in an alarmingly nervous state, but was she necessarily dangerous? He doubted if Mrs. Ayres had left the two girls a moment to themselves during the drive. What possible reason, after all, had he for alarm?

When he heard Sylvia mounting the stairs, and caught a glimpse of a little tray borne carefully, he gave up all hope of Rose's coming down. Presently he went out and walked down the village street, smoking. As he passed out of the yard he glanced up at Rose's windows, and saw the bright light behind the curtains. He felt glad that the girl had a woman like Sylvia to care for her.

As he looked Sylvia's shadow passed between the window and the light. It had, in its shadowy enlargement, a benignant aspect. There was an angelic, motherly bend to the vague shoulders. Sylvia was really in her element. She petted and scolded the girl, whom she found flung upon her bed like a castaway flower, sobbing pitifully.

"What on earth is the matter?" demanded Sylvia, in a honeyed tone, which at once stung and sweetened. "Here you are in the dark, crying and going without your victuals. You ought to be ashamed of yourself."

As she spoke Sylvia struck a match and lit the lamp. Rose buried her face deeper in the bed.

"I don't want any lamp," she gasped.

"Don't want any lamp? Ain't you ashamed of yourself? I should think you were a baby. You are going to have a lamp, and you are going to sit up and eat your supper." Sylvia drew down the white shades carefully, then she bent over the girl. She did not touch her, but she was quivering with maternal passion which seemed to embrace without any physical contact. "Now, what is the matter?" she said.

"Nothing."

"What is the matter?" repeated Sylvia, insistently.

Suddenly Rose sat up. "Nothing is the matter," she said. "I am just nervous." She made an effort to control her face. She smiled at Sylvia with her wet eyes and swollen mouth. She resolutely dabbed at her flushed face with a damp little ball of handkerchief.

Sylvia turned to the bureau and took a fresh handkerchief from the drawer. She sprinkled it with some toilet water that was on the dressing-table, and gave it to Rose. "Here is a clean handkerchief," she said, "and I've put some of your perfumery on it. Give me the other."

Rose took the sweet-smelling square of linen and tried to smile again. "I just got nervous," she said.

"Set down here in this chair," said Sylvia, "and I'll draw up the little table, and I want you to eat your supper. I've brought up something real nice for you."

"Thank you, Aunt Sylvia; you're a dear," said Rose, pitifully, "but—I don't think I can eat anything." In spite of herself the girl's face quivered again and fresh tears welled into her eyes. She passed her scented handkerchief over them. "I am not a bit hungry," she said, brokenly.

Sylvia drew a large, chintz-covered chair forward. "Set right down in this chair," she said, firmly. And Rose slid weakly from the bed and sank into the chair. She watched, with a sort of dull gratitude, while Sylvia spread a little table with a towel and set out the tray.

"There," said she. "Here is some cream toast and some of those new pease, and a little chop, spring lamb, and a cup of tea. Now you just eat every mite of it, and then I've got a saucer of strawberries and cream for you to top off with."

Rose looked hopelessly at the dainty fare. Then she looked at Sylvia. The impulse to tell another woman her trouble got the better of her. If women had not other women in whom to confide, there are times when their natures would be too much for them. "I heard some news this morning," said she. She attempted to make her voice exceedingly light and casual.

"What?"

"I heard about Mr. Allen's engagement."

"Engagement to who?"

"To—Lucy."

"Lucy!"

"Lucy Ayres. She seems to be a very sweet girl. She is very pretty. I hope she will make him very happy." Rose's voice trembled with sad hypocrisy.

"Who told you?" demanded Sylvia.

"She told me herself."

"Did her mother hear it?"

"She did, but I think she did not understand. Lucy spoke in French. She talks French very well. She studied with Miss Farrel, you know. I think Lucy has done all in her power to fit herself to become a good wife for an educated man."

"What did she tell you in French for? Why didn't she speak in English?"

"I don't know."

"Well, I know. She did it so her mother wouldn't hear, and say in English that she was telling an awful whopper. Mr. Allen is no more engaged to Lucy Ayres than I am."

Rose gazed at Sylvia with sudden eagerness. "What makes you think so, Aunt Sylvia?"

"Nothing makes me think what I know. Mr. Allen has never paid any attention to Lucy Ayres, beyond what he couldn't help, and she's made a mountain out of a mole-hill. Lucy Ayres is man-crazy, that's all. You needn't tell me."

"Then you don't think—?"

"I know better. I'll ask Mr. Allen."

"If you asked him it would make it very hard for him if it wasn't so," said Rose.

"I don't see why."

"Mr. Allen is a gentleman, and he could not practically accuse a woman of making an unauthorized claim of that sort," said Rose.

"Well, I won't say anything about it to him if you think I had better not," said Sylvia, "but I must say I think it's pretty hard on a man to have a girl going round telling folks he's engaged to her when he ain't. Eat that lamb chop and them pease while they're hot."

"I am going to. They are delicious. I didn't think I was hungry at all, but to have things brought up this way—"

"You've got to eat a saucer of strawberries afterwards," said Sylvia, happily.

She watched the girl eat, and she was in a sort of ecstasy, which was, nevertheless, troubled. After a while, when Rose had nearly finished the strawberries, Sylvia ventured a remark.

"Lucy Ayres is a queer girl," said she. "I've known all about her for some time. She has been thinking young men were in love with her, when they never had an idea of such a thing, ever since she was so high."

Sylvia indicated by her out-stretched hand a point about a foot and a half from the floor.

"It seems as if she must have had some reason sometimes," said Rose, with an impulse of loyalty towards the other girl. "She is very pretty."

"As far as I know, no young man in East Westland has ever thought of marrying her," said Sylvia. "I think myself they are afraid of her. It doesn't do for a girl to act too anxious to get married. She just cuts her own nose off."

"I have never seen her do anything unbecoming," began Rose; then she stopped, for Lucy's expression, which had caused a revolt in her, was directly within her mental vision.

It seemed as if Sylvia interpreted her thought. "I have seen her making eyes," said she.

Rose was silent. She realized that she, also, had seen poor Lucy making eyes.

"What a girl is so crazy to get married for, anyway, when she has a good mother and a good home, I can't see," said Sylvia, leading directly up to the subject in the secret place of her mind.

Rose blushed, with apparently no reason. "But she can't have her mother always, you know, Aunt Sylvia," said she.

"Her mother's folks are awful long-lived."

"But Lucy is younger. In the course of nature she will outlive her mother, and then she will be all alone."

"What if she is? 'Ain't she got her good home and money enough to be independent? Lucy won't need to lift a finger to earn money if she's careful."

"I always thought it would be very dreadful to live alone," Rose said, with another blush.

"Well, she needn't be alone. There's plenty of women always in want of a home. No woman need live alone if she don't want to."

"But it isn't quite like—" Rose hesitated.

"Like what?"

"It wouldn't seem quite so much as if you had your own home, would it, as if
—" Rose hesitated again.

Sylvia interrupted her. "A girl is a fool to get married if she's got money
enough to live on," said she.

"Why, Aunt Sylvia, wouldn't you have married Uncle Henry if you had had
plenty of money?" asked the girl, exactly as Henry had done.

Sylvia colored faintly. "That was a very different matter," said she.

"But why?"

"Because it was," said Sylvia, bringing up one of her impregnable ramparts
against argument.

But the girl persisted. "I don't see why," she said.

Sylvia colored again. "Well, for one thing, your uncle Henry is one man in a
thousand," said she. "I know every silly girl thinks she has found just that
man, but it's only once in a thousand times she does; and she's mighty lucky
if she don't find out that the man in a thousand is another woman's husband,
when she gets her eyes open. Then there's another thing: nothing has ever
come betwixt us."

"I don't know what you mean."

"I mean we've had no family," said Sylvia, firmly, although her color
deepened. "I know you think it's awful for me to say such a thing, but look
right up and down this street at the folks that got married about the same time
Henry and I did. How many of them that's had families 'ain't had reason to
regret it? I tell you what it is, child, girls don't know everything. It's awful
having children, and straining every nerve to bring them up right, and then to
have them go off in six months in consumption, the way the Masons lost their
three children, two boys and a girl. Or to worry and fuss until you are worn to
a shadow, the way Mrs. George Emerson has over her son, and then have him
take to drink. There wasn't any consumption in the Mason family on either
side in a straight line, but the three children all went with it. And there ain't
any drink in the Emerson family, on her side or his, all as straight as a string,
but Mrs. Everson was a Weaver, and she had a great-uncle who drank himself
to death. I don't believe there's a family anywhere around that hasn't got
some dreadful thing in it to leak out, when you don't expect it, in children.
Sometimes it only leaks in a straight line, and sometimes it leaks sidewise.
You never know. Now here's my family. I was a White, you know, like your
aunt Abrahama. There's consumption in our family, the worst kind. I never
had any doubt but what Henry and I would have lost our children, if we'd had
any."

"But you didn't have any," said Rose, in a curiously naïve and hopeful tone.

"We are the only ones of all that got married about the time we did who didn't have any," said Sylvia, in her conclusive tone.

"But, Aunt Sylvia," said Rose, "you wouldn't stop everybody's getting married? Why, there wouldn't be any people in the world in a short time."

"There's some people in the world now that would be a good sight better off out of it, for themselves and other folks," said Sylvia.

"Then you don't think anybody ought to get married?"

"If folks want to be fools, let them. Nothing I can say is going to stop them, but I'll miss my guess if some of the girls that get married had the faintest idea what they were going into they would stop short, if it sent them over a rail-fence. Folks can't tell girls everything, but marriage is an awful risk, an awful risk. And I say, as I said before, any girl who has got enough to live on is a fool to get married."

"But I don't see why, after all."

"Because she is," replied Sylvia.

This time Rose did not attempt to bruise herself against the elder woman's imperturbability. She did not look convinced, but again the troubled expression came over her face.

"I am glad you relished your supper," said Sylvia.

"It was very nice," replied Rose, absently. Suddenly the look of white horror which had overspread her countenance on the night of her arrival possessed it again.

"What on earth is the matter?" cried Sylvia.

"I almost remembered, then," gasped the girl. "You know what I told you the night I came. Don't let me remember, Aunt Sylvia. I think I shall die if I ever do."

Sylvia was as white as the girl, but she rose briskly. "There's nothing to remember," she said. "You're nervous, but I'm going to make some of that root-beer of mine to-morrow. It has hops in it, and it's real quieting. Now you stop worrying, and wait a minute. I've got something to show you. Here, you look at this book you've been reading, and stop thinking. I'll be back in a minute. I've just got to step into the other chamber."

Sylvia was back in a moment. She never was obliged to hesitate for a second as to the whereabouts of any of her possessions. She had some little boxes in her hand, and one rather large one under her arm. Rose looked at them with interest. "What is it, Aunt Sylvia?" said she.

Sylvia laughed. "Something to show you that belongs to you," she said.

"Why, what have you got that belongs to me, Aunt Sylvia?"

"You wait a minute."

Sylvia and Rose both stood beside the white dressing-table, and Sylvia opened the boxes, one after another, and slowly and impressively removed their contents, and laid them in orderly rows on the white dimity of the table. The lamplight shone on them, and the table blazed like an altar with jewelled fires. Rose gasped. "Why, Aunt Sylvia!" said she.

"All these things belonged to your aunt Abrahama, and now they belong to you," said Sylvia, in a triumphant tone.

"Why, but these are perfectly beautiful things!"

"Yes; I don't believe anybody in East Westland ever knew she had them. I don't believe she could have worn them, even when she was a girl, or I should have heard of them. I found them all in her bureau drawer. She didn't even keep them under lock and key; but then she never went out anywhere, and if nobody even knew she had them, they were safe enough. Now they're all yours."

"But they belong to you, Aunt Sylvia."

Sylvia took up the most valuable thing there, a really good pearl necklace, and held it dangling from her skinny hand. "I should look pretty with this around my neck, shouldn't I?" she said. "I wanted to wear that pink silk, but when it comes to some things I ain't quite out of my mind. Here, try it on."

Rose clasped the necklace about her white, round throat, and smiled at herself in the glass. Rose wore a gown of soft, green China silk, and the pearls over its lace collar surrounded her face with soft gleams of rose and green.

"These amethysts are exquisite," said Rose, after she had done admiring herself. She took up, one after another, a ring, a bracelet, a necklace, a brooch, and ear-rings, all of clear, pale amethysts in beautiful settings.

"You could wear these," she said to Sylvia.

"I guess I sha'n't begin to wear jewelry at my time of life," declared Sylvia. Her voice sounded almost angry in its insistence. "Everything here is yours," she said, and nodded her head and set her mouth hard for further emphasis.

The display upon the dressing-table, although not of great value, was in reality rather unusual. All of the pieces were, of course, old, and there were more semi-precious than precious stones, but the settings were good and the whole enough to delight any girl. Rose hung over them in ecstasy. She had not many jewels. Somehow her income had never seemed to admit of jewels. She was pleased as a child. Finally she hung some pearl ear-rings over her ears by bits of white silk, her ears not being pierced. She allowed the pearl necklace to remain. She clasped on her arms some charming cameo bracelets and a heavy gold one set with a miniature of a lady. She covered her slender fingers with rings and pinned old brooches all over her bosom. She fastened a pearl spray in her hair, and a heavy shell comb. Then she fairly laughed out loud. "There!" said she to Sylvia, and laughed again.

Sylvia also laughed, and her laugh had the ring of a child's. "Don't you feel as if you were pretty well off as you are?" said she.

Rose sprang forward and hugged Sylvia. "Well off!" said she. "Well off! I never knew a girl who was better off. To think of my being here with you, and your being as good as a mother to me, and Uncle Henry as good as a father; and this dear old house; and to see myself fairly loaded down with jewels like a crown-princess. I never knew I liked such things so much. I am fairly ashamed."

Rose kissed Sylvia with such vehemence that the elder woman started back, then she turned again to her mirror. She held up her hands and made the gems flash with colored lights. There were several very good diamonds, although not of modern cut; there was a fairly superb emerald, also pearls and amethysts and green-blue turquoises, on her hands. Rose made a pounce upon a necklace of pink coral, and clasped it around her neck over the pearls.

"I have them all on now," she said, and her laugh rang out again.

Sylvia surveyed her with a sort of rapture. She had never heard of "Faust," but the whole was a New England version of the "Jewel Song." As Marguerite had been tempted to guilty love by jewels, so Sylvia was striving to have Rose tempted by jewels to innocent celibacy. But she was working by methods of which she knew nothing.

Rose gazed at herself in the glass. A rose flush came on her cheeks, her lips pouted redly, and her eyes glittered under a mist. She thrust her shining fingers through her hair, and it stood up like a golden spray over her temples. Rose at that minute was wonderful. Something akin to the gleam of the jewels seemed to have waked within her. She felt a warmth of love and ownership of which she had never known herself capable. She felt that the girl and her jewels, the girl who was the greatest jewel of all, was her very own. For the first time a secret anxiety and distress of mind, which she had confided to no one, was allayed. She said to herself that everything was as it should be. She had Rose, and Rose was happy. Then she thought how she had found the girl when she first entered the room, and had courage, seeing her as she looked now, to ask again: "What was the matter? Why were you crying?"

Rose turned upon her with a smile of perfect radiance. "Nothing at all, dear Aunt Sylvia," she cried, happily. "Nothing at all."

Sylvia smiled. A smile was always somewhat of an effort for Sylvia, with her hard, thin lips, which had not been used to smiling. Sylvia had no sense of humor. Her smiles would never be possible except for sudden and unlooked-for pleasures, and those had been rare in her whole life. But now she smiled, and with her lips and her eyes. "Rose wasn't crying because she thought Mr. Allen was going to marry another girl," she told herself. "She was only crying because a girl is always full of tantrums. Now she is perfectly happy. I am able to make her perfectly happy. I know that all a girl needs in this world to make her happy and free from care is a woman to be a mother to her. I am making her see it. I can make up to her for everything. Everything is as it should be."

She stood gazing at Rose for a long moment before she spoke. "Well," said she, "you look like a whole jewelry shop. I don't see, for my part, how your aunt came to have so many—why she wanted them."

"Maybe they were given to her," said Rose. A tender thought of the dead woman who had gone from the house of her fathers, and left her jewels behind, softened her face. "Poor Aunt Abrahama!" said she. "She lived in this house all her life and was never married, and she must have come to think that all her pretty things had not amounted to much."

"I don't see why," said Sylvia. "I don't see that it was any great hardship to live all her life in this nice house, and I don't see what difference it made about her having nice things, whether she got married or not. It could not have made any difference."

"Why not?" asked Rose, looking at her with a mischievous flash of blue eyes. A long green gleam like a note of music shot out from the emerald on her finger as she raised it in a slight gesture. "To have all these beautiful things put away in a drawer, and never to have anybody see her in them, must have made some difference."

"It wouldn't make a mite," said Sylvia, stoutly.

"I don't see why."

"Because it wouldn't."

Rose laughed, and looked again at herself in the glass.

"Now you had better take off those things and go to bed, and try to go to

126

sleep," said Sylvia.

"Yes, Aunt Sylvia," said Rose. But she did not stir, except to turn this way and that, to bring out more colored lights from the jewels.

Sylvia had to mix bread that night, and she was obliged to go. Rose promised that she would immediately go to bed, and kissed her again with such effusion that the older woman started back. The soft, impetuous kiss caused her cheek to fairly tingle as she went down-stairs and about her work. It should have been luminous from the light it made in her heart.

When Henry came home, with a guilty sense of what he was to do next day, and which he had not courage enough to reveal, he looked at his wife with relief at her changed expression. "I declare, Sylvia, you look like yourself to-night," he said. "You've been looking kind of curious to me lately."

"You imagined it," said Sylvia. She had finished mixing the bread, and had washed her hands and was wiping them on the roller-towel in the kitchen.

"Maybe I did," admitted Henry. "You look like yourself to-night, anyhow. How is Rose?"

"Rose is all right. Young girls are always getting nervous kinks. I took her supper up to her, and she ate every mite, and now I have given her her aunt's jewelry and she's tickled to pieces with it, standing before the looking-glass and staring at herself like a little peacock." Sylvia laughed with tender triumph.

"I suppose now she'll be decking herself out, and every young man in East Westland will be after her," said Henry. He laughed, but a little bitterly. He, also, was not altogether unselfish concerning the proprietorship of this young thing which had come into his elderly life. He was not as Sylvia, but although he would have denied it he privately doubted if even Horace was quite good enough for this girl. When it came to it, in his heart of hearts, he doubted if any but the fatherly love which he himself gave might be altogether good for her.

"Rose is perfectly contented just the way she is," declared Sylvia, turning upon him. "I shouldn't be surprised if she lived out her days here, just as her aunt did."

"Maybe it would be the best thing," said Henry. "She's got us as long as we live." Henry straightened himself as he spoke. Since his resolve to resume his work he had felt years younger. Lately he had been telling himself miserably that he was an old man, that his life-work was over. To-night the pulses of youth leaped in his veins. He was so pleasantly excited that after he and Sylvia had gone to bed it was long before he fell asleep, but he did at last, and just in time for Rose and Horace.

Rose, after Sylvia went down-stairs, had put out her light and sat down beside the window gazing out into the night. She still wore her jewels. She could not bear to take them off. It was a beautiful night. The day had been rather warm, but the night was one of coolness and peace. The moon was just rising. Rose could see it through the leafy branches of an opposite elm-tree. It seemed to be caught in the green foliage. New shadows were leaping out of the distance as the moon increased. The whole landscape was dotted with white luminosities which it was bliss not to explain, just to leave mysteries. Wonderful sweetnesses and fresh scents of growing things, dew-wet, came in her face.

Rose was very happy. Only an hour before she had been miserable, and now her whole spirit had leaped above her woe as with the impetus of some celestial fluid rarer than all the miseries of earth and of a necessity surmounting them. She looked out at the night, and it was to her as if that and the whole world was her jewel-casket, and the jewels therein were immortal, and infinite in possibilities of giving and receiving glory and joy. Rose thought of Horace, and a delicious thrill went over her whole body. Then she thought of Lucy Ayres, and felt both pity and a sort of angry and contemptuous repulsion. "How a girl can do so!" she thought.

Intuitively she knew that what she felt for Horace was a far nobler love than Lucy's. "Love—was it love, after all?" Rose did not know, but she gave her head a proud shake. "I never would put him in such a position, and lie about him, just because—" she said to herself.

She did not finish her sentence. Rose was innately modest even as to her own self-disclosures. Her emotions were so healthy that she had the power to keep them under the wings of her spirit, both to guard and hold the superior place. She had a feeling that Lucy Ayres's love for Horace was in a way an insult to him. After what Sylvia had said, she had not a doubt as to the falsity of what Lucy had told her during their drive. She and Lucy had been on the front seat of the carriage, when Lucy had intimated that there was an understanding between herself and Horace. She had spoken very low, in French, and Rose had been obliged to ask her to repeat her words. Immediately Lucy's mother's head was between the two girls, and the bunch of violets on her bonnet grazed Rose's ear.

"What are you saying?" she had asked Lucy, sharply. And Lucy had lied. "I said what a pleasant day it is," she replied.

"You said it in French."

"Yes, mother."

"Next time say it in English," said Mrs. Ayres.

Of course, if Lucy had lied to her mother, she had lied to her. She had lied in two languages. "She must be a very strange girl," thought Rose. She resolved that she could not go to see Lucy very often, and a little pang of regret shot through her. She had been very ready to love poor Lucy.

Presently, as Rose sat beside the window, she heard footsteps on the gravel sidewalk outside the front yard, and then a man's figure came into view, like a moving shadow. She knew the figure was a man because there was no swing of skirts. Her heart beat fast when the man opened the front gate and shut it with a faint click. She wondered if it could be Horace, but immediately she saw, from the slightly sidewise shoulders and gait, that it was Henry Whitman. She heard him enter; she heard doors opened and closed. After a time she heard a murmur of voices. Then there was a flash of light across the yard, from a lighted lamp being carried through a room below. The light was reflected on the ceiling of her room. Then it vanished, and everything was quiet. Rose thought that Sylvia and Henry had retired for the night. She almost knew that Horace was not in the house. She had heard him go out after supper and she had not heard him enter. He had a habit of taking long walks on fine nights.

Rose sat and wondered. Once the suspicion smote her that possibly, after all, Lucy had spoken the truth, that Horace was with her. Then she dismissed the suspicion as unworthy of her. She recalled what Sylvia had said; she recalled how she herself had heard Lucy lie. She knew that Horace could not be fond of a girl like that, and he had known her quite a long time. Again Rose's young rapture and belief in her own happiness reigned. She sat still, and the moon at last sailed out of the feathery clasp of the elm branches, and the whole landscape was in a pale, clear glow. Then Horace came. Rose started up. She stood for an instant irresolute, then she stole out of her room and down the spiral stair very noiselessly. She opened the front door before Horace could insert his key in the latch.

Horace started back.

"Hush," whispered Rose. She stifled a laugh. "Step back out in the yard just a minute," she whispered.

Horace obeyed. He stepped softly back, and Rose joined him after she had closed the door with great care.

"Now come down as far as the gate, out of the shadows," whispered Rose. "I want to show you something."

The two stole down to the gate. Then Rose faced Horace in full glare of moonlight.

"Look at me," said she, and she stifled another laugh of pure, childish delight.

Horace looked. Only a few of the stones which Rose wore caught the moonlight to any extent, but she was all of a shimmer and gleam, like a creature decked with dewdrops.

"Look at me," she whispered again.

"I am looking."

"Do you see?"

"What?"

"They are poor Aunt Abrahama's jewels. Aunt Sylvia gave them to me. Aren't they beautiful? Such lovely, old-fashioned settings. You can't half see in the moonlight. You shall see them by day."

"It is beautiful enough now," said Horace, with a sort of gasp. "Those are pearls around your neck?"

"Yes, really lovely pearls; and such carved pink coral! And look at the dear old pearl spray in my hair. Wait; I'll turn my head so the moon will show on it. Isn't it dear?"

"Yes, it is," replied Horace, regarding the delicate spray of seed pearls on Rose's head.

"And only look at these bracelets and these rings; and I had to tie the ear-rings on because my ears are not pierced. Would you have them pierced and wear them as they are—I believe ear-rings are coming into vogue again—or would you have them made into rings?"

"Rings," said Horace, emphatically.

"I think that will be better. I fancy the ear-rings dangling make me a little nervous already. See all these brooches, and the rings."

Rose held up her hands and twirled her ring-laden fingers, and laughed again.

"They are pretty large, most of the rings," said she. "There is one pearl and one emerald that are charming, and several of the dearest old-fashioned things. Think of poor Aunt Abrahama having all these lovely things packed away in a bureau drawer and never wearing them."

"I should rather have packed away my name," said Horace.

"So should I. Isn't it awful? The Abrahama is simply dreadful, and the way it comes down with a sort of whack on the White! Poor Aunt Abrahama! I feel

130

almost guilty having all her pretty jewels and being so pleased with them."

"Oh, she would be pleased, too, if she knew."

"I don't know. She and my mother had been estranged for years, ever since my mother's marriage. Would she be pleased, do you think?"

"Of course she would, and as for the things themselves, they are fulfilling their mission."

Rose laughed. "Maybe jewels don't like to be shut up for years and years in a drawer, away from the light," said she. "They do seem almost alive. Look, you can really see the green in that emerald!"

Horace was trembling from head to foot. He could hardly reply.

"Why, you are shivering," said Rose. "Are you cold?"

"No—well, perhaps yes, a little. It is rather cool to-night after the hot day."

"Where have you been?"

"I walked to Tunbury and back."

"That is seven miles. That ought to have warmed you. Well, I think we must go in. I don't know what Aunt Sylvia would say."

"Why should she mind?"

"I don't know. She might not think I should have run out here as I did. I think all these jewels went to my head. Come. Please walk very softly."

Horace hesitated.

"Come," repeated Rose, imperatively, and started.

Horace followed.

The night before they had been on the verge of a love scene, now it seemed impossible, incongruous. Horace was full of tender longing, but he felt that to gratify it would be to pass the impossible.

"Please be very still," whispered Rose, when they had reached the house door. She herself began opening it, turning the knob by slow degrees. All the time she was stifling her laughter. Horace felt that the stifled laughter was the main factor in prohibiting the love-making.

Rose turned the knob and removed her hand as she pushed the door open; then something fell with a tiny tinkle on the stone step. Both stopped.

"One of my rings," whispered Rose.

Horace stooped and felt over the stone slab, and finally his hand struck the tiny thing.

"It's that queer little flat gold one," continued Rose, who was now serious.

A sudden boldness possessed Horace. "May I have it?" he said.

"It's not a bit pretty. I don't believe you can wear it."

Horace slipped the ring on his little finger. "It just fits."

"I don't care," Rose said, hesitatingly. "Aunt Sylvia gave me the things. I don't believe she will care. And there are two more flat gold rings, anyway. She will not notice, only perhaps I ought to tell her."

"If you think it will make any trouble for you—"

"Oh no; keep it. It is interesting because it is old-fashioned, and as far as giving it away is concerned, I could give away half of these trinkets. I can't go around decked out like this, nor begin to wear all the rings. I certainly never should have put that ring on again."

Horace felt daunted by her light valuation of it, but when he was in the house, and in his room, and neither Sylvia nor Henry had been awakened, he removed the thing and looked at it closely. All the inner surface was covered with a clear inscription, very clear, although of a necessity in minute characters—"Let love abide whate'er betide."

Horace laughed tenderly. "She has given me more than she knows," he thought.

Chapter XVI

Henry Whitman awoke the next morning with sensations of delight and terror. He found himself absolutely unable to rouse himself up to that pitch of courage necessary to tell Sylvia that he intended to return to his work in the shop. He said to himself that it would be better to allow it to become an accomplished fact before she knew it, that it would be easier for him. Luckily for his plans, the family breakfasted early.

Directly after he had risen from the table, Henry attempted to slip out of the house from the front door without Sylvia's knowledge. He had nearly reached the gate, and had a sensation of exultation like a child playing truant, when he heard Sylvia's voice.

"Henry!" she called. "Henry Whitman!"

Henry turned around obediently.

"Where are you going?" asked Sylvia.

She stood under the columns of the front porch, a meagre little figure of a woman dressed with severe and immaculate cheapness in a purple calico wrapper, with a checked gingham apron tied in a prim bow at her back. Her hair was very smooth. She was New England austerity and conservatism embodied. She was terrifying, although it would have puzzled anybody to have told why. Certain it was that no man would have had the temerity to contest her authority as she stood there. Henry waited near the gate.

"Where are you going?" asked Sylvia again.

"Down street," replied Henry.

"Whereabouts down street?"

Henry said again, with a meek doggedness, "Down street."

"Come here," said Sylvia.

Henry walked slowly towards her, between the rows of box. He was about three feet away when she spoke again. "Where are you going?" said she.

"Down street."

Sylvia looked at Henry, and he trembled inwardly. Had she any suspicion? When she spoke an immense relief overspread him. "I wish you'd go into the drug store and get me a quarter of a pound of peppermints," said she.

Then Henry knew that he had the best of it. Sylvia possessed what she considered an almost guilty weakness for peppermints. She never bought them herself, or asked him to buy them, without feeling humiliated. Her austere and dictatorial manner vanished at the moment she preferred the request for peppermints.

"Of course I'll get them," said Henry, with enthusiasm. He mentally resolved upon a pound instead of a quarter.

"I don't feel quite right in my stomach, and I think they're good for me," said Sylvia, still abjectly. Then she turned and went into the house. Henry started afresh. He felt renewed compunction at his deceit as he went on. It seemed hard to go against the wishes of that poor, little, narrow-chested woman who had had so little in life that a quarter of a pound of peppermints seemed too much for her to desire.

But Henry realized that he had not the courage to tell her. He went on. He had just about time to reach the shop before the whistle blew. As he neared the shop he became one of a stream of toilers pressing towards the same goal. Most of them were younger than he, and it was safe to assume none were going to work with the same enthusiasm. There were many weary, rebellious faces. They had not yet come to Henry's pass. Toil had not yet gotten the better of their freedom of spirit. They considered that they could think and live to better purpose without it. Henry had become its slave. He was his true self only when under the conditions of his slavery. He had toiled a few years longer than he should have done, to attain the ability to keep his head above the waters of life without toil. The mechanical motion of his hands at their task of years was absolutely necessary to him. He had become, in fact, as a machine, which rusts and is good for nothing if left long inactive. Henry was at once pitiable and terrible when he came in sight of the many-windowed building which was his goal. The whistles blew, and he heard as an old war-horse hears the summons to battle. But in his case the battle was all for naught and there was no victory to be won. But the man was happier than he had been for months. His happiness was a pity and a shame to him, but it was happiness, and sweet in his soul. It was the only happiness which he had not become too callous to feel. If only he could have lived in the beautiful old home, and spent the rest of his life in prideful wrestling with the soil for goodly crops, in tasting the peace of life which is the right of those who have worked long!

But it all seemed too late. When a man has become welded to toil he can never separate himself from it without distress and loss of his own substance of individuality. What Henry had told Sidney Meeks was entirely true: good-fortune had come too late for him to reap the physical and spiritual benefit from it which is its usual dividend. He was no longer his own man, but the man of his life-experience.

When he stood once more in his old place, cutting the leather which smelled to him sweeter than roses, he was assailed by many a gibe, good-natured in a way, but still critical.

"What are you to work again for, Henry?" "You've got money enough to live on." "What in thunder are you working for?"

One thing was said many times which hit him hard. "You are taking the bread out of the mouth of some other man who needs work; don't you know it, Henry?" That rankled. Otherwise Henry, at his old task, with his mind set free by the toil of his hands, might have been entirely happy.

"Good Lord!" he said, at length, to the man at his side, a middle-aged man with a blackened, sardonic face and a forehead lined with a scowl of rebellion, "do you suppose I do it for the money? I tell you it's for the work."

"The work!" sneered the other man.

"I tell you I've worked so long I can't stop, and live."

The other man stared. "Either you're a damned fool, or the men or the system

—whatever it is that has worked you so long that you can't stop—ought to go to—" he growled.

"You can't shake off a burden that's grown to you," said Henry.

The worker on Henry's other side was a mere boy, but he had a bulging forehead and a square chin, and already figured in labor circles.

"As soon try to shake off a hump," he said, and nodded.

"Yes," said Henry. "When you've lived long enough in one sort of a world it settles onto your shoulders, and nothing but death can ease a man from the weight of it."

"That's so," said the boy.

"But as far as keeping the bread from another man goes—" said Henry. Then he hesitated. He was tainted by the greed for unnecessary money, in spite of his avowal to the contrary. That also had come to be a part of him. Then he continued, "As far as that goes, I'm willing to give away—a—good part of what I earn."

The first man laughed, harshly. "He'll be for giving a library to East Westland next, to make up to men for having their money and freedom in his own pockets," he said.

"I 'ain't got so much as all that, after all," said Henry. "Because my wife has had a little left to her, it don't follow that we are millionaires."

"I guess you are pretty well fixed. You don't need to work, and you know it. You ought to be ashamed of yourself. There's my wife's brother can't get a job."

"Good reason why," said the boy on the other side. "He drinks."

"He drinks every time he gets out of work and gets clean discouraged," retorted the man.

"Well," said the boy, "you know me well enough to know that I'm with my class every time, but hanged if I can see why your wife's brother 'ain't got into a circle that there's no getting him out of. We've got to get out of work sometimes. We all know it. We've got to if we don't want humps on all our shoulders; and if Jim can't live up to his independence, why, he's out of the running, or, rather, in his own running so neither God nor man can get him out of it. You know the time that last strike was on he was in the gutter every day, when he could beg enough money to keep him there. Now, we can't have that sort of thing. When a man's got so he can't work nor fight neither, why, he's up against it. If Henry here gave up his job, Jim couldn't get it, and you know it."

135

Henry went on. He hardly heard now what they were saying. His mind was revelling in its free flights of rebellion against everything. Henry, for a man who kept the commandments, was again as wicked as he could be, and revelling in his wickedness. He was like a drinker returned to his cups. His joy was immense, but unholy. However, the accusation that he was taking bread from another man who needed it more than he still rankled. He could, after all, rise somewhat above mere greed. He resolved that he would give, and no one should know of his giving, to the family of the man Jim who had no work.

During the morning Henry did not trouble himself about Sylvia and what she would think about it all. Towards noon, however, he began to dread going home and facing her. When he started he felt fairly cowardly. He stopped at the drug store and bought a pound of peppermints.

Albion Bennet waited on him. Albion Bennet was an intensely black-haired man in his forties. His black hair was always sleek with a patent hair-oil which he carried in his stock. He always wore a red tie and an old-fashioned scarf-pin set with a tiny diamond, and his collars were made of celluloid.

"I have gone back to the hotel to board," he informed Henry, while tying up the parcel. He colored a little under his black, bristling cheeks as he spoke.

"I thought you left," said Henry.

"So I did. I went to board at the Joneses', but—I can't stand a girl right in my face and eyes all the time. When I want to get married, and see the right one, then I want to do the courting; but hang it if I can stand being courted, and that's what I've been up against ever since I left the hotel, and that's a fact. Susy Jones was enough, but when it came to Fanny Elliot getting thick with her, and both of them on hand, it was too much. But I stuck it out till Susy began to do the cooking and her mother made me eat it."

"I have heard Miss Hart wasn't a very good cook," said Henry.

"Well, she ain't anything to brag of; but say, a man can stand regulation cooking done bad, but when it comes to new-fangled messes done bad, so a man don't know what he's eating, whether it's cats or poisonous mushrooms, I draw the line. Miss Hart's bread is more generally saleratusy and heavy, but at least you know it's heavy bread, and I got heavy stuff at the Joneses and didn't know what it was. And Miss Hart's pies are tough, but you know you've got tough pies, and at the Joneses' I had tough things that I couldn't give a name to. Miss Hart's doughnuts are greasy, but Lord, the greasy things at the Joneses' that Susy made! At least you know what you've got when you eat a greasy doughnut, and if it hurts you you know what to tell the doctor, but I had to give it up. I'd rather have bad cooking and know what it is than bad

136

cooking and know what it isn't. Then there were other things. I like, when I get home from the store, to have a little quiet and read my paper, and Susy and Fanny, if I didn't stay in the parlor, were banging the piano and singing at me all the time to get me down-stairs. So I've gone back to the hotel, and I'm enough sight better off. Of course, when that matter of Miss Farrel came up I left. A man don't want to think he may get a little arsenic mixed in with the bad cooking, but now I'm convinced that's all right."

"How do you know?" asked Henry, paying for the peppermints. "I never thought Miss Hart had anything to do with it myself, but of course she wasn't exactly acquitted, neither she nor the girl. You said yourself that she bought arsenic here."

"So she did, and it all went to kill rats," said Albion. "Lots of folks have bought arsenic here to kill rats with. They didn't all of them poison Miss Farrel." Albion nodded wisely and mysteriously. "No, Lucinda's all right," he said. "I ain't at liberty to say how I know, but I do know. I may get bad cooking at the hotel, but I won't get no arsenic."

Henry looked curiously at the other man. "So you've found out something?" he said.

"I ain't at liberty to say," replied Albion. "It's a pretty nice day, ain't it? Hope we ain't going to have such a hot summer as last, though hot weather is mighty good for my business, since I put in the soda-fountain."

Henry, walking homeward with his package of peppermints, speculated a little on what Albion Bennet had said; then his mind reverted to his anxiety with regard to Sylvia, and her discovery that he had returned to the shop. He passed his arm across his face and sniffed at his coat-sleeve. He wondered if he smelled of leather. He planned to go around to the kitchen door and wash his hands at the pump in the yard before entering the house, but he could not be sure about the leather. He wondered if Rose would notice it and be disgusted. His heart sank as he neared home. He sniffed at his coat-sleeve again. He wondered if he could possibly slip into the bedroom and put on another coat for dinner before Sylvia saw him. He doubted if he could manage to get away unnoticed after dinner. He speculated, if Sylvia asked him where he was going again, what he could say. He considered what he could say if she were to call him to account for his long absence that forenoon.

When he reached the house he entered the side yard, stopped at the pump, washed his hands and dried them on his handkerchief, and drank from the tin cup chained to the pump-nose. He thought he might enter by the front door and steal into his bedroom and get the other coat, but Sylvia came to the side door.

"Where in the world have you been?" she said. Henry advanced, smiling, with the peppermints. "Why, Henry," she cried, in a voice of dismay which had a gratified ring in it, "you've been and bought a whole pound! I only said to buy a quarter."

"They're good for you," said Henry, entering the door.

Sylvia could not wait, and put one of the sweets in her mouth, and to that Henry owed his respite. Sylvia, eating peppermint, was oblivious to leather.

Henry went through into the bedroom and put on another coat before he sat down at the dinner-table.

Sylvia noticed that. "What did you change your coat for?" said she.

Henry shivered as if with cold. "I thought the house seemed kind of damp when I came in," he said, "and this coat is some heavier."

Sylvia looked at him with fretful anxiety. "You've got cold. I knew you would," she said. "You stayed out late last night, and the dew was awful heavy. I knew you would catch cold. You had better stop at the drug store and get some of those pellets that Dr. Wallace puts up."

Again was Henry's way made plain for him. "Perhaps I had," said he, eagerly. "I'll go down and get some after dinner."

But Horace innocently offered to save him the trouble. "I go past the drug store," said he. "Let me get them."

But Sylvia unexpectedly came to Henry's aid. "No," she said. "I think you had better not wait till Mr. Allen comes home from school. Dr. Wallace says those pellets ought to be taken right away, just as soon as you feel a cold, to have them do any good."

Henry brightened, but Rose interposed. "Why, I would love to run down to the drug store and get the medicine," she said. "You lie down after dinner, Uncle Henry, and I'll go."

Henry cast an agonizing glance at Horace. The young man did not understand in the least what it meant, but he came to the rescue.

"The last time I took those pellets," he said, "Mr. Whitman got them for me. It was one Saturday, and I was home, and felt the cold coming on, and I lay down, just as you suggest Mr. Whitman's doing, and got asleep, and awoke with a chill. I think that if one has a cold the best thing is to keep exercising until you can get hold of a remedy. I think if Mr. Whitman walks down to the drug store himself and gets the pellets, and takes one, and keeps out in the open air afterwards, as it is a fine day, it will be the very best thing for him."

"That is just what I think myself," said Henry, with a grateful look at Horace.

Henry changed his coat again before leaving, on the plea that it was better for him to wear a lighter one when walking and the heavier one when he was in the house. He and Horace walked down the street together. They were out of sight of the house when Henry spoke.

"Mrs. Whitman don't know it yet," said he, "but there's no reason why you shouldn't. I 'ain't got any cold. I'll get the pellets to satisfy her, but I 'ain't got any cold. I wanted to get out again and not tell her, if I could help it. I didn't want a fuss. I'm going to put it off as long as I can. Mrs. Whitman's none too strong, and when anything goes against her she's all used up, and I must save her as long as possible."

Horace stared at Henry with some alarm. "What on earth is it?" he said.

"Nothing, only I have gone back to work in the shop."

Horace looked amazed. "But I thought—"

"You thought we had enough so I hadn't any need to work, and you are right," said Henry, with a pathetic firmness. "We have got property enough to keep us, if nothing happens, as long as we live, but I had to go back to that infernal treadmill or die."

Horace nodded soberly. "I think I understand," said he.

"I'm glad you do."

"But Mrs. Whitman—"

"Oh, poor Sylvia will take it hard, and she won't understand. Women don't understand a lot of things. But I can't help it. I'll keep it from her for a day or two. She'll have to hear of it before long. You don't think Rose will mind the leather smell?" concluded Henry.

"I wouldn't worry about that. There is nothing very disagreeable about it," Horace replied, laughing.

"I will always change my coat and wash my hands real particular before I set down to the table," said Henry, wistfully. Then he added, after a second's hesitation: "You don't think she will think any the less of me? You don't suppose she won't be willing to live in the house because I work in the shop?"

"You mean Rose—Miss Fletcher?"

"Yes; of course she's been brought up different. She don't know anything about people's working with their hands. She's been brought up to think they're beneath her. I suppose it's never entered into the child's head that she would live to set at the same table with a man who works in a shoe-shop. You don't suppose it will set her against me?"

"I think even if she has been brought up differently, as you say, that she has a great deal of sense," replied Horace. "I don't think you need to worry about that."

"I'm glad you don't. I guess it would about break Sylvia's heart to lose her now, and I've got so I set a good deal by the child myself. Mr. Allen, I want to ask you something."

Henry paused, and Horace waited.

"I want to ask you if you've noticed anything queer about Sylvia lately," Henry said, at last.

Horace looked at him. "Do you mean in her looks or her manners?"

"Both."

Horace hesitated in his turn. "Now you speak of it—" he began.

"Well," said Henry, "speak out just what you think."

"I have not been sure that there was anything definite," Horace said, slowly. "I have not been sure that it was not all imagination on my part."

"That's just the way I've been feeling," Henry said, eagerly. "What is it that you've been noticing?"

"I told you I am not sure that it is not all imagination, but—"

"What?"

"Well, sometimes your wife has given me the impression that she was brooding over something that she was keeping entirely to herself. She has had a look as if she had her eyes turned inward and was worrying over what she saw. I don't know that you understand what I mean by that?"

Henry nodded. "That's just the way Sylvia's been looking to me."

"I don't know but she looks as well as ever."

"She's grown thin."

"Maybe she has. Sometimes I have thought that, but what I have noticed has been something intangible in her manner and expression, that I thought was there one minute and was not at all sure about the next. I haven't known whether the trouble, or difference, as perhaps I had better put it, was with her or myself."

Henry nodded still more emphatically. "That's just the way it's seemed to me, and we 'ain't either of us imagined it. It's so," said he.

"Have you any idea—"

"No, I haven't the least. But my wife's got something on her mind, and she's had something on her mind for a long time. It ain't anything new."

"Why don't you ask her?"

"I have asked her, and she says that of course she's got something on her mind, that she ain't a fool. You can't get around Sylvia. She never would tell anything unless she wanted to. She ain't like most women."

Just then Horace turned the corner of the street leading to his school, and the conversation ceased, with an enjoinder on his part to Henry not to be disturbed about it, as he did not think it could be anything serious.

Henry's reply rang back as the two men went their different ways. "I don't suppose it can be anything serious," he said, almost angrily.

Horace, however, was disposed to differ with him. He argued that a woman of Sylvia Whitman's type does not change her manner and grow introspective for nothing. He was inclined to think there might be something rather serious at the bottom of it all. His imagination, however, pictured some disease, which she was concealing from all about her, but which caused her never-ceasing anxiety and perhaps pain.

That night he looked critically at her and was rather confirmed in his opinion. Sylvia had certainly grown thin, and the lines in her face had deepened into furrows. She looked much older than she had done before she had received her inheritance. At the same time she puzzled Horace by looking happier, albeit in a struggling sort of fashion. Either Rose or the inheritance was the cause of the happiness. Horace was inclined to think it was Rose, especially since she seemed to him more than ever the source of all happiness and further from his reach.

That night he had found in the post-office a story of whose acceptance he had been almost sure, accompanied by the miserable little formula which arouses at once wrath and humiliation. Horace tore it up and threw the pieces along the road. There was a thunder-shower coming up. It scattered the few blossoms remaining on the trees, and many leaves, and the bits of the civilly hypocritical note of thanks and rejection flew with them upon the wings of the storm wind.

Horace gazed up at the clouds overhead, which looked like the rapids of some terrible, heavenly river overlapping each other in shell-like shapes and moving with intense fury. He thought of Rose, and first hoped that she was in the house, and then reflected that he might as well give up all hope of ever marrying her. The returned manuscript in his pocket seemed to weigh down his very soul. He recalled various stories which he had read in the current magazines of late, and it seemed to him that his compared very favorably with them. He tried to think of the matter judicially, as if the rejected story were not his own, and felt justified in thinking well of it. He had a sickening sense of being pitted against something which he could not gainsay, which his own convictions as to the privilege of persons in authority to have their own opinions forbade him to question.

"The editors had a perfect right to return my story, even if it is every whit as worthy of publication, even worthier, than anything which has appeared in their magazine for a twelvemonth," he told himself.

He realized that he was not dependent upon the public concerning the merit of his work—he could not be until the work appeared in print—but he was combating the opinions (or appealing to them) of a few men whose critical abilities might be biassed by a thousand personal matters with which he could not interfere. He felt that there was a broad, general injustice in the situation, but absolute right as to facts. These were men to whom was given the power to accept or refuse. No one could question their right to use that power. Horace said to himself that he was probably a fool to entertain for a moment any hope of success under such conditions.

"Good Lord! It might depend upon whether the readers had indigestion," he thought; and at the same time he accepted the situation with a philosophic pride of surrender.

"It's about one chance in a good many thousand," he told himself. "If I don't get the chance some other fellow does, and there's no mortal way but to make the best of it, unless I act like a fool myself." Horace was exceedingly alive to the lack of dignity of one who kicked against the pricks. He said to himself that if he could not marry Rose, if he could not ask her why, he must accept his fate, not attack it to his own undoing, nor even deplore it to his ignominy.

In all this he was, rather curiously, leaving the girl and her possible view of the matter entirely out of the question. Horace, while he was not in the least self-deprecatory, and was disposed to be as just in his estimate of himself as of other men, was not egotistical. It did not really occur to him that Rose's fancy, too, might have been awakened as his own had been, that he might cause her suffering. It went to prove his unselfishness that, upon entering the house, and seeing Rose seated beside a window with her embroidery, his first feeling was of satisfaction that she was housed and safe from the fast-gathering storm.

Rose looked up as he entered, and smiled.

"There's a storm overhead," remarked Horace.

"Yes," said Rose. "Aunt Sylvia has just told me I ought not to use a needle, with so much lightning. She has been telling me about a woman who was sewing in a thunder-storm, and the needle was driven into her hand." Rose laughed, but as she spoke she quilted her needle into her work and tossed it on a table, got up, and went to the window.

"It looks almost wild enough for a cyclone," she said, gazing up at the rapid scud of gray, shell-like clouds.

"Rose, come right away from that window," cried Sylvia, entering from the dining-room. "Only last summer a woman in Alford got struck standing at a window in a tempest."

"I want to look at the clouds," said Rose, but she obeyed.

Sylvia put a chair away from the fireplace and out of any draught. "Here," said she. "Set down here." She drew up another chair close beside Rose and sat down. There came a flash of lightning and a terrible crash of thunder. A blind slammed somewhere. Out in the great front yard the rain swirled in misty columns, like ghostly dancers, and the flowering shrubs lashed the ground. Horace watched it until Sylvia called him, also, to what she considered a place of safety. "If you don't come away from that window and set on the sofa I shall have a conniption fit," she said. Horace obeyed. As he sat down he thought of Henry, and without stopping to think, inquired where he was.

"He went down to Mr. Meeks's," replied Sylvia, with calm decision.

Horace stared at her. He wondered if she could possibly be lying, or if she really believed what she said.

He did not know what had happened that afternoon; neither did Rose. Rose had gone out for a walk, and while Sylvia was alone a caller, Mrs. Jim Jones, had come. Mrs. Jim Jones was a very small, angry-looking woman. Nature had apparently intended her to be plump and sweet and rosy, and altogether comfortable, but she had flown in the face of nature, like a cross hen, and had her own way with herself.

It was scarcely conceivable that Mrs. Jim Jones could be all the time in the state of wrath against everything in general which her sharp tongue and her angry voice evinced, but she gave that impression. Her little blond face looked like that of a doll which has been covered with angry pin-scratches by an ill-tempered child. Whenever she spoke these scratches deepened.

Mrs. Jim Jones could not bring herself to speak of anything without a show of temper, whether she really felt it or not. She fairly lashed out at Sylvia when the latter inquired if it was true that Albion Bennet had left her house and returned to the hotel.

"Yes, it is true, and thank the Lord for His unspeakable mercy to the children of men. I couldn't have stood that man much longer, and that's the gospel truth. He ate like a pig, so there wasn't a mite of profit in it. And he was as fussy as any old maid I ever saw. If I have to choose between an old maid and an old batch for a boarder, give me the old maid every time. She don't begin to eat so much, and she takes care of her room. Albion Bennet about ruined my spare chamber. He et peanuts every Sunday, and they're all ground into the carpet. Yes, I'm mighty glad to get rid of him. Let alone everything else, the way he pestered my Susy was enough to make me sick of my bargain. There that poor child got so she tagged me all over the house for fear Albion Bennet would make love to her. I guess Susy ain't going to take up with a man like Albion Bennet. He's too old for her anyhow, and I don't believe he makes much out of his drug store. I rather guess Susy looks higher than that. Yes, he's gone, and it's 'good riddance, bad rubbish.'"

"If you feel so about it I'm glad he's gone back to Lucinda," said Sylvia. "She didn't have many steady boarders, and it did sort of look against her, poor thing, with all the mean talk there's been."

"I guess there wasn't quite so much smoke without a little fire," said Mrs. Jim Jones, and her small face looked fairly evil.

Then Sylvia was aroused. "Now, Mrs. Jones, you know better," said she. "You know as well as you want to that Lucinda Hart was no more guilty than you and I were. We both went to school with her."

Mrs. Jim Jones backed down a little. There was something about Sylvia Whitman when she was aroused that a woman of Mrs. Jones's type could not face with impunity. "Well, I don't pretend to know," said she, with angry sullenness.

"You pretended to know just now. If folks don't know, it seems to me the best thing they can do is to hold their tongues, anyhow."

"I am holding my tongue, ain't I? What has got into you, Sylvia Whitman?"

"No, you didn't hold your tongue when you said that about there not being so much smoke without some fire."

"Well, there always is fire when there's smoke, ain't there?"

"No, there ain't always, not on the earth. Sometimes there's smoke that folks' wicked imaginations bring up out of the other place. I do believe that."

"Why, Sylvia Whitman, how you do talk! You're almost swearing."

"Have it swearing if you want to," said Sylvia. "I know I'm glad that Albion Bennet has gone back to Lucinda's. Everybody knows how mortal scared he is of his own shadow, and if he's got grit enough to go back there it's enough to about satisfy folks that there wasn't anything in the story."

"Well, it's 'good riddance, bad rubbish,' as far as I'm concerned," said Mrs. Jim Jones. There had been on her face when she first entered an expression of peculiar malignity. Sylvia knew it of old. She had realized that Mrs. Jones had something sweet for her own tongue, but bitter for her, in store, and that she was withholding it as long as possible, in order to prolong the delight of anticipation. "You've got two boarders, ain't you?" inquired Mrs. Jim Jones.

"I've got one boarder," replied Sylvia, with dignity, "and we keep him because he can't bear to go anywhere else in East Westland, and because we like his company."

"I thought Abrahama White's niece—"

"She ain't no boarder. She makes her home here. If you think we'd take a cent of money from poor Abrahama's own niece, you're mistaken."

"I didn't know. She takes after her grandmother White, don't she? She was mortal homely."

Then Sylvia fairly turned pale with resentment. "She doesn't look any more like old Mrs. White than your cat does," said she. "Rose is a beauty; everybody says so. She's the prettiest girl that ever set foot in this town."

"Everybody to their taste," replied Mrs. Jim Jones, in the village formula of contempt. "I heard Mr. Allen, your boarder, was going to marry her," she added.

"He ain't."

"I'm glad to hear it from headquarters," said Mrs. Jim Jones. "I said I couldn't believe it was true."

"Mr. Allen won't marry any girl in East Westland," said Sylvia.

"Is there anybody in Boston?" asked Mrs. Jim Jones, losing her self-possession a little.

Sylvia played her trump card. "I don't know anything—that is, I ain't going to say anything," she replied, mysteriously.

Mrs. Jim Jones was routed for a second, but she returned to the attack. She had not yet come to her particular errand. She felt that now was the auspicious moment. "I felt real sorry for you when I heard the news," said she.

Sylvia did not in the least know what she meant. Inwardly she trembled, but she would have died before she betrayed herself. She would not even disclose her ignorance of what the news might be. She did not, therefore, reply in words, but gave a noncommittal grunt.

"I thought," said Mrs. Jim Jones, driven to her last gun, "that you and Mr. Whitman had inherited enough to make you comfortable for life, and I felt real bad to find out you hadn't."

Sylvia turned a little pale, but her gaze never flinched. She grunted again.

"I supposed," said Mrs. Jim Jones, mouthing her words with intensest relish, "that there wouldn't be any need for Mr. Whitman to work any more, and when I heard he was going back to the shop, and when I saw him turn in there this morning, I declare I did feel bad."

Then Sylvia spoke. "You needn't have felt bad," said she. "Nobody asked you to."

Mrs. Jim Jones stared.

"Nobody asked you to," repeated Sylvia. "Nobody is feeling at all bad here. It's true we've plenty, so Mr. Whitman don't need to lift his finger, if he don't want to, but a man can't set down, day in and day out, and suck his thumbs when he's been used to working all his life. Some folks are lazy by choice, and some folks work by choice. Mr. Whitman is one of them."

Mrs. Jim Jones felt fairly defrauded. "Then you don't feel bad?" said she, in a crestfallen way.

"Nobody feels bad here," said Sylvia. "I guess nobody in East Westland feels bad unless it's you, and nobody wants you to."

After Mrs. Jim Jones had gone, Sylvia went into her bedroom and sat down in a rocking-chair by the one window. Under the window grew a sweetbrier rose-bush. There were no roses on it, but the soothing perfume of the leaves came into the room. Sylvia sat quite still for a while. Then she got up and went into the sitting-room with her mouth set hard.

When Rose had returned she had greeted her as usual, and in reply to her question where Uncle Henry was, said she guessed he must be at Mr. Meeks's; there's where he generally was when he wasn't at home.

It did not occur to Sylvia that she was lying, not even when, later in the afternoon, Horace came home, and she answered his question as to her husband's whereabouts in the same manner. She had resolved upon Sidney

Meeks's as a synonyme for the shoe-shop. She knew herself that when she said Mr. Meeks's she in reality meant the shoe-shop. She did not worry about others not having the same comprehension as herself. Sylvia had a New England conscience, but, like all New England consciences, it was susceptible of hard twists to bring it into accordance with New England will.

The thunder-tempest, as Sylvia termed it, continued. She kept glancing, from her station of safety, at the streaming windows. She was becoming very much worried about Henry. At last she saw a figure, bent to the rainy wind, pass swiftly before the side windows of the sitting-room. She was on her feet in an instant, although at that minute the room was filled with blue flame followed by a terrific crash. She ran out into the kitchen and flung open the door.

"Come in quick, for mercy's sake!" she called. Henry entered. He was dripping with rain. Sylvia did not ask a question. "Stand right where you are till I bring you some dry clothes," she said.

Henry obeyed. He stood meekly on the oil-cloth while Sylvia hurried through the sitting-room to her bedroom.

"Mr. Whitman has got home from Mr. Meeks's, and he's dripping wet," she said to Horace and Rose. "I am going to get him some dry things and hang the wet ones by the kitchen stove."

When she re-entered the kitchen with her arms full, Henry cast a scared glance at her. She met it imperturbably.

"Hurry and get off those wet things or you'll catch your death of cold," said she.

Henry obeyed. Sylvia fastened his necktie for him when he was ready for it. He wondered if she smelled the leather in his drenched clothing. His own nostrils were full of it. But Sylvia made no sign. She never afterwards made any sign. She never intimated to Henry in any fashion that she knew of his return to the shop. She was, if anything, kinder and gentler with him than she had been before, but whenever he attempted, being led thereto by a guilty conscience, to undeceive her, Sylvia lightly but decidedly waved the revelation aside. She would not have it.

That day, when she and Henry entered the sitting-room, she said, so calmly that he had not the courage to contradict her: "Here is your uncle Henry home from Mr. Meeks's, and he was as wet as a drowned rat. I suppose Mr. Meeks didn't have any umbrella to lend. Old bachelors never do have anything."

Henry sat down quietly in his allotted chair. He said nothing. It was only when the storm had abated, when there was a clear streak of gold low in the west, and all the wet leaves in the yard gave out green and silver lights, when

Sylvia had gone out in the kitchen to get supper and Rose had followed her, that the two men looked at each other.

"Does she know?" whispered Horace.

"If she does know, and has taken a notion never to let anybody know she knows, she never will," replied Henry.

"You mean that she will never mention it even to you?"

Henry nodded. He looked relieved and scared. He was right. He continued to work in the shop, and Sylvia never intimated to him that she knew anything about it.

Chapter XVII

When Henry had worked in the shop before Sylvia's inheritance, he had always given her a certain proportion of his wages and himself defrayed their housekeeping bills. He began to do so again, and Sylvia accepted everything without comment. Henry gradually became sure that she did not touch a dollar of her income from her new property for herself. One day he found on the bureau in their bedroom a book on an Alford savings-bank, and discovered that Sylvia had opened an account therein for Rose. Sylvia also began to give Rose expensive gifts. When the girl remonstrated, she seemed so distressed that there was nothing to do but accept them.

Sylvia no longer used any of Abrahama White's clothes for herself. Instead, she begged Rose to take them, and finally induced her to send several old gowns to her dressmaker in New York for renovation. When Rose appeared in these gowns Sylvia's expression of worried secrecy almost vanished.

The time went on, and it was midsummer. Horace was spending his long vacation in East Westland. He had never done so before, and Sylvia was not pleased by it. Day after day she told him that he did not look well, that she thought he needed a change of air. Henry became puzzled. One day he asked Sylvia if she did not want Mr. Allen to stay with them any longer.

"Of course I do," she replied.

"Well, you keep asking him why he doesn't go away, and I began to think you didn't," said Henry.

"I want him to stay," said Sylvia, "but I don't want any foolishness."

"Foolishness?" said Henry, vaguely.

It was a very hot afternoon, but in spite of the heat Rose and Horace were afield. They had been gone ever since dinner. It was Saturday, and Henry had come home early from the shop. The first question he asked had been concerning the whereabouts of the young people. "Off together somewhere," Sylvia had replied. Then the conversation had ensued.

"Yes, foolishness," repeated Sylvia, with a sort of hysterical violence. She sat out on the front porch with some mending, and she sewed feverishly as she spoke.

"I don't know what you mean by foolishness, I guess, Sylvia."

Henry sat on the porch step. He wore a black mohair coat, and his thin hair was well brushed.

"It does seem," said Sylvia, "as if a young man and a young woman might live in the same house and behave themselves."

Henry stared at her. "Why, Sylvia, you don't mean—"

"I mean just what I said—behave themselves. It does seem sometimes as if everything any girl or young man thought of was falling in love and getting married," Sylvia said—"falling in love and getting married," with a bitter and satirical emphasis.

"I don't see," said Henry, "that there is very much against Mr. Allen and Rose's falling in love and getting married. I think he might do worse, and I think she might. Sometimes I've looked at the two of them and wondered if they weren't just made for each other. I can't see quite what you mean, Sylvia? You don't mean to say that you don't want Mr. Allen ever to get married?"

"He can marry whoever he wants to," said Sylvia, "but he sha'n't marry her."

"You don't mean you don't want her ever to get married?"

"Yes, I do mean just that."

"Why, Sylvia, are you crazy?"

"No, I ain't crazy," replied Sylvia, doggedly. "I don't want her to get married, and I'm in the right of it. She's no call to get married."

"I don't see why she 'ain't got a call as well as other girls."

"She 'ain't. Here she's got a good home, and everything she needs, and more, too. She's got money of her own that she had when she come here, plenty of it. I'm going over to Alford to-morrow and see if I can't find some things in the stores there for her that I think she'll like. And I'm going to get Jim Jones —he's a good hand—to see if he can't get a good, safe horse and pretty carriage for her, so she can ride out."

Henry stared. "I dunno as I can take care of a horse, Sylvia," he said, doubtfully.

"Nobody wants you to. I can get Billy Hudson to come. He can sleep in the chamber over the kitchen. I spoke to his mother about it, and she's tickled to pieces. She says he's real handy with horses, and he'll come for fifteen dollars a month and his board. Rose is going to have everything she wants."

"Does she want a horse and carriage?"

"I shouldn't think of it if I didn't s'pose she did."

"What made me ask," said Henry, "was, I'd never heard her speak of it, and I knew she had money enough for anything if she did want it."

"Are you grudging my spending money her own aunt left on her?"

Henry looked reproachfully at his wife. "I didn't quite deserve that from you, Sylvia," he said, slowly.

Sylvia looked at him a moment. Her face worked. Then she glanced around to be sure nobody saw, and leaned over and touched the shoulder of Henry's mohair coat with a little, skinny hand. "Henry," she said, pitifully.

"What, Sylvia?"

"You know I didn't mean anything. You've always been generous about money matters. We 'ain't never had ill feeling about such a thing as that. I shouldn't have spoke that way if I hadn't been all wrought up, and—" Suddenly Sylvia thrust her hand under her white apron and swept it up to her face. She shook convulsively.

"Now, Sylvia, of course you didn't mean a blessed thing. I've known you were all wrought up for a long time, but I haven't known what about. Don't take on so, Sylvia."

A little, hysterical sob came from Sylvia under the apron. Her scissors fell from her lap and struck the stone slab on which Henry was sitting. He picked them up. "Here are your scissors, Sylvia," said he. "Now don't take on so. What is it about? What have you got on your mind? Don't you think it would do you good to tell me?"

"I wish," sobbed Sylvia, "that Abrahama White had left her property where it belonged. I wish we'd never had a cent of it. She didn't do right, and she laid the burden of her wrong-doing onto us when she left us the property."

"Is that what's troubling you, Sylvia?" said Henry, slowly. "If that's all," he continued, "why—"

But Sylvia interrupted him. She swept the apron from her face and showed it grimly set. There was no trace of tears. "That ain't troubling me," said she. "Nothing's troubling me. I'm kind of nervous, that's all, and I hate to set still and see foolishness. I don't often give way, and I 'ain't nothing to give way for. I'm jest all wrought up. I guess there's going to be a thunder-tempest. I've felt jest like it all day. I wish you'd go out in the garden and pick a mess of green corn for supper. If you're a mind to you can husk it, and get that middling-sized kettle out from under the sink and put the water on to boil. I suppose they'll be home before long now. They ain't quite got to going without their victuals."

Henry rose. "I'd admire to get the corn," said he, and went around the house towards the kitchen. Left to herself, Sylvia let her work fall in her lap. She stared at the front yard and the street beyond and the opposite house, dimly seen between waving boughs, and her face was the face of despair. Little, commonplace, elderly countenance that it seemed, it was strengthened into tragedy by the terrible stress of some concealed misery of the spirit. Sylvia sat very stiffly, so stiffly that even the work in her lap, a mass of soft muslin, might have been marble, with its immovable folds. Sylvia herself looked petrified; not a muscle of her face stirred. She was suffering the keenest agony upon earth, that agony of the spirit which strikes it dumb.

She had borne it for months. She had never let slip the slightest hint of it. At times she had managed to quiet it with what she knew to be sophistries. She had been able to imagine herself almost happy with Rose and the new passion for her which had come into her life, but that passion was overgrown by her secret, like some hideous parasite. Even the girl's face, which was so beloved, was not to be seen without a pang to follow upon the happiness. Sylvia showed, however, in spite of her face of utter despair, an odd strength, a courage as if for battle.

After awhile she heard Henry's returning footsteps, and immediately her face and whole body relaxed. She became flesh, and took up her needlework, and Henry found her sewing placidly. The change had been marvellous. Once more Sylvia was a little, commonplace, elderly woman at her commonplace task. Even that subtle expression which at times so puzzled Henry had disappeared. The man had a sensation of relief as he resumed his seat on the stone step. He was very patient with Sylvia. It was his nature to be patient with all women. Without realizing it, he had a tenderness for them which verged on contempt. He loved Sylvia, but he never lost sight of the fact that she was a woman and he a man, and therefore it followed, as a matter of course, that she was by nature weaker and, because of the weakness, had a sweet inferiority. It had never detracted from his love for her; it had increased it. There might not have been any love in the beginning except for that.

Henry was perhaps scarcely capable of loving a woman whom he might be compelled to acknowledge as his superior. This elderly New-Englander had in him none of the spirit of knight-errantry. He had been a good, faithful husband to his wife, but he had never set her on a pedestal, but a trifle below him, and he had loved her there and been patient with her.

But patience must breed a certain sense of superiority. That is inevitable. Henry's tender patience with Sylvia's moods and unreason made him see over her character, as he could see over her physical head. Lately this sense of mystery had increased, in a way, his comprehension of his own stature. The more mysterious Sylvia became, and the more Henry's patience was called into action, the taller he appeared to himself to become.

While he had been getting the corn out in the garden, and preparing it to be cooked, he had reflected upon Sylvia's unaccountable emotion and her assertion that there was no reason for it, and he realized his masculine height. He knew that it would have been impossible for him to lose control of himself and then declare that there was no cause; to sway like a reed driven by the wind.

Henry was rather taken by this idea. When he had returned to his station on the porch he was thinking how women were reeds driven by the winds of their emotions, and really, in a measure, irresponsible. If he had again found Sylvia with her apron over her face, he was quite prepared to be very tender, but he was relieved to see that the paroxysm had passed. He did not smile as he sat down, neither did Sylvia. It was rather unusual for them to smile at each other, but they exchanged looks of peaceful accord, which really meant more than smiles.

"Well," said Henry, "the kettle's on the stove."

"How much corn did you get?"

"Well, I allowed three ears apiece. They're pretty good size. I thought that was about right."

Sylvia nodded.

"The corn's holding out pretty well," said Henry. "That other later kind will be ready by the time the lima beans are ripe."

"That 'll go nice for succotash," said Sylvia, taking another stitch.

"That's what I was thinking," said Henry.

He sat staring out upon the front yard, and he was in reality thinking, with pleasant anticipations, of the succotash. Now that he was back in his old track at the shop, his appetite was better, and he found himself actually dreaming about savory dishes like a boy. Henry's pleasures in life were so few and simple that they had to go a long way, and lap over onto his spiritual needs from his physical ones.

Sylvia broke in upon his visions of succotash. She was straining her eyes to see the road beyond the front yard. "What time is it?" she asked. "Do you know?"

"It was half-past five by the kitchen clock."

"They ain't in sight yet." Sylvia stared and frowned at the distance. "This house does set too far back," she said, impatiently.

"Now, Sylvia, I wouldn't give up a mite of this front yard."

"I'd give it all up if I could see folks go past. A woman wants to see something out of the window and from the doorstep besides flowers and box and trees."

Sylvia glared at the yard, which was beautiful. The box grew lustily, framing beds of flowers and clusters of radiant bushes. There were two perfectly symmetrical horse-chestnut-trees, one on each side of the broad gravel walk. The yard looked like some wonderful map wherein the countries were made of flowers, the design was so charmingly artificial and prim.

"It's awful set, I think," said Sylvia. "I'd rather have flowers growing where they want to instead of where they have to. And I never did like box. Folks say it's unhealthy, too."

"It's been here for years, and the people who belonged here have never been short-lived," said Henry. "I like it."

"I don't," said Sylvia. She looked at the road. "I don't see where they can be."

"Oh, they'll be along soon. Don't worry, Sylvia."

"Well," said Sylvia, in a strident voice, "I'm going in and get supper, and when it's ready we'll set down and eat it. I ain't going to wait one minute. I'm just sick of this kind of work."

Sylvia got up, and her scissors dropped again onto the step. Henry picked them up. "Here are your scissors," said he.

Sylvia took them and went into the house with a flounce. Henry heard a door slam and dishes rattle. "She's all wrought up again," he thought. He felt very tall as he pitied Sylvia. He was sorry for her, but her distress over such a matter as the young folks' being late seemed to him about as much to be taken seriously as the buzzing of a bumblebee over a clump of lilies in the yard.

He was watching the bumblebee when he heard the front gate click, and thought with relief that the wanderers had returned, then Sidney Meeks came into view from between the rows of box. Sidney came up the walk, wiping his forehead with a large red handkerchief, and fanning himself with an obsolete straw hat.

"Hullo," said Henry.

"How are you?" said Meeks. "It's a corking hot day."

"Yes, it is pretty hot, but I think it's a little cooler than it was an hour ago."

"Try walking and you won't think so."

"Set down," said Henry, pointing to the chair Sylvia had just vacated. "Set down and stay to supper."

"I don't say I won't stay to supper, but I've got an errand first. I've struck a new idea about wine. Haven't you got a lot of wild grapes down back here?"

"Yes, back of the orchard."

"Well, I've got an idea. I won't say what it is now. I want to see how it turns out first. Does Sylvia use wild grapes?"

"No, I know she won't. There are going to be bushels of Concords and Delawares."

"Well, I want you to go down with me and let me look at your wild grape-vines. I suppose the grapes must be set long ago. I just want to see how many there are. I suppose I can make a deal with you for some?"

"You can have them, and welcome. I know Sylvia will say so, too."

"Well, come along. We can go around the house."

Henry and Meeks skirted the house and the vegetable garden, then crossed a field, and found themselves at one side of the orchard. It was a noble old orchard. The apple, pear, and peach trees, set in even rows, covered three acres. Between the men and the orchard grew the wild grapes, rioting over an old fence. Henry began to say there was a gap in the fence farther down, but the lawyer's hand gripped his arm with sudden violence, and he stopped short. Then he as well as Meeks heard voices. They heard the tones of a girl, trembling with sweetness and delight, foolish with the blessed folly of life and youth. The voice was so full of joy that at first it sounded no more articulate than a bird's song. It was like a strophe from the primeval language of all languages. Henry and Meeks seemed to understand, finally, what the voice said, more from some inner sympathy, which dated back to their youth and chorded with it, than from any actual comprehension of spoken words.

This was what the sweet, divinely foolish girl-voice said: "I don't know what you can see in me to love."

There was nothing in the words; it was what any girl might say; it was very trite, but it was a song. Celestial modesty and pride were in it, and joy which looked at itself and doubted if it were joy.

Then came the man's voice, and that sang a song also foolish and trite, but divine and triumphant and new as every spring.

Henry and Meeks saw gradually, as they listened, afraid to move lest they be heard. They saw Horace and Rose sitting on the green turf under an apple-tree. They leaned against its trunk, twisted with years of sun and storm, and the green spread of branches was overhead, and they were all dappled with shade and light like the gold bosses of a shield. The man's arm was around the girl, and they were looking at each other and seeing this world and that which is to come.

Suddenly Meeks gave Henry's arm another violent clutch. He pointed. Then they saw another girl standing in the tangle of wild grapes. She wore a green muslin gown, and was so motionless that it was not easy to discern her readily. She was listening and watching the lovers, and her young face was terrible. It was full of an enormous, greedy delight, as of one who eats ravenously, and yet there was malignity and awful misery and unreason in it. Her cheeks were flushed and her blue eyes glittered. It was evident that everything she heard and saw caused her the most horrible agony and a more horrible joy. She was like a fanatic who dances in fire.

Meeks and Henry looked at her for a long minute, then at each other. Henry nodded as if in response to a question. Then the two men, moving by almost imperceptible degrees, keeping the utmost silence, hearing all the time that love duet on the other side of the grape-vines, got behind the girl. She had been so intent that there had been no danger of seeing them. Horace and Rose were also so intent that they were not easily reached by any sight or sound outside themselves.

Meeks noiselessly and firmly clasped one of Lucy Ayres's arms. It was very slender, and pathetically cold through her thin sleeve. Henry grasped the other. She turned her wild young face over her shoulder, and saw them, and yielded. Between them the two men half carried, half led the girl away across the fields to the road. When they were on the road Henry released his grasp of her arm, but Meeks retained his. "Will you go quietly home?" said he, "or shall Mr. Whitman and I go with you?"

"I will go," Lucy replied, in a hoarse whisper.

Meeks looked keenly at her. "Now, Lucy," he said, in a gentle voice, "there's no use; you've got to go home."

"Yes," said Henry. "Go home to your ma, right away, like a good girl."

Lucy remained motionless. Her poor young eyes seemed to see nothing.

"Good Lord!" sighed Meeks, wiping his forehead with his disengaged hand. "Well, come along, Lucy. Now, Lucy, you don't want to make a spectacle of yourself on the street. I think we must go home with you, because I can see right in your eyes that you won't budge a step unless we make you, but we don't want to walk holding on to you. So now you just march along ahead, and we'll keep behind you, and we won't have all the town up in arms."

Lucy said nothing. Meeks wiped his forehead again, freed her, and gave her a gentle shove between her shoulders. "Now, march," said he.

Lucy began to walk; the two men kept behind her. Presently they met a boy, who evidently noticed nothing unusual, for he leaped past, whistling.

"Thank the Lord it isn't far," muttered Meeks, wiping his forehead. "It's d—n hot."

Lucy walked on quite rapidly after awhile. They were nearly in sight of her home when Mrs. Ayres met them. She was almost running, and was pale and out of breath.

"Lucy," she began, "where—?" Then she realized that Meeks and Henry were with the girl.

"Henry, you just keep an eye on her," said Meeks. Then he spoke to Mrs. Ayres with old-fashioned ceremony. "Madam," he said, "will you be so kind as to step aside? I have a word I would like to say to you."

Mrs. Ayres, with a scared glance at Lucy, complied.

"Just this way a moment," he said. "Now, madam, I have a word of advice which you are at liberty to take or not. Your daughter seems to be in a dangerously nervous state. I will tell you plainly where we found her. It seems that Mr. Allen and Miss Fletcher have fallen in love with each other, and have come to an understanding. We happened upon them, sitting together very properly, as lovers should, in the apple orchard back of Mr. Whitman's, and your daughter stood there watching them. She is very nervous. If you take my advice you will lose no time in getting her away."

Mrs. Ayres stood and listened with a cold, pale dignity. She waited until Meeks had entirely finished, then she spoke slowly and evenly.

"Thank you, Mr. Meeks," she said. "Your advice is very good, so good that I have proved it by anticipating you. My daughter is in a very nervous condition. She never fully recovered from a severe attack of the grip."

Mrs. Ayres lied, and Meeks respected her for it.

"We are to start before long for St. Louis, where my brother lives," continued Mrs. Ayres. "I am going to rent my house furnished. My brother is a widower, and wishes us to make our home with him, and we may never return here. I was obliged to go on an errand to the store, and when I came home I missed Lucy and was somewhat anxious. I am very much obliged to you. We are going away, and I have no doubt that an entire change of scene will restore my daughter entirely. Yesterday she had a sick headache, and is still suffering somewhat from it to-day."

"That woman lied like a gentleman," Meeks said to Henry when they were on their way home. "Good Lord! I was thankful to her."

Henry was regarding him with a puzzled look. "Do you think the poor girl is in love with Mr. Allen, too?" he asked.

"I think she is in love with love, and nothing will cure that," said Meeks.

Chapter XVIII

Henry looked more and more disturbed as they went down the street. "I declare, I don't know what Sylvia will say," he remarked, moodily.

"You mean about the pretty little love-affair?" said Meeks, walking along fanning himself with his hat.

"Yes, she'll be dreadful upset."

"Upset; why?"

"It beats me to know why. Who ever does know the why of a woman?"

"What in creation is the fellow, anyhow?" said Meeks, with a laugh. "Are all the women going daft over him? He isn't half bad looking, and he's a good sort, but I'm hanged if I can see why he should upset every woman who looks at him. Here we've just escorted that poor Ayres girl home. I declare, her face made me shiver. I was glad there wasn't any pond handy for her. But if you mean to say that your good, sensible old wife—"

"Get out! You know better," cried Henry, impatiently. "You know Sylvia better than that. She sets a lot by Mr. Allen; I do myself; but, as far as that goes, she'd give her blessing if he'd marry any girl but Rose. That's where the hitch comes in. She doesn't want him to marry her."

"Thinks he isn't good enough?"

"I don't believe it's that. I don't know what it is. She says she don't want Rose to marry anybody."

"Good Lord! Sylvia doesn't expect a girl with a face like that, and money to boot, to be an old maid! My only wonder is that she hasn't been snapped up before now."

"I guess Rose has had chances."

"If she hasn't, all the men who have seen her have been stone blind."

"I don't know what has got into Sylvia, and that's the truth," Henry said. "I never saw her act the way she does lately. I can't imagine what has got into her head about Rose that she thinks she mustn't get married."

"Maybe Sylvia is in love with the girl," said Meeks, shrewdly.

"I know she is," said Henry. "Poor Sylvia loves her as if she was her own daughter, but I have always understood that mothers were crazy to have their daughters married."

"So have I, but these popular ideas are sometimes nonsense. I have always heard that myself."

"Sylvia and I have been happy enough together," said Henry. "It can't be that her own life as a married woman makes her think it a better plan to remain single."

"That's stuff."

"It seems so to me. Well, all the reason I can think of is, Sylvia has come to set so much by the girl that she's actually jealous of her."

"Do you suppose they'll tell her to-night?" asked Meeks.

Henry regarded him with an expression of actual terror. "Seems as if they might wait, and let Sylvia have her night's sleep," he muttered.

"I guess I won't stay to supper," said Meeks.

"Stay, for the Lord's sake."

Meeks laughed. "I believe you are afraid, Henry."

"I hate to see a woman upset over anything."

"So do I, for that matter. Do you think my staying might make it any better?"

"Yes, it might. Here we are in sight of the house. You ain't going to back out?"

Meeks laughed again, although rather uneasily. "All right," he said.

When he and Henry entered they found Sylvia moving nervously about the sitting-room. She was scowling, and her starched apron-strings were rampant at her slim back.

"Well," she said, with a snap, "I'm glad somebody has come. Supper's been ready for the last quarter of an hour, and I don't know but the corn is spoiled. How do you do, Mr. Meeks? I'll be glad to have you stay to supper, but I don't know as there's a thing fit to eat."

"Oh, I'll risk it," Sidney said. "You can't have anything worse than I've got at home. I had to go to Alford about that confounded Ames case. I had a dinner there that wasn't fit for a dog to eat, and I'm down to baker's bread and cheese."

"Where have *you* been?" demanded Sylvia of Henry. He cast an appealing glance at Meeks. The two men stood shoulder to shoulder, as if confronted by a common foe of nervous and exasperated feminity.

"I'm to blame for that," said Meeks. "I wanted to see if you had any wild grapes to spare, and I asked Henry to go down to the orchard with me. I suppose you can spare me some of those wild grapes?"

"Take all you want, and welcome," said Sylvia. "Now, I'll put supper on the table, and we'll eat it. I ain't going to wait any longer for anybody."

After Sylvia had gone, with a jerk, out of the room, the two men looked at each other. "Couldn't you give Allen a hint to lay low to-night, anyhow?" whispered Meeks.

Henry shook his head. "They'll be sure to show it some way," he replied. "I don't know what's got into Sylvia."

"It seems a pretty good sort of match, to me."

"So it does to me. Of course Rose has got more money, and I know as well as I want to that Horace has felt a little awkward about that; but lately he's been earning extra writing for papers and magazines, and it was only last Monday he told me he'd got a steady job for a New York paper that wouldn't interfere with his teaching. He seemed mighty tickled about it, and I guess he made up his mind then to go ahead and get married."

"Come to supper," cried Sylvia, in a harsh voice, from the next room, and the two men went out at once and took their seats at the table. Rose's and Horace's places were vacant. "I'd like to know what they think," said Sylvia, dishing up the baked beans. "They can eat the corn cold. It's just as good cold as it is all dried up. Here it is six o'clock and they ain't come yet."

"These are baked beans that are baked beans," said Meeks.

"Yes, I always have said that Sylvia knows just how to bake beans," said Henry. "I go to church suppers, and eat other folks' baked beans, but they 'ain't got the knack of seasoning, or something."

"It's partly the seasoning and partly the cooking," said Sylvia, in a somewhat appeased voice.

"This is brown bread, too," said Meeks. His flattering tone was almost fulsome.

Henry echoed him eagerly. "Yes, I always feel just the same about the brown bread that Sylvia makes," he said.

But the brown bread touched a discordant tone.

Sylvia frowned. "Mr. Allen always wants it hot," said she, "and it 'll be stone cold. I don't see where they went to."

"Here they are now," said Henry. He and Meeks cast an apprehensive glance at each other. Voices were heard, and Horace and Rose entered.

"Are we late?" asked Rose. She smiled and blushed, and cast her eyes down before Sylvia's look of sharp inquiry. There was a wonderful new beauty about the girl. She fairly glowed with it. She was a rose indeed, full of sunlight and dew, and holding herself, over her golden heart of joy, with a divine grace and modesty.

Horace did not betray himself as much. He had an expression of subdued triumph, but his face, less mobile than the girl's, was under better control. He took his place at the table and unfolded his napkin.

"I am awfully sorry if we have kept you waiting, Mrs. Whitman," he said, lightly, as if it did not make the slightest difference if she had been kept waiting.

Sylvia had already served Rose with baked beans. Now she spoke to Horace. "Pass your plate up, if you please, Mr. Allen," she said. "Henry, hand Mr. Allen the brown bread. I expect it's stone cold."

"I like it better cold," said Horace, cheerfully.

Sylvia stared at him, then she turned to Rose. "Where on earth have you been?" she demanded.

Horace answered for her. "We went to walk, and sat down under a tree in the orchard and talked; and we hadn't any idea how the time was passing," he said.

Henry and Meeks cast a relieved glance at each other. It did not appear that an announcement was to be made that night. After supper, when Meeks left,

Henry strolled down the street a little way with him.

"I'm thankful to have it put off to-night, anyhow," he said. "Sylvia was all wrought up about their being late to supper, and she wouldn't have got a mite of sleep."

"You don't think anything will be said to-night?"

"No, I guess not. I heard Sylvia tell Rose she'd better go to bed right after supper, and Rose said, 'Very well, Aunt Sylvia,' in that way she has. I never saw a human being who seems to take other people's orders as Rose does."

"Allen told me he'd got to sit up till midnight over some writing," said Meeks. "That may have made a difference to the girl. Reckon she knew spooning was over for to-day."

Henry looked back at the house. There were two lighted windows on the second floor. "Rose is going to bed," he said. "That light's in her room."

"She looked happy enough to dazzle one when she came in, poor little thing," said Meeks. In his voice was an odd mixture of tenderness, admiration, and regret. "You've got your wife," he said, "but I wonder if you know how lonely an old fellow like me feels sometimes, when he thinks of how he's lived and what he's missed. To think of a girl having a face like that for a man. Good Lord!"

"You might have got married if you'd wanted to," said Henry.

"Of course; could get married now if I wanted to, but that isn't the question. I don't know what I'm such a d—n fool as to tell you for, only it's like ancient history, and no harm that I can see for either the living or the dead. There was a time when, if Abrahama White had worn a face like that for me—well— Poor girl, she got her heart turned the way it wasn't meant to go. She had a mean, lonesome life of it. Sometimes now, when I go into that house where she lived so many years, I declare, the weight of the burden she had to bear seems to be on me. It was a cruel life for a woman, and here's your wife wanting that girl to live the same way."

"Wouldn't she have you after Susy got married?" asked Henry. The words sounded blunt, but his voice was tender.

"Didn't ask her. I don't think so. She wasn't that kind of woman. It was what she wanted or nothing with her, always was. Guess that was why I felt the way I did about her."

"She was a handsome girl."

"Handsome! This girl you've got is pretty enough, but there never was such a beauty as Abrahama. Sometimes when I call her face back before my eyes, I declare it sounds like women's nonsense, but I wonder if I haven't done better losing such a woman as that than marrying any other."

"She was handsome," Henry said again, in his tone of futile, wondering sympathy.

When Henry had left Sidney and returned home, he found, to his horror, that Sylvia was not down-stairs. "She's up there with the girl, and Rose 'll tell her," he thought, uneasily. "She can't keep it to herself if she's alone with another woman."

He was right. Sylvia had followed the girl to her room. She was still angry with Rose, and filled with a vague suspicion, but she adored her. She was hungry for the pleasure of unfastening her gown, of seeing the last of her for the day. When she entered she found Rose seated beside the window. The lamp was not lit.

Sylvia stood in the doorway looking into the shadowy room. "Are you here?" she asked. She meant her voice to be harsh, but it rang sweet with tenderness.

"Yes, Aunt Sylvia."

"Where are you?"

"Over here beside the window."

"What on earth are you setting in the dark for?"

"Oh, I just thought I'd sit down here a few minutes. I was going to light the lamp soon."

Sylvia groped her way to the mantel-shelf, found the china match-box, and struck a match. Then she lit the lamp on the bureau and looked at the girl. Rose held her face a little averted. The lighting of the room had blotted out for her the soft indeterminateness of the summer night outside, and she was a little afraid to look at Sylvia with the glare of the lamp full upon her face.

"You'll get cold setting there," said Sylvia; "besides, folks can look right in. Get up and I'll unhook your dress."

Rose got up. Sylvia lowered the white window-shade and Rose stood about for her gown to be unfastened. She still kept her face away from the older woman. Sylvia unfastened the muslin bodice. She looked fondly at the soft, girlish neck when it was exposed. Her lips fairly tingled to kiss it, but she put the impulse sternly from her.

"What were you and Mr. Allen talking about so long down in the orchard?" said she.

"A good many things—ever so many things," said Rose, evasively.

Sylvia saw the lovely, slender neck grow crimson. She turned the girl around with a sudden twist at the shoulders, and saw the face flushing sweetly under its mist of hair. She saw the pouting lips and the downcast eyes.

"Why don't you look at me?" she said, in a hard whisper.

Rose remained motionless.

"Look at me."

Rose raised her eyelids, gave one glance at Sylvia, then she dropped them again. She was all one soft, rosy flush. She smiled a smile which she could not control—a smile of ecstasy.

Sylvia turned deadly pale. She gasped, and held the girl from her, looking at her pitilessly. "You don't mean it?" she exclaimed.

Then Rose spoke with a sudden burst of emotion. "Oh, Aunt Sylvia," she said, "I thought I wouldn't tell you to-night. I made him promise not to tell to-night, because I was afraid you wouldn't like it, but I've got to. I don't feel right to go to bed and not let you know."

"Then it's so?"

Rose gave her a glance of ineffable happiness and appeal for sympathy.

"You and him are planning to get married?"

"Not for a year; not for a whole year. He's absurdly proud because he's poor, and he wants to make sure that he can earn more than his teacher's salary. Not for a whole year."

"You and him are planning to get married?"

"I wasn't sure till this afternoon," Rose whispered. She put her arms around Sylvia, and tried to nestle against her flat bosom with a cuddling movement of her head, like a baby. "I wasn't sure," she whispered, "but he—told me, and—

now I am sure."

Then Rose wept a little, softly, against Sylvia's thin breast. Sylvia stood like a stone. "Haven't you had all you wanted here?" she asked.

"Oh, Aunt Sylvia, you know I have. You've been so good to me."

"I had got my plans made to put in a bath-room," said Sylvia. "I've got the carpenters engaged, and the plumber. They are going to begin next week."

"You've been as good as can be to me, Aunt Sylvia."

"And I'm on the lookout for a carriage and horse you can drive, and I've been planning to have some parties for you. I've tried to think of everything that would make you feel happy and contented and at home."

"Oh, you have; I know you have, dear Aunt Sylvia," murmured Rose.

"I have done all I knew how," repeated Sylvia, in a stony fashion. She put the girl gently away and turned to go, but Rose caught her arm.

"Aunt Sylvia, you aren't going like this!" she cried. "I was afraid you wouldn't like it, though I don't know why. It does seem that Horace is all you could ask, if I were your very own daughter."

"You are like my very own daughter," said Sylvia, stiffly.

"Then why don't you like Horace?"

"I never said anything against him."

"Then why do you look so?"

Sylvia stood silent.

"You won't go without kissing me, anyway, will you?" sobbed Rose.

This time she really wept with genuine hurt and bewilderment.

Sylvia bent and touched her thin, very cold lips to Rose's. "Now go to bed," she said, and moved away, and was out of the room in spite of Rose's piteous cry to her to come back.

Henry, after he had entered the house and discovered that Sylvia was up-stairs with Rose, sat down to his evening paper. He tried to read, but could not get further than the glaring headlines about a kidnapping case. He was listening always for Sylvia's step on the stair.

At last he heard it. He turned the paper, with a loud rustle, to the continuation of the kidnapping case as she entered the room. He did not even look up. He appeared to be absorbed in the paper.

Sylvia closed the hall door behind her noiselessly; then she crossed the room and closed the door leading into the dining-room. Henry watched her with furtive eyes. He was horribly dismayed without knowing why. When Sylvia had the room completely closed she came close to him. She extended her right hand, and he saw that it contained a little sheaf of yellowed newspaper clippings pinned together.

"Henry Whitman," said she.

"Sylvia, you are as white as a sheet. What on earth ails you?"

"Do you know what has happened?"

Henry's eyes fell before her wretched, questioning ones. "What do you mean, Sylvia?" he said, in a faint voice.

"Do you know that Mr. Allen and Rose have come to an understanding and are going to get married?"

Henry stared at her.

"She has just told me," said Sylvia. "Here I have done everything in the world I could for her to make her contented."

"Sylvia, what on earth makes you feel so? She is only going to do what every girl who has a good chance does—what you did yourself."

"Look at here," said Sylvia, in an awful voice.

"What are they?"

"I found them in a box up in the garret. They were cut from newspapers years ago, when Rose was nothing but a child, just after her mother died."

"What are they? Don't look so, Sylvia."

"Here," said Sylvia, and Henry took the little yellow sheaf of newspaper clippings, adjusted his spectacles, moved the lamp nearer, and began to read.

He read one, then he looked at Sylvia, and his face was as white as hers. "Good God!" he said.

Sylvia stood beside him, and their eyes remained fixed on each other's white face. "I suppose the others are the same," Henry said, hoarsely.

Sylvia nodded. "Only from different papers. It's terrible how alike they are."

"So you've had this on your mind?"

Sylvia nodded grimly.

"When did you find them?"

"We'd been living here a few days. I was up in the garret. There was a box."

Henry remained motionless for a few moments. Then he sighed heavily, rose, and took Sylvia by the hand. "Come," he said.

"What are you going to do?"

"Come."

Sylvia followed, dragging back a little at her husband's leading hand, like a child. They passed through the dining-room into the kitchen. "There's a fire in the stove, ain't there?" said Henry, as they went.

Sylvia nodded again. She did not seem to have many words for this exigency.

Out in the kitchen Henry moved a lid from the stove, and put the little sheaf of newspaper clippings, which seemed somehow to have a sinister aspect of its own, on the bed of live coals. They leaped into a snarl of vicious flame. Henry and Sylvia stood hand in hand, watching, until nothing but a feathery heap of ashes remained on top of the coals. Then he replaced the lid and looked at Sylvia.

"Have you got any reason to believe that any living person besides you and I knows anything about this?" he asked.

Sylvia shook her head.

"Do you think Miss Farrel knew?"

Sylvia shook her head again.

"Do you think that lawyer out West, who takes care of her money, knows?"

"No." Sylvia spoke in a thin, strained voice. "This must be what she is always afraid of remembering," she said.

"Pray God she never does remember," Henry said. "Poor little thing! Here she is carrying a load on her back, and if she did but once turn her head far enough to get a glimpse of it she would die of it. It's lucky we can't see the other side of the moon, and I guess it's lucky we haven't got eyes in the backs of our heads."

"You wondered why I didn't want her to get married to him," said Sylvia.

Henry made an impatient motion. "Look here, Sylvia," he said. "I love that young man like my own son, and your feeling about it is rank idiocy."

"And I love her like my own daughter!" cried Sylvia, passionately. "And I don't want to feel that she's marrying and keeping anything back."

"Now, look here, Sylvia, here are you and I. We've got this secret betwixt us, and we've got to carry it betwixt us, and never let any living mortal see it as long as we both live; and the one that outlives the other has got to bear it alone, like a sacred trust."

Sylvia nodded. Henry put out the kitchen lamp, and the two left the room, moving side by side, and it was to each of them as if they were in reality carrying with their united strength the heavy, dead weight of the secret.

Chapter XIX

Henry, after the revelation which Sylvia had made to him, became more puzzled than ever. He had thought that her secret anxiety would be alleviated by the confidence she had made him, but it did not seem to be. On the contrary, she went about with a more troubled air than before. Even Horace and Rose, in the midst of their love-dream, noticed it.

One day Henry, coming suddenly into the sitting-room, found Rose on her knees beside Sylvia, weeping bitterly. Sylvia was looking over the girl's head with a terrible, set expression, as if she were looking at her own indomitable will. For the first time Henry lost sight of the fact that Sylvia was a woman. He seemed to see her as a separate human soul, sexless and free, intent upon her own ends, which might be entirely distinct from his, and utterly unknown to him.

Rose turned her tear-wet face towards him. "Oh, Uncle Henry," she sobbed, "Aunt Sylvia is worrying over something, and she won't tell me."

"Nonsense," said Henry.

"Yes, she is. Horace and I both know she is. She won't tell me what it is. She goes about all the time with such a dreadful face, and she won't tell me. Oh, Aunt Sylvia, is it because you don't want me to marry Horace?"

Sylvia spoke, hardly moving her thin lips. "I have nothing whatever against your marriage," she said. "I did think at first that you were better off as you were, but now I don't feel so."

"But you act so." Rose stumbled to her feet and ran sobbing out of the room.

Henry turned to his wife, who sat like a statue. "Sylvia, you ought to be ashamed of yourself," he said, in a bewildered tone. "Here you are taking all the pleasure out of that poor child's little love-affair, going about as you do."

"There are other things besides love-affairs," said Sylvia, in a strange, monotonous tone, almost as if she were deaf and dumb, and had no knowledge of inflections. "There are affairs between the soul and its Maker that are more important than love betwixt men and women."

Sylvia did not look at Henry. She still gazed straight ahead, with that expression of awful self-review. The thought crossed Henry's mind that she was more like some terrible doll with a mechanical speech than a living woman. He went up to her and took her hands. They were lying stiffly on her lap, in the midst of soft white cambric and lace—some bridal lingerie which she was making for Rose. "Look here, Sylvia," said Henry, "you don't mean that you are fretting about—what you told me?"

"No," said Sylvia, in her strange voice.

"Then what—?"

Sylvia shook off his hands and rose to her feet. Her scissors dropped with a thud. She kept the fluffy white mass over her arm. Henry picked up the scissors. "Here are your scissors," said he.

Sylvia paid no attention. She was looking at him with stern, angry eyes.

"What I have to bear I have to bear," said she. "It is nothing whatever to you. It is nothing whatever to any of you. I want to be let alone. If you don't like to see my face, don't look at it. None of you have any call to look at it. I am doing what I think is right, and I want to be let alone."

She went out of the room, leaving Henry standing with her scissors in his hand.

After supper that night he could not bear to remain with Sylvia, sewing steadily upon Rose's wedding finery, and still wearing that terrible look on her face. Rose and Horace were in the parlor. Henry went down to Sidney Meeks's for comfort.

"Something is on my wife's mind," he told Sidney, when the two men were alone in the pleasant, untidy room.

"Do you think she feels badly about the love-affair?"

"She says that isn't it," replied Henry, gloomily, "but she goes about with a face like grim death, and I don't know what to make of it."

"She'll tell finally."

"I don't know whether she will or not."

"Women always do."

"I don't know whether she will or not."

"She will."

Henry remained with Meeks until quite late. Sylvia sewed and sewed by her sitting-room lamp. Her face never relaxed. She could hear the hum of voices across the hall.

After awhile the door of the parlor was flung violently open, and she heard Horace's rushing step upon the stair. Then Rose came in, all pale and tearful.

"I have told him I couldn't marry him, Aunt Sylvia," she said.

Sylvia looked at her. "Why not?" she asked, harshly.

"I can't marry him and have you feel so dreadfully about it."

"Who said I felt dreadfully about it?"

"Nobody said so; but you look so dreadfully."

"I can't help my looks. They have nothing whatever to do with your love-affairs."

"You say that just to pacify me, I know," said Rose, pitifully.

"You don't know. Do you mean to say that you have dismissed him?"

"Yes, and he is horribly angry with me," moaned Rose.

"I should think he would be. What right have you to dismiss a man to please another woman, who is hardly any relation to you? I should think he would be mad. What did he do?"

"He just slammed the door and ran."

Sylvia laid her work on the table and started out of the room with an angry stride.

"Where are you going?" asked Rose, feebly, but she got no reply.

Soon Sylvia re-entered the room, and she had Horace by the arm. He looked stern and bewildered. Sylvia gave him a push towards Rose.

"Now look at here, both of you," she said. "Once for all, I have got nothing to say against your getting married. I am worrying about something, and it is nobody's business what it is. I am doing right. I am doing what I know is right, and I ain't going to let myself be persuaded I ain't. I have done all I could for Rose, and I am going to do more. I have nothing against your getting married. Now I am going into the parlor to finish this work. The lamp in there is better. You can settle it betwixt you."

Sylvia went out, a long line of fine lace trailing in her wake. Horace stood still where she had left him. Rose looked at him timidly.

"I didn't know she felt so," she ventured, at last, in a small voice.

Horace said nothing. Rose went to him, put her hand through his arm, and laid her cheek against his unresponsive shoulder. "I did think it would about kill her if it went on," she whispered. "I think I was mistaken."

"And you didn't mind in the least how much I was hurt, as long as she wasn't," said Horace.

"Yes, I did."

"I must say it did not have that appearance."

Rose wept softly against his rough coat-sleeve. "I wanted to do what was right, and she looked so dreadfully; and I didn't want to be selfish," she sobbed.

Horace looked down at her, and his face softened. "Oh Rose," he said, "you are all alike, you women. When it comes to a question of right or wrong, you will all lay your best-beloved on the altar of sacrifice. Your logic is all wrong, dear. You want to do right so much that the dust of virtue gets into your eyes of love and blinds them. I should come first with you, before your aunt Sylvia, and your own truth and happiness should come first; but you wanted to lay them all at her feet—or, rather, at the feet of your conscience."

"I only wanted to do what was right," Rose sobbed again.

"I know you did, dear." Horace put his arm around Rose. He drew her to a chair, sat down, and took her on his knee. He looked at her almost comically, in return for her glance of piteous appeal.

"Don't laugh at me," she whispered.

Horace kissed her. "I am not laughing at you, but at the eternal feminine, dear," he said. "There is something very funny about the eternal feminine. It is so earnest on the wrong tack, and hurts itself and others so cruelly, and gets no thanks for it."

"I don't know what you mean. I don't like your talking so to me, Horace. I only meant to do what was right."

"I won't talk so any more, darling."

"I don't think I have much of the eternal feminine about me, Horace."

"Of course not, sweetheart."

"I love you, anyway," Rose whispered, and put up her face to be kissed again, "and I didn't want to hurt you. I only wanted to do my duty."

"Of course you did, sweetheart. But now you think your duty is to marry me, don't you?"

170

Rose laughed, and there was something angelic and innocent about that laugh of the young girl. Horace kissed her again, then both started. "She is talking to herself in there," whispered Rose. "Horace, what do you suppose it is about? Poor Aunt Sylvia must be worrying horribly about something. What do you think it is?"

"I don't know, darling," replied Horace, soberly.

They both heard that lamentable murmur of a voice in the other room, but the doors were closed and not a word could be understood.

Sylvia was sewing rapidly, setting the most delicate and dainty stitches, and all the time she was talking carrying on a horrible argument, as if against some invisible dissenter.

"Ain't I doing everything I can?" demanded Sylvia. "Ain't I, I'd like to know? Ain't I bought everything I could for her? Ain't I making her wedding-clothes by hand, when my eyes are hurting me all the time? Ain't I set myself aside and given her up, when God knows I love her better than if she was my own child? Ain't I doing everything? What call have I to blame myself? Only to-day I've bought a lot of silver for her, and I'm going to buy a lot more. After the underclothes are done I'm going about the table linen, though she don't need it. I ain't using a mite of her aunt Abrahama's. I'm saving it all for her. I'm saving everything for her. I've made my will and left all her aunt's property to her. What have I done? I'm doing right; I tell you I'm doing right. I know I'm doing right. Anybody that says I ain't, lies. They lie, I say. I'm doing right. I—"

Henry opened the door. He had just returned from Sidney Meeks's. Sylvia was sewing quietly.

Henry looked around the room. "Why, who were you talking to?" he asked.

"Nobody," replied Sylvia, taking another stitch.

"I thought I heard you talking."

"How could I be talking when there ain't anybody here to talk to?"

Chapter XX

It was not quite a year afterwards that the wedding-day of Rose and Horace was set. It was July, shortly after the beginning of the summer vacation. The summer was very cool, and the country looked like June rather than July. Even the roses were not gone.

The wedding was to be in the evening, and all day long women worked decorating the house. Rose had insisted on being married in the old White homestead. She was to have quite a large wedding, and people from New York and Boston crowded the hotel. Miss Hart was obliged to engage three extra maids. Hannah Simmons had married the winter before. She had married a young man from Alford, where she now lived, and came over to assist her former mistress. Lucinda had a look of combined delight and anxiety. "It's almost as bad as when they thought we'd committed murder," she said to Hannah.

"It was queer how we found that," said Hannah.

"Hush," said Lucinda. "You remember what we agreed upon after we'd told Albion Bennet that we'd keep it secret."

"Of course I remember," said Hannah; "but there ain't any harm in my reminding you how queer it was that we found the arsenic, that the poor thing had been taking to make her beautiful complexion, in her room."

"It was awful," said Lucinda. "Poor soul! I always liked her. People ought to be contented with what God has given them for complexions."

"I wonder if she would have looked very dreadful if she hadn't taken it," Hannah said, ruminatingly. She was passing the kitchen looking-glass as she spoke, and glanced in it. Hannah considered that her own skin was very rough. "I suppose," said she, "that it would never have happened if she had been careful. I suppose lots of women do use such things."

Lucinda cast a sharp glance at Hannah. "It's downright wicked fooling with them," said she. "I hope you won't get any such ideas into your head."

"No, I sha'n't," replied Hannah. "I'm married."

"I heard pretty straight this morning," said Lucinda, "that Lucy Ayres had got married out West, and had done real well."

"I'm mighty glad of it," said Hannah, sharply. "She was crazy enough to get married when she was here."

Lucinda echoed her as sharply. "Guess you're right," she said. "Albion Bennet told me some things. I shouldn't think she'd make much of a wife, if she has got a pretty face."

"She's just the kind to settle down and be a real sensible woman, after she's found out that she's on the earth and not in the clouds," returned Hannah, with an air of wisdom.

Then Albion Bennet came into the kitchen for some hot water for shaving. He was going to the wedding, and had closed his store early, and was about to devote a long time to preparations. Lucinda, also, was going. She had a new

172

black silk for the occasion.

When Albion left the kitchen he beckoned her to follow him. She made an excuse and went out into the corridor. "What is it?" she said to Albion, who was waiting, holding his pitcher of hot water.

"Nothing," said he, "only I was over to Alford this morning and—I bought some violets. I thought you'd like to wear them to the wedding."

Lucinda stared at him. "What for?" asked she.

Albion fidgeted and his pitcher of hot water tilted.

"Look out, you're spilling the water," said Lucinda. "What for?"

"I—thought you might like to wear them, you know," said Albion. He had never before given violets to a woman, and she had never had any given her by a man.

"Thank you," she said, faintly.

"I've ordered a hack to come for me at half-past seven, and—I thought maybe you'd like to ride with me," said Albion, further.

Lucinda stared. "What for?" she said again.

"I thought you might like to ride."

Then Lucinda colored. "Why, folks would talk," said she.

"Let them. I don't care; do you?"

"Albion Bennet, I'm a lot older than you. I ain't old enough to be your mother, but I'm a good deal older than you."

"I don't care," said Albion. "I know how old you are. I don't care. I'd enough sight rather have you than those young things that keep racing to my store. When I get you I shall know what I've got, and when I've got them I shouldn't know. I'd rather have heavy bread, or dry bread, and know it was bread, than new-fangled things that ain't a mite more wholesome, and you don't know what you've got. I don't know how you feel, Lucinda, but I ain't one who could ever marry somebody he hadn't summered and wintered. I've summered and wintered you, and you've summered and wintered me. I don't know how much falling in love there is for either of us, but I reckon we can get on together and have a good home, and that's what love-making has to wind up in, if the mainspring don't break and all the works bust. I'm making quite a little lot from my store. I suppose maybe the soda and candy trade will fall off a little if I get married, but if it does I can take a young clerk to draw it. You won't have to work so hard. You can let some of this big hotel, and keep rooms enough for us, and I'll hire a girl for the kitchen and you can do fancy-work."

"Land!" said Lucinda. "I can do the work for only two."

"You're going to have a hired girl," said Albion, firmly. "I know of one I can get. She's a real good cook. Are you going in the hack with me, Lucinda?"

Lucinda looked up at him, and her face was as the face of a young girl. She had never had an offer, nor a lover. Albion Bennet looked very dear to her.

"Good land!" said Albion, "you act as if you were a back number, Lucinda. You look as young as lots of the young women. You don't do up your hair quite like the girls that come for soda and candy, but otherwise—"

"I can do up my hair like them, if I want to," said Lucinda. "It's thick enough. I suppose I 'ain't fussed because I didn't realize that anybody but myself ever thought about it one way or the other."

"Then you'll go in the hack?" said Albion.

Lucinda made a sudden, sharp wheel about. "I sha'n't get ready to go in a hack if I don't hurry and get these biscuits made for supper," said she, and was gone.

It is odd how individuality will uprear itself before its own consciousness, in the most adverse circumstances. Few in all the company invited to the wedding wasted a thought upon Albion Bennet and Lucinda Hart, but both felt as if they were the principal figures of it all. Lucinda really did merit attention. She had taken another rôle upon her stage of life. The change in her appearance savored of magic. Albion kept looking at her as if he doubted his very eyes. Lucinda did not wear the black silk which she had made for the occasion. She had routed out an old lavender satin, which she had worn years ago and had laid aside for mourning when her father died. It was made in one of those quaint styles which defy fashion. Lucinda had not changed as to her figure. She hesitated a little at the V-shape of the neck. She wondered if she really ought not to fill that in with lace, but she shook her head defiantly, and fastened around her neck a black velvet ribbon with a little pearl pin. Then she tucked Albion's violets in the lavender satin folds of her waist. Her hair was still untouched with gray, and she had spoken the truth when she had said she could arrange it like a girl. She had puffed it low over her temples and given it a daring twist in the back.

Albion fairly gasped when he saw her. "Lord!" said he, "why ain't you been for candy and soda to the store, too?"

Few people at the wedding noticed Lucinda and Albion, but they noticed each other to that extent that all save themselves seemed rather isolated from them.

Albion whispered to Lucinda that she would make a beautiful bride, and she looked up at him, and they were in love.

They stood well back. Neither Lucinda nor Albion were pushing. Lucinda considered that her wonderful city boarders belonged in the front ranks, and Albion shared her opinion. It was a beautiful wedding. The old house was transformed into a bower with flowers and vines. Musicians played in the south room, which was like a grove with palms. There was a room filled with the wedding-presents, and the glitter of cut glass and silver seemed almost like another musical effect.

The wedding was to be at eight o'clock. Everybody was there before that time. Meeks and Henry stood together in the hall by the spiral staircase, which was wound with flowers and vines. Henry wore a dress-suit for the first time in his life. Meeks wore an ancient one, in which he moved gingerly. "I believe I weigh fifty pounds more than I did when the blamed thing was made," he said to Henry, "and the broadcloth is as thin as paper. I'm afraid to move."

Henry looked very sober. "What's the matter, Henry?" asked Sidney.

"It's Sylvia."

"Sylvia? I thought—"

"Yes, I thought, too, that she had got what was on her mind off it, but she hasn't. I don't know what ails her. She ain't herself. I'm worried to death about her."

Then the wedding-march was played and the bridal party came down the stairs. Rose was on the arm of the lawyer who had acted as her trustee. He was to give her away. The task had been an impossible one for Henry to undertake, although he had been the first one thought of by Rose. Henry had told Meeks, and the two had chuckled together over it. "The idea of a man from a shoe-shop giving away a bride in real lace at a swell wedding," said Henry.

"She was the right sort to ask you, though," said Meeks.

"Bless her little heart," said Henry, "she wouldn't care if Uncle Henry smelled strong enough of leather to choke out the smell of the flowers. But I ain't going to make a spectacle of myself at my time of life. If I stand that dress-suit I shall do well. Sylvia is going to wear black lace with a tail to it. I know somebody will step on it."

Sylvia, in her black lace, came down the stairs in the wake of the bridal party. She did not seem to see her husband as she passed him.

175

"By Jove!" said the lawyer, in a whisper. "What does ail her, Henry? She looks as if she was going to jump at something."

Henry did not answer. He made his way as quickly as possible after Sylvia, and Sidney kept with him.

Horace and Rose, in her bridal white, stood before the clergyman. The music had ceased. The clergyman opened his mouth to begin the wedding-service, when Sylvia interrupted him. She pushed herself like a wedge of spiritual intent past the bridal pair and the bridesmaids and best man, and stood beside the clergyman. He was a small, blond man, naturally nervous, and he fairly trembled when Sylvia put her hand on his arm and spoke.

"I have something to say," said she, in a thin, strained voice. "You wait."

The clergyman looked aghast at her. People pressed forward, craning their necks to hear more distinctly. Some tittered from nervousness. Henry made his way to his wife's side, but she pushed him from her.

"No," she said. "Stand back, Henry, and listen with the others. You had nothing to do with it. You ain't concerned in it."

Then she addressed the assembly. "This man, my husband," she said, "has known nothing of it. I want you all to understand that before I begin." Sylvia fumbled in the folds of her black lace skirt, while the people waited. She produced a roll of paper and held it up before them. Then she began her speech.

"I want," said she, "before all this company, before my old friends, and the friends of these two young people who are about to be married, to make my confession. I have not had the courage before. I have courage now, and this is the fitting time and place, since it metes out the fittest punishment and shame to me, who deserve so much. You have assembled here to-night thinking that you were to be at my house at this wedding. It is not so. It is not my house. None of this property is mine. I have known it was not mine since a little while after we came to live here. I have known it all belonged to Rose Fletcher, Abrahama White's own niece. After Rose came to live with us, I tried to put salve on my conscience by doing every single thing I could for her. When my husband went to work again, I spent every cent that came from her aunt's property on Rose. I gave her all her aunt's jewelry. I tried to salve over my conscience and make it seem right—what I had done, what I was doing. I tried to make it seem right by telling myself that Rose had enough property of her own and didn't need this, but I couldn't do it. I have been in torment, holding wealth that didn't belong to me, that has gnawed at my very heart all the time. Now I am going to confess. Here is Abrahama White's last will and testament. I found it in a box in the garret with some letters.

176

Abrahama wrote letters to her sister asking her to forgive her, and telling her how sorry she was, and begging her to come home, but she never sent one of them. There they all were. She had tried to salve her conscience as I have tried to salve mine. She couldn't do it, either. She had to give it up, as I am doing. Then she made her will and left all her property to Rose."

Sylvia unfolded the roll of paper and began reading. The will was very short and concise. It was as follows:

"I, Abrahama White, being in sound mind and understanding, and moved thereunto by a desire to make my peace with God for my sins before I give up this mortal flesh, declare this to be my last will and testament. I give and bequeath to my niece, Rose Fletcher, the daughter of my beloved sister, deceased, my entire property, real and personal, to her and her heirs forever. And I hereby appoint Sidney Meeks, Esquire, as my executor.

"(Signed) Abrahama White."

Sylvia read the will in her thin, strained voice, very clearly. Every word was audible. Then she spoke again. "I have kept it secret all this time," said she. "My husband knew nothing of it. I kept it from him. I tried to hide from God and myself what I was doing, but I could not. Here is the will, and Miss Rose Fletcher, who stands before you, about to be united to the man of her choice, is the owner of this house and land and all the property which goes with it."

She stopped. There was a tense silence. Then Sidney Meeks spoke. "Mrs. Whitman," he said, "may I trouble you for the date of that document you hold, and also for the names of the witnesses?"

Sylvia looked at Sidney in bewilderment, then she scrutinized the will. "I don't see any date," she said, at last, "and there is no name signed except just Abrahama's."

Meeks stepped forward. "Ladies and gentlemen," he said, "Mrs. Whitman has, I am pleased to say, been under quite unnecessary anxiety of spirit. The document which she holds is not valid. It is neither dated nor signed. I have seen it before. The deceased lady, Miss Abrahama White, called me in one morning, shortly before her death, and showed me this document, which she had herself drawn up, merely to make her wishes clear to me. She instructed me to make out a will under those directions, and I was to bring it to her for her signature, and produce the proper witnesses. Then, the next day, she called me in to inform me that there had been a change in her plans since she had heard of her niece's having a fortune, and gave me directions for the later will, which was properly made out, signed, witnessed, and probated after Miss White's decease. Mrs. Whitman is the rightful heir; but since she has labored under the delusion that she was not, I am sure we all appreciate her

177

courage and sense of duty in making the statement which you have just heard from her lips."

Sylvia looked at the lawyer, and her face was ghastly. "Do you mean to say that I have been thinking I was committing theft, when I wasn't, all this time?" said she.

"I certainly do."

Henry went to Sylvia and took hold of her arm, but she did not seem to heed him. "I was just as guilty," said she, firmly, "for I had the knowledge of sin in my heart and I held it there. I was just as guilty."

She stared helplessly at the worthless will which she still held. A young girl tittered softly. Sylvia turned towards the sound. "There is no occasion to laugh," said she, "at one who thought she was sinning, and has had the taste of sin in her soul, even though she was not doing wrong. The intention was there."

Sylvia stopped. Rose had both arms around her, and was kissing her and whispering. Sylvia pushed her gently away. "Now," she said to the minister, "you can go on with your marrying. Even if Mr. Meeks had told me before what he has just told me here in your presence, I should have had to speak out. I've carried it on my shoulders and in my heart just as long as I could and live and walk and speak under it, let alone saying my prayers. I don't say I haven't got to carry it now, for I have, as long as I live; but telling you all about it was the only way I could shift a little of the heft of it. Now I feel as if the Lord Almighty was helping me carry the burden, and always would. That's all I've got to say. Now you can go on with your marrying."

Sylvia stepped back. There was a hush, then a solemn murmur of one voice, broken at intervals by other hushes and low responses.

When it was over, and the bridal pair stood in the soft shadow of their bridal flowers—Rose's white garment being covered with a lace-like tracery of vines and bride roses, and her head with its chaplet of orange-blossoms shining out clearly with a white radiance from the purple mist of leaves and flowers, which were real, yet unreal, and might have been likened to her maiden dreams—Henry and Sylvia came first to greet them.

Henry's dress-suit fitted well, but his shoulders, bent with his life-work over the cutting-table, already moulded it. No tailor on earth could overcome the terrible, triumphant rigidity of that back fitted for years to its burden of toil. However, the man's face was happy with a noble happiness. He simply shook hands, with awkward solemnity, with the two, but in his heart was great, unselfish exultation.

"This man," he was saying to himself, "has work to do that won't grind him down and double him up, soul and body, like a dumb animal. He can take care of his wife, and not let her get bent, either, and the Lord knows I'm thankful."

He felt Sylvia's little nervous hand on his arm, and a great tenderness for her was over him. He had not a thought of blame or shame on her account.

Instead, he looked at Rose, blooming under her bridal flowers, not so much smiling as beaming with a soft, remote radiance, like a star, and he said to himself: "Thank the Lord that she will never get so warped and twisted as to what is right and wrong by the need of money to keep soul and body together, that she will have to do what my wife has done, and bear such a burden on her pretty shoulders."

It seemed to Henry that never, not even in his first wedded rapture, had he loved his wife as he loved her that night. He glanced at her, and she looked wonderful to him; in fact, there was in Sylvia's face that night an element of wonder. In it spirit was manifest, far above and crowning the flesh and its sordid needs. Her shoulders, under the fine lace gown, were bent; her very heart was bent; but she saw the goal where she could lay her burden down.

The music began again. People thronged around the bride and groom. There were soft sounds of pleasant words, gentle laughs, and happy rejoinders. Everybody smiled. They witnessed happiness with perfect sympathy. It cast upon them rosy reflections. And yet every one bore, unseen or seen, the burden of his or her world upon straining shoulders. The grand, pathetic tragedy inseparable from life, which Atlas symbolized, moved multiple at the marriage feast, and yet love would in the end sanctify it for them all.

THE END